Praise for the *Monk* Novels by Lee Goldberg

Mr. Monk Goes to Hawaii

"An entertaining and ruefully funny diversion that stars one of television's best-loved characters, and because it's a mystery novel, it will stick long after you've forgotten the plot of the latest *Monk* episode."
—*Honolulu Star-Bulletin*

Mr. Monk Goes to the Firehouse

"The first in a new series is always an occasion to celebrate, but Lee Goldberg's TV adaptations double your pleasure. . . . *Mr. Monk Goes to the Firehouse* brings everyone's favorite OCD detective to print. Hooray!"
—*Mystery Scene*

Acclaim for Lee Goldberg's previous mysteries

"Can books be better than television? You bet they can—when Lee Goldberg's writing them."
—Lee Child

"A nifty creative take on the tradition of great amateur sleuths with a cast of quirky characters."
—Stuart M. Kaminsky

"A clever, high-octane whodunit that moves like a bullet train."
—Janet Evanovich

continued . . .

"Well plotted and beautifully rendered."
—Margaret Maron, Edgar, Agatha, and Macavity Award–winning author of the Deborah Knott mysteries

"Elegant writing, wry humor, a suspenseful premise, [and] a fast-paced plot."
—Aimee and David Thurlo, authors of the Ella Clah, Sister Agatha, and Lee Nez mystery series

"A clever, twisting tale." —Lisa Gardner

"A riveting mystery . . . wonderful stuff!"
—Paul Bishop, two-time LAPD Detective of the Year and head of the West Los Angeles Sex Crimes and Major Assault Crimes Units, and author of *Twice Dead*, *Chalk*, and *Whispers*

"Sly humor, endearing characters, tricky plots."
—Jerrilyn Farmer

"A swift saga with colorful homicides, glamorous locales, and clever puzzles."
—Walter Wager, author of *Telefon*, *Twilight's Last Gleaming*, and *58 Minutes*

"Intricate plots and engaging characters . . . page-turning entertainment." —Barbara Seranella

"A devilish plot sense, sophisticated humor, and a smooth writing style . . . he's as good as anyone writing in the genre today."

—Donald Bain, coauthor of the *Murder, She Wrote* series

"Just what the doctor ordered, a sure cure after a rash of blah mysteries . . . more plot twists than a strand of DNA."

—Elaine Viets, author of *Murder Unleashed*

"Fast-paced, tightly constructed mysteries. . . . You'll read them in great big gulps!" —Gregg Hurwitz

MR. MONK
AND THE BLUE FLU

A Novel by

Lee Goldberg

Based on the television series created by

Andy Breckman

A SIGNET BOOK

SIGNET
Published by New American Library, a division of
Penguin Group (USA) Inc., 375 Hudson Street,
New York, New York 10014, USA
Penguin Group (Canada), 90 Eglinton Avenue East, Suite 700, Toronto,
Ontario M4P 2Y3, Canada (a division of Pearson Penguin Canada Inc.)
Penguin Books Ltd., 80 Strand, London WC2R 0RL, England
Penguin Ireland, 25 St. Stephen's Green, Dublin 2,
Ireland (a division of Penguin Books Ltd.)
Penguin Group (Australia), 250 Camberwell Road, Camberwell, Victoria 3124,
Australia (a division of Pearson Australia Group Pty. Ltd.)
Penguin Books India Pvt. Ltd., 11 Community Centre, Panchsheel Park,
New Delhi - 110 017, India
Penguin Group (NZ), cnr Airborne and Rosedale Roads, Albany,
Auckland 1310, New Zealand (a division of Pearson New Zealand Ltd.)
Penguin Books (South Africa) (Pty.) Ltd., 24 Sturdee Avenue,
Rosebank, Johannesburg 2196, South Africa

Penguin Books Ltd., Registered Offices:
80 Strand, London WC2R 0RL, England

First published by Signet, an imprint of New American Library,
a division of Penguin Group (USA) Inc.

ISBN 978-0-7394-7758-8

Printed in the United States of America

PUBLISHER'S NOTE

This is a work of fiction. Names, characters, places, and incidents either are the product of the author's imagination or are used fictitiously, and any resemblance to actual persons, living or dead, business establishments, events, or locales is entirely coincidental.

The publisher does not have any control over and does not assume any responsibility for author or third-party Web sites or their content.

To Valerie and Madison,
my Natalie and Sharona

ACKNOWLEDGMENTS

I would like to thank Dr. D. P. Lyle, William Rabkin, T. J. MacGregor, Janet Markham, Pat Tierney, David Mack, Tony Fennelly, Sheila Lowe, Hal Glatzer, Karen Tannert, Michael Siverling, Eve Simson, Aubrey Nye Hamilton, Jim Doherty, Paul Bishop, Lee Lofland, and Barbara Fahringer for their invaluable technical assistance on astrology, medicine, geography, police procedure, and dental fillings, among other things. Any mistakes in the book are entirely my fault and shouldn't be held against the fine people mentioned above.

Special thanks, as always, to my friend Andy Breckman, creator of *Monk*, and his incredibly talented staff—Stefanie Preston, Tom Scharpling, David Breckman, Hy Conrad, Joe Toplyn, Daniel Dratch, Jonathan Collier, and Blair Singer—for their inspiration, enthusiasm, and support. And to Gina Maccoby and Kerry Donovan, without whom there would be no *Monk* books for me to write and you to enjoy.

I would love to hear from you. Please stop by www.leegoldberg.com and say hello. We validate parking.

1

Mr. Monk Takes a Walk in the Park

The corpse might as well have been in a minefield, surrounded by razor wire, and guarded by trigger-happy snipers. There was no way Adrian Monk would go near it.

Monk stood on the red gravel jogging path that ran around McKinley Park at Vermont and Twentieth on Potrero Hill. He wore one of his six identical wool coats, one of his twelve identical off-white shirts (tieless and buttoned up to the collar), one of his twelve identical pairs of pleated brown slacks (specially tailored for him with eight belt loops instead of the usual seven), and one of his twelve identical pairs of brown leather shoes (Hush Puppies buffed to a shine each night).

He held a pair of binoculars up to his eyes. From where he stood he had a clear view west across the Mission District and Noe Valley to Sutro Tower, which rose out of the fog that always seemed to surround the Twin Peaks in the morning.

But that wasn't what he was looking at.

His binoculars were trained on the dead young woman sprawled only ten yards below him. The weedy area around her body was cordoned off with yellow crime scene tape that was twined around several trees.

The woman was twisted at an unnatural angle, her mouth open in a silent, frozen scream. Her shirt was hiked up, revealing the pale skin of her flat stomach and her tattooed lower back. The tattoo was a plus sign, with little matching plus signs in each of the four quadrants of the larger one. She was wearing Lycra shorts that showed off her long, muscled legs.

She was a jogger. The two previous victims were also joggers. And like them, she'd been strangled.

I'm not a cop or a medical examiner, but I'd picked up a little basic knowledge about homicide investigation over the years as Monk's assistant. Even I could tell from the bruising around her neck that someone had throttled her.

But my imagination wouldn't leave it at that. I put myself in her shoes. Or *shoe*, I should say, since she was missing her left one, just like the other victims who had been killed over the last month.

She had been jogging along the path in the early-morning stillness, enjoying the quiet and the view, her breathing steady and deep. And then he attacked her, knocking her off her feet. He wrapped his hands tightly around her throat. Her lungs ached for air. Her heart pumped madly. Her head and chest felt like they were going to burst.

She had suffered horribly.

I got scared just thinking about it, and I wasn't even in any danger.

It's that kind of overactive imagination that would make me a lousy cop. Since I'm not one, and have no official status with the police, I tend to keep my mouth shut at crime scenes and be as unobtrusive as possible. I feel like I'm in the way and that if I speak up, it will only call attention to the fact that I'm someplace where I really shouldn't be.

Capt. Leland Stottlemeyer chewed on a toothpick and studied the body. Maybe he was imagining the same stuff I was. Maybe he was wondering what the victim had been like, whether she could carry a tune or how her face changed when she smiled. Maybe he was asking himself why his wife left him and if there was anything he could do to get her back. Or maybe he was just trying to decide where to eat lunch. Cops can be amazingly dispassionate about death.

Lt. Randy Disher was standing beside him, busily scrawling something in his notebook. My guess was that he was doodling, because there wasn't anything for him to take notes on. Not yet, anyway. And while he was good at running down facts, and eager to please his captain, deduction wasn't his strength.

The truth is, they were both waiting for Monk, the brilliant detective and my boss, to share his observations or, better yet, solve the murder right then and there. It wasn't that crazy a thing for them to hope for. Monk had done it before. That's why the SFPD paid him to consult on the trickiest homicide cases. He used to be a cop himself once until his obsessive-compulsive disorder made staying on the force impossible for him.

I stood beside Monk. Behind us, several uniformed officers and crime scene techs were going over the playground and jogging path, searching for clues.

Stottlemeyer looked up at us expectantly. "Are you going to be joining us?"

"I don't think so," Monk said.

"The body is down here, Monk."

"Yes, I can see that."

Monk grimaced with disgust, lowering his binoculars. But it wasn't the body that made him uncomfortable; it was where it was located—right in the middle of a dog park. There were no dogs in the park now, but when we arrived some officers were still cleaning up the evidence that dogs had been there, if you catch my drift.

"This is the crime scene." Stottlemeyer pointed to the body.

"So is this," Monk said.

"The crime scene is where the body is," Stottlemeyer said.

"I beg to differ," Monk said.

"You can't investigate the murder from up there."

"I can't investigate the murder if I'm dead."

"Standing here isn't going to kill you," Stottlemeyer said.

"If I had to stand there," Monk said, "I would kill myself."

"We've cleaned up all the dog poop," Stottlemeyer said. "I guarantee you won't step in anything."

"The ground is saturated with it," Monk said. "This entire park should be dug up, put in a rocket, and sent into deep space."

Stottlemeyer sighed. There was no way he was going to win this one; he had to know that. "Okay, fine. What can you tell me?"

"The killer was hiding in the playground equipment over in the sandbox." Monk gestured behind himself to a fortlike structure that was part slide, part jungle gym. "When the victim ran past on the track, he tackled her, pinned her to the ground, and killed her. She was easy to overcome because she was already winded from running. He took her left shoe and then rolled her off the edge of the hill into the toxic-waste dump."

"Dog park," Stottlemeyer said.

"Same thing," Monk said.

"I've got the mayor, the chief, and the news media all over me on these killings, and we've got nothing. I don't even know who this poor woman is. She's not carrying any ID," Stottlemeyer said. "I need you to tell me something I don't already know. Have you got anything at all?"

Monk sighed. "Not really."

Stottlemeyer sighed. "Damn."

"Except she's from Russia, probably the Republic of Georgia, where she was active in the United National Movement, which favors closer ties with the European Union. So did she. She married a Jewish man from Eastern Europe."

Stottlemeyer and Disher shared a stunned look. I was pretty stunned, too.

"Is that all?" Stottlemeyer asked dryly.

"Her shoes are new," Monk said.

Disher glanced down at the body. "How do you know that?"

"The soles aren't worn down and the leather isn't creased yet," Monk said. "The only dirt on the laces is the red dust from the track."

"That's very observant," Stottlemeyer said, "but I think Randy meant how did you know the other stuff?"

"One of her teeth is capped with steel, which you see a lot in Soviet dentistry."

"I don't see much Soviet dentistry," Stottlemeyer said. "I guess I need to get out more."

"The tattoo on her back is the five crosses, adopted as the symbol of resistance by the Georgian nationalist movement in 1991. It became part of the Georgian flag in 2004," Monk said. "She's wearing a gold wedding ring on her right hand, which is a common practice in Eastern European countries, particularly among the Jewish faith. You'll notice the ring has a slight reddish tint because Russian gold has a higher copper content than Western gold."

"You saw all that from up there?" Stottlemeyer asked.

"I had these." Monk held up his binoculars.

Stottlemeyer shook his head. "I'm standing right over the body and I couldn't see half that stuff."

"It's okay, sir," Disher said. "I didn't even see three-quarters of it."

Stottlemeyer gave him a look. "I feel so much better now."

Disher smiled. "I'm glad I could be there for you."

One of the things that amazed me about Monk was that he knew all about things like Soviet dental fillings or the copper content of gold from different regions, but if someone had a gun to his head he wouldn't be able to name one of the judges on *American Idol* or tell you what a Big Mac was. I often wondered how he decided what obscure knowledge was worth knowing and what wasn't. After all, which was he more likely to come across, a Big Mac carton or the Georgian flag?

Monk rolled his shoulders and tilted his head like he was working a kink out in his neck. But I knew that wasn't it. What was irritating him was a detail, some fact that didn't fit where it was supposed to. Stottlemeyer noticed it, too.

"What's bugging you, Monk?"

"She's a brunette in her twenties," Monk said. "And almost six feet tall."

"That's obvious," Stottlemeyer said. "Even to me."

"She's buff," Monk said.

"She's in good shape; that's true."

"The first victim was a blonde in her early thirties and kind of flabby," Monk said. "The second victim was a short Asian young woman in her late teens."

"They were all female joggers who were strangled and had their left running shoe taken," Stottlemeyer said. "What's your point?"

"I think we should call the killer the Foot Maniac," Disher said. We all looked at him. "Since he takes their left shoe."

"No," Stottlemeyer said.

"How about the Foot Strangler?"

"You can't strangle a foot," I said.

"The Foot Phantom," Disher said.

"No," Stottlemeyer said firmly.

"We need to call him something, Captain."

"How about 'the perp'?" I said.

"How about the Foot Fiend?"

"How about you put a sock in it," Stottlemeyer said, and glanced up at Monk. "What are you getting at, Monk?"

"Why these women?"

Stottlemeyer shrugged. "They were the women who happened to be jogging by when nobody else was around. They were in the wrong place at the wrong time."

Monk shook his head. "I don't think so. He picked these three women for a specific reason. They have something in common that we're missing."

"I checked the first two victims out thoroughly," Disher said. "One was married; the other was single. They didn't know each other. They didn't live in the same part of the city. They didn't work in the same professions. And they were wearing different brands of running shoes."

"There must be a pattern," Monk insisted.

"Not everything in life has a pattern," Stottlemeyer said. "Sometimes life is messy."

"It shouldn't be," Monk said.

"It is," Stottlemeyer said.

"We should fix that," Monk said. "Isn't that our job?"

"I suppose you could say that," Stottlemeyer said.

It certainly was for Monk. He craved order, and there was nothing more disorderly than a murder. My theory is that for him, solving the crime was simply a matter of organizing the facts until they fit into the places where they belonged. In other words, he wasn't really investigating homicides; he was cleaning up a mess. And he probably wouldn't stop until he cleaned up the mess at the center of his own seemingly orderly life—the unsolved murder of his wife, Trudy.

Stottlemeyer turned to Disher. "Take some officers and canvass the neighborhood. See if anybody knows a young Russian woman. You might also check with immigration and missing persons for a woman matching her description."

"Will do," Disher said.

"The killer will probably have red gravel and dog . . ." Monk couldn't bring himself to say the word.

"Poop," I said.

". . . on his shoes," Monk continued. "You should put out an APB."

"And say what?" Disher said. " 'Be on the lookout for a man with dog poop on his shoes'?"

Monk nodded. "I see your point."

"You do?" Stottlemeyer said.

"I was being ridiculous," Monk said.

"I never thought I'd hear you say that," Stottlemeyer said. "That's showing real progress, Monk."

"We should alert Homeland Security," Monk said.

Stottlemeyer sighed. Some things never changed.

"I'll add that to my to-do list." Disher started to go.

"One more thing, Randy," Stottlemeyer said. "Check the credit card statements of all the victims for recent purchases at shoe stores or department stores. Maybe they all shopped at the same place."

"That's quite a list," Disher said. "I could use a hand."

"Get all the help you need."

"What will you be doing?" Disher asked pointedly.

"Captain stuff," Stottlemeyer said, his eyes daring Disher to push it beyond that.

"Right," Disher said, and hurried off.

Monk motioned over the officer who'd loaned him the binoculars. His name was Milner and, if not for the wedding ring he was wearing, I might have been interested in his first name, too.

"Thank you for loaning me these." Monk returned the binoculars to Officer Milner, then waved his hand at me for a disinfectant wipe. I dug into my purse for one and gave it to him.

"My pleasure, sir," Officer Milner said. For a moment, I thought he might salute. His uniform was perfectly starched, and he moved with an almost military bearing. Perhaps that was what attracted me to him. "It's amazing how you noticed all those little details."

"Those are good binoculars," Monk said, wiping his hands.

"You're just being modest," Officer Milner said.

"Yes," Monk said. "I am."

We started back toward my Jeep. Stottlemeyer met us there.

"Listen, I need to give you a heads-up on something," he said quietly, obviously not wanting to draw much attention.

"Oh, sweet Mother of God," Monk gasped, backing away.

"What?" Stottlemeyer said.

Monk hunched over and covered his face with his hands. I leaned close to him and whispered in his ear, "What's wrong, Mr. Monk?"

"I don't know how to tell him," Monk said.

"Tell him what?"

"He stepped in it," Monk said.

"In what?"

"It," Monk said gravely.

I looked back at Stottlemeyer, then down at his shoes. The captain followed my gaze. He'd stepped in dog crap.

"Oh, hell." He started to scrape the sole of his right shoe against the edge of the curb.

"No!" Monk shrieked. "Are you insane? There are innocent bystanders all around you."

Stottlemeyer started to put his foot back on the ground and Monk shrieked again. So the captain stood on one foot, his other leg bent at the knee, the dirty foot held off the ground behind him.

Monk addressed the police officers and crime scene techs. "Everybody stand back. Way back. For your own good. We don't want any collateral damage."

"Okay, Monk," the captain said in a low voice. "What would you like me to do?"

Stottlemeyer was adept at handling Monk, more so than me sometimes, and was eager to quickly defuse the situation.

"Don't move," Monk said, and rushed over to the crime scene van.

"I'm not," Stottlemeyer said. "So much for trying to be discreet."

"What's up?" I asked.

"Monk has to hear this," Stottlemeyer said.

Monk came back with several large evidence bags and handed them to me.

"What am I supposed to do with these?" I asked.

Monk looked Stottlemeyer in the eye. "We're going to get through this together. I won't abandon you, Captain."

"I appreciate that, Monk."

"Listen to me carefully, follow my instructions to the letter, and you'll be all right. Take your shoe off very slowly and place it in the bag."

Stottlemeyer bent down.

"Wait!" Monk yelled, startling Stottlemeyer and almost causing him to lose his balance.

"What?" Stottlemeyer snapped angrily.

"Gloves," Monk said.

Scowling and hopping on one foot, Stottlemeyer reached into his pocket, put on a pair of rubber gloves, then slowly removed his shoe.

"What I wanted to tell you is that the rank and file in the department have been working without a contract for over a year now," the captain said. "The city wants to make deep cuts in our pay, medical benefits, and pension contributions. Our union reps have been trying to talk sense to them for months, but the city won't budge on their demands."

Stottlemeyer handled his shoe, for Monk's benefit, as if it were nitroglycerin, gently sliding it into the bag that I held open in front of him.

"Seal the bag," Monk said.

I did.

"The point is," Stottlemeyer said, "negotiations collapsed this morning. Both sides walked away from the table."

Monk waved the forensic tech over and motioned for him to take the bag from me.

"Take it to a remote location at least fifty miles from the nearest populated area and burn it," Monk instructed the tech, then turned back to Stottlemeyer. "Now the sock."

The tech went off to make arrangements with NASA to have the bag launched into deep space.

The captain groaned and took off his sock. I held open another bag and he dropped the sock into it. I gave the bag to him.

"You think there might be a strike?" I asked.

"It's against the law for police officers to strike," Stottlemeyer said. "But I hear a nasty strain of the flu is going around."

Monk covered his nose and mouth with his hands and staggered backward. "May God have mercy on your soul."

"It's not an actual flu, Monk. It's the Blue Flu," Stottlemeyer said. "It's what happens when all the officers call in sick even though they aren't."

"Why would they want to do that?" Monk said.

"To make a statement to management," Stottlemeyer said. "It's the only leverage we have if we can't strike. It could happen in the next day or so, but you didn't hear it from me."

"Why are you telling us?" I asked.

"Because it means you might not work for a while," Stottlemeyer said.

"What about the criminals?" Monk asked. "Are they going to take a sick day, too?"

"I wish they would," Stottlemeyer said, and hopped on one foot back to his car.

2

Mr. Monk Goes Shopping

The local newscasts that night led with the announcement that negotiations between the police officers' union and city negotiators had reached an impasse. It appeared the failure of the talks only hardened the resolve on both sides not to budge from their positions.

San Francisco mayor Barry Smitrovich vowed to bring the city's budget under control and not bow to pressure to make concessions to the police officers.

"Everyone in this city is going to have to make some painful sacrifices," Smitrovich said, standing behind a podium erected outside his family's popular seafood restaurant on Fisherman's Wharf. "That includes our police officers, who have enjoyed higher salaries and better medical and pension benefits than most of their fellow city employees. We can't afford that any longer."

Smitrovich was a heavyset, balding man with a bulbous nose, big hands, and a perpetual blush. He looked to me like he'd be a lot more comfortable on a fishing trawler than standing in a suit behind that podium.

"We all appreciate the hard work, dedication, and courage of our city's police force. It is the finest in the nation. But we can't ignore the fiscal realities facing this city," he said. "Let me remind the fine men and women in blue that they have sworn to uphold the law, including those that forbid them from striking and putting the public's safety at risk."

Biff Nordoff, leader of the police union and an ex-cop himself, had a face like a tire tread. You could see every year he'd spent on the force. He gave a statement in front of a police car.

"When you're a cop on the street, you expect your partner to be there to watch your back, to look out for you, to support you, to keep you safe," Nordoff said. "Today our partner, the city of San Francisco, said they weren't going to do that anymore. They said they didn't carc if our families are cared for, if our kids get an education, if we will be secure in our old age. And yet they want us to put our lives on the line without anyone watching our back. That's just wrong."

That story was followed by KGO-TV reporter Margo Cole, who had more synthetic parts than the Bionic Woman, reporting live from Potrero Hill. She stared gravely into the camera with her fish lips. Her grim expression probably had more to do with her Botox injections than the story she was reporting.

"The killer who has been preying on female joggers has claimed a third victim, identified as Serena Mirkova, twenty-three, a recent immigrant from the Republic of Georgia. She was found this morning in McKinley Park."

Margo repeated details on the other killings and underscored the police department's lack of progress on the case, although there was a shot of Stottlemeyer, looking stiff and uncomfortable on camera, saying that the department was pursuing several potential leads. Then it was back to Margo for the final word.

"The killer's reign of terror is driving women off the streets after nightfall. They are shuddering in fear behind their locked doors and windows, wondering when or if the police will finally catch the Golden Gate Strangler."

Well, at least now the killer had a name.

Margo didn't mention anything about the missing running shoes because the police were holding back that detail from the media.

The next morning 70 percent of the city's police force called in sick, and several sources in city government told the *San Francisco Chronicle* that they feared the city could be swept by a crime wave.

I figured that was just inflammatory rhetoric spread by City Hall in an effort to turn public opinion against the cops. But as much as I supported Stottlemeyer and Disher, I was worried that the sick-out did leave average citizens like myself more vulnerable than usual.

Luckily, I got paid my pitiful salary whether Monk was on a case or not. I wasn't simply his investigative assistant—I was also his driver, his secretary, his spokeswoman, his personal shopper, and his Sherpa through the urban jungle of San Francisco.

The one thing I wasn't was his maid. But I didn't have to worry about his ever asking me to do his dishes, sweep his floor, or clean his windows because he enjoyed doing those tasks himself way too much. In fact, I often had to restrain him from cleaning my house, too.

It's not that I wouldn't appreciate his taking over all my housework. I hate housework, can't afford a maid, and never have enough time do all the things that need doing. The problem is that he's overzealous where tidiness is concerned.

Believe it or not, there's such a thing as a house that's *too* clean and *too* orderly.

The one time I let him straighten up my place, it looked like a model home afterward, and not in a good way. There was none of the domestic disorder that naturally comes from living in a house and that makes a home, well, homey. He made it creepy. Not only that, it smelled like a hospital.

I also like to have some privacy, which isn't easy when you're a single mother raising a twelve-year-old daughter. The last thing I wanted was Monk rummaging around in my closet.

Since Monk had no investigation to occupy his time, and he'd cleaned his place as much as he could without opening his walls and buffing the studs, I took him shopping with me. Julie needed new school clothes, and there was a big clearance sale at the Nordstrom in the San Francisco Centre mall.

Julie was unbelievably brand-conscious. I could buy a pair of jeans for ten dollars at Wal-Mart, slice them up with a knife, and run over them with my car, and they'd look just like the jeans she wanted that cost $150. But no, she had to have the name brand or face becoming a social outcast, forever exiled to the geek corner of the cafeteria. Or so she claimed.

I wanted my daughter to know that who you are is more than the sum of the designer trademarks that you wear, but it was a losing battle. If her clothes and shoes didn't scream Von Dutch or Juicy, Hard Tail or Paul Frank, True Religion or Nike, she refused to be seen in public.

The only way I could afford the clothes and shoes that she absolutely had to have was to wait like a vulture for the big sales and then pounce the moment the stores opened, which is what I was doing with Monk.

While I sorted through the clearance items, wrestling with other desperate, henpecked mothers over pants, blouses, running shoes, and T-shirts, Monk was occupied at one of the carousels of bargain blouses, which were arranged in groups according to size.

The arrangement of blouses wasn't good enough for him. He didn't like the blouses all mixed up like that. He organized them by brand, color, and pattern, then by sizes within those groups. Any blouses without a match in brand, color, or design he set aside in a section (more like a purgatory) of their own.

I was glancing at Monk when a hugely pregnant woman snatched a blouse from right in front of me, the last one in Julie's size. The woman looked like she was about to deliver twins, or perhaps quadruplets, at any moment.

"That's mine," I said.

"That's funny, lady, since it's in my hand and not yours."

"I had it in front of me," I said.

"The whole table is in front of you," she said. "Does that mean all of the blouses on it are yours too?"

Her purse slid off her shoulder onto the floor. When she bent over to pick it up, I was half tempted to kick her in the butt, but I restrained myself. I knew what it was like to be pregnant. The hormones can turn you into a monster. Maybe she was a sweet, good-natured woman when she wasn't knocked up.

She walked away and I saw Monk looking at her, too. From the expression on his face, he didn't seem any fonder of her than I was. He went back to organizing the carousel and I continued searching for values.

I ended up finding a Juicy jacket, a pair of Von Dutch pants, a couple of Paul Frank T-shirts, and a pair of running shoes that altogether cost less than any one of those items would individually at their original prices.

I felt so good about my shopping prowess that I took Monk to the Nordstrom café for a snack, my treat. It wasn't particularly magnanimous of me, since I knew that all he'd order was a bottle of Sierra Springs water.

On the way to the café he nearly collided with an old man who came around a pillar wheeling an oxygen tank behind him. He was wheezing, the tiny tubes from the tank running up to his nose. Now that I saw him up close, he wasn't as old as I thought he was, maybe in his sixties. His grizzled cheeks were sunken and his eyes were fierce.

"Pardon us," I said, and hurried along.

But Monk didn't move. He was examining the man as if he were another species.

"Smoke three packs a day for thirty years and you can have one of these, too," the man wheezed, and knocked his knuckles against the tank.

Monk cocked his head and narrowed his eyes. I went back, tugged him by the sleeve, and led him into the café. We sat at the bar, where a flat-screen TV was tuned to the midday news. I ordered Monk his water and got myself a coffee and a strawberry tart.

I noticed that the pregnant woman was in the café too, sitting at table, eating a piece of cake. It looked like she hadn't bought the blouse after all. I was tempted to run back to the kids' department and look for it.

Monk was still staring at the old man with the oxygen tank, who was walking through the aisles in the men's department outside the café.

"Stop staring," I said. "It isn't polite."

"I'm not staring," Monk said. "I'm observing."

"Could you at least try to be subtle about it?"

Monk smiled. "That's like asking a snake if he can slither."

He picked up a menu, held it in front of his face, and peered over the edge, observing the old man and then observing the pregnant woman and then observing a nun who was sipping a cup of coffee and idly toying with the cross around her neck. By trying to be subtle, he'd made himself even more obvious. People were staring at *him* now.

I decided to ignore him and glanced at the TV. Mayor Smitrovich was holding a press conference from City Hall. I thought it might be news about the Blue Flu, so I asked the bartender to crank up the volume so I could hear what the Mayor was saying.

". . . which is why I'm announcing a two-hundred-and-fifty-thousand-dollar reward for any information from the public leading to the arrest and conviction of the Golden Gate Strangler," the mayor said. "Please call the number on your screen if you can help in any way."

I plucked the menu from Monk's hands and gestured to the TV. "Listen to this."

"We can't let one man terrorize the city," Smitrovich was saying. "Especially now, when our police force has abandoned their responsibility to our citizens with their illegal walkout."

I jotted the phone number on a napkin. "This could be a big opportunity for you, Mr. Monk."

And for me, too. If he got the $250,000 reward, he could give me a fat raise and I wouldn't have to wait for clearance sales to buy my daughter clothes.

"I'm not eligible for the reward," Monk said. "I'm already on the case. I'm a city employee."

"You were. Now you're just a private citizen who is going to get a quarter of a million dollars for solving the murders."

But Monk wasn't listening to me anymore. He was staring at the old man. "He's still standing."

"Good for him," I said. "He's a fighter."

"He should be flat on his back by now."

"Mr. Monk, I'm surprised at you. Where's your compassion?"

Monk slid off his stool and marched over to the old man. I gathered up my bags and chased after him.

"Okay, gramps, the jig is up," Monk said, blocking the man's path.

"The jig?" the old man wheezed.

"You're going down." Monk jabbed his finger at the man's face.

"Get out of my way." The old man pushed past him, but Monk put his foot in front of the wheels of the oxygen tank trolley, stopping it.

"The only place you're going is jail," Monk said.

"Leave me alone," the old man yelled, yanking his trolley free.

Monk pulled his sleeves down over his hands and embraced the tank, holding it tight. The old man tugged, but Monk refused to let go.

"Give it up, geezer," Monk said.

I stood between the two of them and looked at Monk. "What are you doing?

"He's a fake," Monk said. "Call security."

But I didn't have to. Two beefy guys with matching earpieces and identical ill-fitting jackets approached out of nowhere. One of them spoke up.

"I'm Ned Wilton, store security. What's the problem here?"

Wilton was an African-American man with a barrel chest and a military buzz cut. He looked like a weight lifter turned Secret Service agent.

"Isn't it obvious?" the old man said, gasping for breath. "I'm being attacked by this lunatic."

"He's part of a shoplifting ring," Monk said.

The old man started coughing. Wilton glanced at him, then back at Monk.

"Did you see this man steal any items?"

"No," Monk said. Wilton's jaw muscles tightened. I wondered if worked on those muscles at the gym, too.

"Then why do you think he's a shoplifter?"

"Look at the gauge on his oxygen tank," Monk said. "It's empty."

The old man abruptly collapsed on the floor and began to gasp for breath, clutching at his chest. The other security guy crouched at his side. "We'd better call an ambulance."

Wilton nodded, and the other man spoke into a radio he had pulled out of his jacket pocket.

"It's an act," Monk said. "The gauge has been at zero for at least five minutes, and you saw him wrestling with me over the tank. If he really had emphysema, his skin would be blue by now."

The old man was having spasms, writhing and choking on the floor. A crowd of horrified shoppers was beginning to gather. Wilton broke out in a sweat.

"I think he's dying," the other security guy said.

Monk ignored him. "The tank is full of stolen merchandise. The lining of the tank jams the security tags, allowing him to go in and out of the store without setting off the sensors."

The old man gurgled. His legs twitched. Even Wilton wasn't buying the performance now.

Wilton unlatched the top of the tank. It was stuffed to the rim with designer clothing.

The old man stopped flopping and sighed with resignation. "Oh, hell," he said.

"Your days of villainy are over," Monk said.

"Thank you, sir," Wilton said to Monk. "We appreciate the assist. I think we've got it covered now."

"Then you know about the pregnant lady," Monk said.

"What pregnant lady?"

Monk motioned to the woman in the café, who was standing up at her table and heading out. "The one who isn't pregnant."

She glanced at us and must have seen something on our faces she didn't like. She bolted. Without even thinking, I charged after her. It was no contest. I took her down with a flying tackle, a skill I learned from my brother.

We hit the ground hard. Her tummy pack burst open like a piñata, spilling clothes and toiletries all over the floor. The woman snarled at me, and I snarled right back. I grabbed the blouse she'd taken from me and I held it up in my fist victoriously.

You don't want to get between a mother, her daughter, and a Juicy blouse at 80 percent off the regular price.

Monk and Wilton rushed over. Wilton restrained the woman and called for more backup on his radio. I got to my feet.

"Nice tackle," Monk said.

"How did you know she wasn't pregnant?" I asked.

"She walked straight and didn't waddle. And when she dropped her purse, she bent at the waist to pick it up."

I didn't notice that, and I was standing right behind her at the time. I guess I was blinded by righteous shopper indignation.

Wilton looked back at Monk. "Anybody else we should know about?"

"The nun in the café," Monk said.

She was still sitting at the table, pretending not to notice us, toying with her cross.

"She's wearing a habit from the order of Saint Martha of Bethany, but she's got a crucifix around her neck with a figure of Jesus on it," Monk said. "The nuns of that order wear a simple gold cross. She's the ringleader and the lookout."

A half dozen other security personnel showed up, and Wilton sent two of them into the café to apprehend the non-nun.

"This was fun," Monk said. "We should go shopping more often."

I folded the blouse and headed toward the nearest cashier. I didn't want to get arrested for shoplifting. "You're very observant, Mr. Monk."

"No," Monk said with a satisfied smile. "I stare."

3

Mr. Monk and the Straight Answer

I hid my purchases for Julie in my room. She had a report card coming up in a few days, and I decided to save the new clothes and shoes as a reward for the good grades I knew she was going to get.

Saturday morning, the mother of one of Julie's friends called and offered to take the kids to the movies, one of those Lindsay Lohan sequels to a Disney remake. She invited me to come along too, but I bowed out. I was looking forward to a few hours of peace. Plus, I was going to owe that mother a Saturday off. That was how it worked and, believe me, the moms kept track.

No sooner was Julie out the door than Stottlemeyer called. I figured he was looking for Monk, and that it meant there was another murder to investigate. So much for my free day.

"Monk isn't here," I said. "It's Saturday, so he's probably outside scrubbing his sidewalk."

"I'm not looking for Monk," Stottlemeyer said. "I was thinking you might be free for a coffee or something." Before I could reply, he quickly added, "I'm not asking you out."

"Of course not," I said. Then I cringed, thinking of all the different, hurtful ways he could take that. His wife had just left him, so his self-confidence must have been in the toilet as it was. The last thing he needed was me making him feel like the least desirable man on earth. "I mean, not that you aren't datable. You've very datable. What I meant was that I knew you didn't mean it the way it could have been meant, know what I mean?"

"Yeah," he said. "This was a bad idea. Forget I called. This never happened."

When Karen walked out on Stottlemeyer, I told him to call me if he needed anything. It was a safe offer to make, since I knew the captain would never take me up on it. For one thing, Stottlemeyer was a cop, so he had to be tough, stoic, and invulnerable, because to be anything else would be a sign of weakness (which is probably one of the reasons his marriage tanked, but what do I know?). For another thing, we weren't friends. The only connection we really had was our concern and affection for Adrian Monk.

Obviously, I was wrong.

"Wait, it's okay," I said. "A coffee sounds great. Really great. I was looking for an excuse not to do laundry, wash the dishes, and pay bills. Where would you like to meet?"

We met at a coffeehouse and newsstand down the block from me. The place was filled with ratty couches and armchairs, which I'm sure the owner thought gave it a homey, *Friends*-like feel. Instead it felt like we were having coffee in a crummy apartment. But the coffee was good and the place was close by.

Stottlemeyer looked almost as worn down as the furniture: hair askew, puffy eyes, wrinkled clothes. I wanted to hug him, but that's the mother in me. I want to hug everybody who looks the least bit unhappy. I never had that urge until Julie was born. Instead we shook hands.

He mumbled a "How are you?" and we made some unmemorable small talk while we ordered our coffee and pastries and found a table. Then there was a long, awkward moment of silence while we blew on our coffees and tried to ignore the long, awkward moment of silence.

"I'm beginning to understand Monk a whole lot better," he finally said.

"Why is that?"

"He always had his problems, but when he was with Trudy, he found a balance. He could function. But after he lost her, he lost himself," Stottlemeyer said. "He fell apart. He tries desperately to organize every little detail of the world around him because he thinks if he succeeds, he can put himself back together again."

"You've always known that," I said.

"Yeah, but not like I know it now," Stottlemeyer said.

"Why is that?"

"I'm alone," he said. "You'd think I wouldn't mind, considering."

"Considering what?"

"My wife used to tell me I was in my own little world, shutting her and everybody else out," he said. "She said that it was like living in the house alone. But it's not. I know the difference."

"Now you do," I said, and regretted it the instant the words came out of my mouth.

He nodded. "Yeah, I guess I do."

"I'm sorry," I said.

"Don't be," Stottlemeyer said. "I'm lucky I stayed married as long as I did, given my profession. I see the worst side of humanity every day. I thought I was protecting her from it. Do you think if I told her everything, if I came home and vomited up my day, she'd still be with me?"

I shrugged.

He stared into his coffee. "Up until now, I always had the job to keep me busy, to occupy my time. The thing is, Natalie, I don't know how to be alone."

"You aren't," I said. "You still have your family and friends."

"Is that what people told you when your husband died?"

"Your wife isn't dead."

"She might as well be," he said. "And each time I see her and she walks away, I die a little, too."

"Have you told her that?"

"She knows," Stottlemeyer said.

I wasn't going to argue the point. I didn't know him or Karen well enough to judge whether he was right.

"So you're afraid you're going to turn into Mr. Monk?"

"As a matter of fact, yes, I am," he said. "Only without the part where I become brilliant at solving crimes."

"That's not going to happen."

"Natalie, you know what I did last night? I shined my shoes. I *never* shine my shoes."

"Did you measure the laces to be sure they were even? Did you place them in their original, mint-condition shoe boxes and arrange them by color?"

"No," he said.

"Then you aren't Monk," I said.

"It sure felt Monkish to me," Stottlemeyer said. "I took one look at my shoes this morning, went outside, and rubbed mud all over them."

Okay, now *that* was strange. But I kept my opinion to myself.

"Shining your shoes, cleaning your pantry, whatever—it's the little things, the mundane rituals and responsibilities of life, that get you through the worst of it," I said. "You're functioning even if you feel like you're not. I think it's part of healing. And then one day, you wake up and the sadness isn't so heavy and your garage is organized. It's like a bonus."

He seemed to mull that over for a while; then he sighed. "Thanks, Natalie. I appreciate this."

"Anytime, Captain," I said, purposely keeping it formal. I didn't want him rebounding in my direction. "What are you going to do now?"

He shrugged. "Start cleaning my garage, I guess."

My cell phone rang. It was Monk. And I couldn't believe what he told me.

"I'll be right over," I said. I snapped the phone shut and stared at Stottlemeyer.

"What is it?" he asked.

"The mayor wants to see Mr. Monk," I said. "Do you think the mayor wants him to work on a case?"

I saw the possibility of Monk's getting the reward for the capture of the Golden Gate Strangler disappearing along with any hope of my getting a raise.

"He knows Monk won't work with any cop but me," Stottlemeyer said. "And that no cop but me will work with Monk."

"Then what could it be?"

"Maybe he wants Monk to negotiate with the police union," Stottlemeyer said.

"Why would the mayor want him to do that?"

"Can you think of a better way to break the will of the union negotiators?" Stottlemeyer said. "After an hour in a room with Monk, they'll either shoot him or shoot themselves."

The San Francisco City Hall was built not long after the 1906 earthquake to scream to the world that the city was back—bigger, stronger, and more opulent than ever.

The building's Beaux Arts flourishes, Doric columns, and Grand Baroque copper dome meant you'd never mistake it for anything but a capitol of some kind. As if the grand dome wasn't grand enough, it was topped with an ornate steeple and a torch that lit up at night whenever the city council met.

The building always struck me as garish and pompous, rather than majestic and imposing. I guess that's fitting for a place that houses mostly politicians and bureaucrats.

But standing in Mayor Smitrovich's office, I felt like I was in an aquarium. There were tarpon, swordfish, and dorados mounted on the walls, their mouths agape, forever twisting in midthrash. A pair of window cleaners worked outside, peering in at us from the other side of the glass behind the mayor. All that was missing to make the effect complete was a ceramic mermaid and a castle for us to swim around. We introduced ourselves.

"It's a real pleasure to finally meet you, Mr. Monk," Smitrovich said, coming around the desk and shaking Monk's hand. "I'm a big fan."

I handed Monk a moist towelette.

"Really?" Monk said, wiping his hand.

"I truly appreciate your tireless efforts on behalf of this city."

"That's such a relief. I was beginning to think you were ignoring all my letters," Monk said. "It's about time someone in authority ended our city's shame and turned Lombard from the world's crookedest street to the straightest."

"You want to *straighten* Lombard?" the mayor said.

"Whoever approved that street should have been beaten with his T square," Monk said. "It's a good thing he was stopped before every street in the city looked like Lombard. It's astonishing to me that nobody has ever bothered to correct it."

"You know how it is, Mr. Monk," the mayor

said. "There are so many other pressing issues that demand our attention."

"What could be more important than that?"

"Actually," the mayor said, "that's why I asked you here today."

"You're not straightening Lombard?"

"Not just yet."

"I know you'll face some opposition from a wacko minority of hippies and beatniks. But I'll back you one hundred percent."

"That's reassuring, because I truly need your support," the mayor said. "It's clear to me that we both share a deep and abiding love for this great city."

"It can't be great as long as the world's crookedest street is here," Monk said. "What would be great is a city with the world's *straightest* street. Just think of all the tourists who would come here to see it."

"Millions of tourists *do* come to see Lombard Street," the mayor said.

"To ridicule us," Monk said. "Where do you think the phrase 'those crazy Americans' comes from? Lombard Street. Fix the street and they'll never say it again."

"Right now, I'm more concerned about the lack of police officers reporting to work. Most of the patrol officers are on the job; it's the detectives and supervisory personnel who aren't showing up," the mayor said. "It's creating a serious public-safety issue. We don't have the manpower to investigate major felonies. You know how important the first forty-eight hours are in an investigation. Tracks are getting cold. Something must be done about this, especially with this strangler on the loose. They couldn't have picked a worse time to pull this crap."

"You could drop your demands for big cuts in police salaries and benefits," I said. "I bet that would bring the detectives back to work."

"Sure, I could give the police officers what they want," the mayor said, shooting me an angry look before shifting his gaze back to Monk, "but then where would the money come from to straighten Lombard Street?"

Monk glanced at me. "He has a point."

"No, he doesn't," I said. "With all due respect, Mr. Smitrovich, these people lay their lives on the line for us. We owe them a decent wage, affordable medical care, and a comfortable retirement."

"And what should I tell the sewer workers, the schoolteachers, and the firefighters who aren't enjoying the same benefits, Miss Teeger? And what do I tell the citizens who want new schools and cleaner, safer, *straighter* streets?"

The last bit was clearly for Monk's benefit, but Monk wasn't paying attention. He was tipping this way and that, trying to peer around the mayor.

The mayor looked over his shoulder to see what was distracting Monk. All he saw were the two window cleaners, running their blades across the glass, wiping away the soap.

"You didn't invite Mr. Monk down here to give him the city's party line on the labor negotiations," I said. "You want something from him."

"That's true, I do," the mayor said, addressing

Monk. "I'd like your help solving the city's homicides."

But Monk was busy waving at the window cleaners. They waved back. Monk waved again. They waved back. Monk waved again and they ignored him.

"Mr. Monk consults for the police because of his special relationship with Captain Stottlemeyer," I said. "He's not going to work for another detective."

I looked at Monk for confirmation, but now he was wiping the air with his hand palm-out in front of him. The window cleaners finally understood and soaped the window again. Monk smiled approvingly as they wiped it with their blades.

"I don't want him to work for any other detectives," the mayor said. "I want *them* to work for *him*."

"I don't understand," I said.

"I want to reinstate him to the San Francisco Police Department," the mayor said, "and promote him to captain of the homicide division."

"Is this some kind of joke?" I asked. "Because if it is, it's cruel."

"I'm completely serious," the mayor said.

Monk marched over to the window and tapped on the glass. "You missed a spot."

The window cleaners shrugged. They couldn't hear him. He mimed spraying the window and wiping the glass in front of him again. They shook their heads no.

I looked at the mayor. "Now I know you're joking."

"He's got a better solve rate than all the detectives in the homicide department put together, and at a fraction of the cost. With Monk at the helm, the homicide department could do the same job, or better than, they've been doing, with at least half as many men. Besides, I think he's ready for command."

"Are we talking about the same man?" I said. "Look at him."

Monk shook his head at the cleaners and pointed to the spot they had just cleaned. The two cleaners started hoisting their platform up to the next floor. Monk banged on the glass.

"Get back down here," Monk yelled.

The mayor smiled. "I see a man with an incredible eye for detail and a commitment to sticking with a task until it's done right."

Monk turned to me. I hoped he'd finally say something about the mayor's outrageous offer.

"I need a wipe," Monk said.

"Excuse us for a moment," I said to the mayor, then went over to Monk and handed him a wipe. "Did you hear what the mayor just said?"

Monk tore open the packet, took out the wipe, and began scrubbing the glass with it.

"What are you doing?" I asked.

Monk looked at his wipe and shook his head. "Silly me, the shmutz was inside."

He turned to the mayor and held up the wipe. "Crisis solved. You can relax now."

"Then you'll take the job?" the mayor said.

"What job?" Monk asked.

"Captain of the homicide division," the mayor said.

Monk looked at the wipe in astonishment, then at me. "This was all I had to do? All these years I've been working to get back in and it comes down to this?"

"Mr. Monk," I said quietly, so the mayor couldn't hear me. "He's taking advantage of you. He's using you as a ploy to break the strike. You'll be a scab."

Monk winced with revulsion. "A scab? That sounds disgusting."

"They are," I said. "You'd be relieving some of the pressure on the city and undermining the officers' efforts to get a better contract."

"But he's offering me my badge," Monk said.

"He's offering you Captain Stottlemeyer's job," I said.

Monk handed me the dirty wipe, then faced the mayor. "I want the job, but not at the captain's expense."

"You'd just be filling in until this labor situation is resolved, commanding a handful of other reinstated detectives who, for various reasons, had to leave the department," the mayor said. "But if you do a good job, and I know you will, this temporary assignment could become a permanent position at another division. I know you want to support the captain, but think about all those crimes going unsolved. Do you want people getting away with murder?"

Monk looked at me. "How can I say no?"

"Repeat after me," I said. *"No."*

Monk considered that for a moment, then turned to the mayor. "I'll do it."

4

Mr. Monk Takes Command

Before we left his office, Mayor Smitrovich gave Monk a badge and me a stack of personnel files on Monk's team of detectives. I was more than a little leery about them. They'd been booted from the force. That meant they could be corrupt or inept. They could be alcoholics or drug addicts. They could be certifiably insane. Or they could be all of the above.

How much could Monk really depend on them? Or trust them?

Monk certainly couldn't expect to get support from any of the competent, able-bodied cops who were still on the job. The officers had to know that if Monk and his motley crew of detectives succeeded, the rank and file would end up with lower wages and lost benefits. And the cops who'd walked out, especially Stottlemeyer and Disher, were going to look at what Monk was doing as a flat-out betrayal.

Even if Monk's reinstatement continued after the contract dispute was resolved, his fellow cops would never forget—or forgive—how he got his badge back. He'd be ostracized. He'd be an outsider in the department he so desperately wanted to be a part of again.

But whatever worries I had about the task ahead, Monk certainly didn't share them. He practically skipped out of the building into the Civic Center Plaza, his gold badge in his hand. I wouldn't have been surprised if he broke into song.

To be honest, I was pissed at him, and not just because he was blithely ignoring the pitfalls of his decision.

I'm a die-hard liberal, and while I wasn't 100 percent behind the police sick-out, I was a big believer in supporting labor unions.

There weren't any actual picket lines, but I felt as if we'd crossed one anyway. And I was pretty sure Stottlemeyer and Disher and anybody else in blue would feel the same way.

And yet I knew Monk had only two goals in life: to get his badge back and to solve his wife's murder. For a long time, both seemed hopelessly out of his reach. And now the mayor was offering to make one of those dreams come true. I knew what that badge meant to Monk. It was an acknowledgment to himself and the world that he'd finally put his life back together after years of lonely struggle.

Monk was right: How could he possibly say no? Who was I to begrudge him this opportunity?

Nobody.

I was his employee. My job, literally, was to support him. No one else was going to; that was for sure.

So I tried to put my anger and frustration aside and focus on what I was paid to do, which was to make his life easier.

I found a bench in the plaza and sat down to go through the files.

Monk stood off to one side, silently admiring his badge, seeing how it caught the light. I think he was trying to convince himself that it was real.

I opened up the first personnel file. The rugged, grim face of Jack Wyatt stared back at me with flinty eyes and gritted teeth. It was as if he were having a colonoscopy while the picture was taken.

Wyatt was a veteran detective in his forties with an amazing case-closure rate and a body count to match it. His violent, unconventional methods earned him the nickname "Mad Jack" on the street and within the department. According to the file, he once ended a high-speed chase with a suspected serial killer by lobbing a hand grenade into the guy's car. (I couldn't find any explanation for why Jack was carrying around explosives.)

It wasn't until the city lost several lawsuits arising from Wyatt's cases that his violent behavior and complete disregard for civil rights finally caught up with him. His badge was yanked three years ago. Since then, he'd been working as what was euphemistically called a "security consultant" in hot spots like Iraq and Afghanistan.

What a charming guy.

There was no picture of Cynthia Chow in her personnel file and not a lot of information, either.

Someone had taken a Magic Marker and blacked out any names, dates, locations, and identifying details because her cases were still classified. That was because Chow spent much of her police career undercover, leading a dangerous double life where the slightest mistake or miscalculation could get her killed.

To survive undercover, she had to live in a constant state of paranoia, which came naturally for her. It gradually became clear as I read that she was a paranoid schizophrenic. She saw conspiracies everywhere and believed that she was under constant surveillance. That much, at least, was true. Her superiors got increasingly concerned by her erratic behavior and kept a very close eye on her, telling her it was all part of the case. It wasn't.

After the resolution of her last undercover case, she was put into therapy and reassigned to homicide. But her paranoid delusions only got worse. By the time she was relieved of her badge, she claimed the government was listening to her thoughts, and space aliens were trying to impregnate her.

The file didn't say what she'd been doing since then. That had been redacted, too.

Frank Porter's file was actually several bulging folders strapped together with thick rubber bands. He'd spent forty-five years on the force, the last two decades in the homicide division.

There were two pictures of him in the file. One was a faded black-and-white photo of a gangly young officer with a crew cut, presumably taken at his graduation from the academy. The other picture was in color and showed a heavier man with jowls, bags under his eyes, and a wide, garish tie that was cinched too tight around his thick neck.

He'd earned an impressive number of commendations over the years for his steady, dependable police work. He probably would still be at a desk in the homicide department if health problems and "the clear onset of senility" hadn't forced him to retire last year.

I closed the files, snapped the rubber bands back into place, and reviewed what I'd learned. Monk's team of crack detectives was comprised of a violent sociopath, a paranoid schizophrenic, and a senile old man.

Monk was in deep trouble.

"You should take a look at these files," I said.

"I don't think so," Monk said.

"There are things you need to know about these detectives the mayor has assigned to you."

"I already know everything I need to know. They're police officers."

"You don't understand. These are some deeply troubled people. They were thrown off the force because they were incapable of functioning in their jobs."

"So was I," Monk said.

He gave his badge one more fond look, then slipped it into his inside jacket pocket.

Sure, he was happy, but the giddy glee had waned, and I saw a hint in his downcast eyes of the sadness he always carried with him. That was when I realized that although he didn't know any of these detectives, he probably understood them better than anyone else.

And maybe, just maybe, he was exactly the right person to lead them.

The homicide division was almost empty and surprisingly quiet when we arrived. A couple of uniformed officers were answering phones, but that was all that was happening. Take away the uniforms and the guns, and it could have been lunch hour in an accountant's office.

Monk touched each desk lamp he passed as he made his way to the captain's office. I've never understood why he needed to tap a row of identical objects, like parking meters and streetlights, and keep a running count. Maybe it calmed him down. Maybe it created the illusion that there was actually some order in the chaotic world around him.

He stopped in the doorway to the captain's office and gazed at the clutter—the stacks of files (of cases past and present), the assorted coffee mugs (some used as pencil holders), the photographs (of Stottlemeyer's family and fellow cops), the knickknacks (like the acrylic paperweight that held a bullet taken from the captain's shoulder), and the spare overcoat, jacket, shirt, and tie Stottlemeyer always kept on the coatrack.

The clutter had increased in recent months. Since the captain's marriage had crumbled, the office had become his home. I was surprised he hadn't moved his bedroom set in.

"I can't work in here," Monk said.

I nodded. It was going to be a monumental chore to organize the office to Monk's liking. It could take months and every available officer on the force working twenty-four/seven to make it happen. It might even require the complete demolition of the building.

"I'm sure it can be straightened up," I said.

He shook his head. "No, this is the captain's office."

"You're the captain now."

Monk walked away, heading across the squad room and down the corridor to the interrogation rooms. He entered the first one he came to. I followed him inside.

The room was stark and cold and dimly lit. The walls were the same gunmetal gray as the metal desk and the matching stiff-backed metal chairs.

Monk sat down in one of the chairs and faced the mirror, which, of course, hid the observation room.

"This will do," he said.

"Do as what?"

"My office," he said.

"Don't you think it's a little sterile?"

He smiled. "Yes, I do."

A young female officer stepped into the room. "Excuse me, Captain Monk?"

Monk looked up, an expression of disbelief on his face. "Captain Monk?"

"You are Captain Monk, aren't you?" the officer asked.

"I'm not sure," he said.

"He is," I said, and introduced myself as his assistant.

"I'm Officer Susan Curtis," she said. "I've been temporarily assigned to clerical duties in the homicide division."

"How unusual that they'd pick a female officer for that," I said.

"Yeah, what a surprise," she said ruefully. "A real incentive not to catch the flu."

It was a bonding moment between the two of us. Well, I *hoped* it was. We needed to have an officer on our side, or, at the very least, one who didn't loathe us for being scabs.

"Is there anything you need, sir?"

"I need a hundred-page, spiral-bound notepad with exactly forty-two spirals. The pages should be white with thirty-four blue lines spaced an eighth of an inch apart. I'll also need four paper clips, two square erasers, a desk lamp like the ones outside, a telephone, and ten unsharpened number two pencils."

Officer Curtis left. Monk looked up at me. I looked back at him. There was a very uncomfortable silence.

"What do I do now?" he said meekly.

"You're the cop, not me."

"Give me a hint," he said.

I sighed. "I suppose you could ask for the file on the Golden Gate Strangler case, go over the crime lab reports, and check to see if Lieutenant Disher discovered whether the victims all bought shoes from the same store."

"Good idea," Monk said. "You should get right on that."

"I'm not a cop," I reminded him.

"I can deputize you."

"No, you can't."

"Yes, I can."

"This isn't the Old West and you aren't the town sheriff rounding up a posse."

"Perhaps you've forgotten who you're dealing with," Monk said. "I'm a captain in the homicide division of the San Francisco Police Department."

"Then start acting like it," I said and walked out, nearly colliding with Frank Porter in the hall.

The retired detective hobbled into the squad room, with a young woman following two steps behind him, dragging her feet as if she were carrying a two-hundred-pound pack on her bony shoulders.

Porter wore an oversize cardigan sweater, a checkered shirt, and corduroy pants with crumbs caught in the ridges. His head reminded me of a vacant lot, dry and empty, with weedy patches of rangy hair. Drool spilled over the edge of his thin, chapped lips like water over an earthen dam.

"Frank Porter, reporting for duty." He offered me his age-spotted hand.

"I'm Natalie Teeger, Captain Monk's assistant." I shook his hand lightly, feeling all twenty-seven brittle bones under his thin skin like twigs wrapped in tissue. "I'm not a police officer."

"Technically, neither am I. This is my granddaughter Sparrow," Porter said. "I guess you could say she's my assistant. She looks out for me."

Sparrow shrugged. "Beats slinging burgers at McDonald's."

"I hear you," I said.

Sparrow was barely out of her teens, wore too

much eyeliner, had a dozen studs lining each of her ears, and was working really hard to radiate boredom and discontent. I knew the look. I'd perfected it when I was her age.

I excused myself and hunted Monk down. He wasn't in the interrogation room anymore. I found him in the evidence room, sitting at a table, looking at three right-foot running shoes that must have been recovered from the dead women. Each shoe was in a plastic evidence bag, and they were laid out in front of him in a vertical row.

"I can't live with this," Monk said.

It was true that three innocent women had been killed, but this wasn't the first time Monk had dealt with murder. I didn't understand why these deaths were affecting him so strongly.

"What happened to those women is a terrible thing," I agreed. "But is this really any different from the other murder cases you've solved?"

"I've never seen such depravity. This is a crime against nature," he said. "Wasn't it enough to take their lives? Did he have to take one of their shoes, too? He's upset the entire balance of the universe."

"By taking *three* shoes?"

"Shoes come in sets of two; that's the natural order," Monk said. "Until those shoes are recovered and this madman is caught, life as we know it is over."

"So you're saying that not only do you have to catch a killer—you have to restore the balance of the entire universe."

"It's my awesome responsibility now."

"At least you're not putting too much pressure

on yourself," I said. "One of your detectives is here."

Monk rose from the table and pointed at the shoes. "*That* is going to haunt my every waking moment."

"I believe it," I said.

"And my unawake moments," he said as he walked out. "And the nanoseconds in between."

I followed Monk into the squad room, where he strode right up to Porter and Sparrow with a smile on his face.

"Hello, Frank," Monk said. "It's been a long time."

"You two know each other?" I asked.

"Frank is one of the best investigators I've ever met," Monk said. "He can follow a paper trail to the tree it was milled from."

I'd never heard Monk lavish such praise on anyone's detective skills. Except his own, of course. I'd also never heard him use such a colorful metaphor. Or any metaphor, for that matter.

"Really?" I asked. "To the actual tree?"

"Of course," Monk said. "Why else would I have said it?"

"I thought it might be a figure of speech."

Monk looked at me as if I were insane.

"I haven't had a bowel movement in three days," Porter announced. "I need an enema."

"Now?" Monk's voice trembled.

"I can't think when I'm stuffed up."

"No one is asking you to think." Monk looked at me. "Did you ask him to think?"

Porter narrowed his eyes at Monk. "I remember

you. You're the nut job who kept reorganizing my desk."

Monk smiled. "Those were good times."

"He's afraid of milk," Porter said to Sparrow.

"You are?" she said, momentarily showing interest in something besides looking uninterested. "Why?"

"It's a bodily fluid in a glass that some twisted person intends to drink." Monk cringed just thinking about it. "It's unnatural."

"It's the most natural thing on earth," Sparrow said. "Babies suckle their mother's breasts for milk. That's what breasts are for."

"I breast-fed Julie," I said.

Monk flushed with embarrassment and looked away from me.

"Maybe you were breast-fed, Mr. Monk," I said.

"That's impossible. I wouldn't drink my own bodily fluids—why would I drink someone else's?"

"Breasts aren't just a fashion accessory," Sparrow said. I was beginning to like this kid. Until she lifted her shirt and flashed Monk.

I thought Monk might scream. I noticed that her ears weren't the only thing she'd pierced.

Porter slapped the desktop. "What's my assignment?"

Monk filled Porter in on the Golden Gate Strangler case and asked him to double-check the victims' credit card purchases. He also asked Porter to put together a board with all the crime scene photos and a map indicating where each murder took place.

"Gladly," Porter said. "And you are?"

"Adrian Monk."

"I remember you," Porter said, and glanced at Sparrow. "He's afraid of milk."

Sparrow sighed—the sound was infused with all the frustration, boredom, and weariness she could possibly muster. She almost broke out in a sweat from the effort.

Officer Curtis walked up and handed Monk a slip of paper. "There's been a homicide in Haight-Ashbury. There's a detective waiting for you at the scene."

"Who's the victim?" Monk asked.

"Allegra Doucet, an astrologer," Officer Curtis said. "You'd think she would have seen it coming."

5

Mr. Monk and the Astrologer

Ever since the mid-1960s, Haight-Ashbury has been mythologized as ground zero of the counterculture movement, home of psychedelic drugs, free-spirited sex, flower children, and the Grateful Dead. A lot of effort went into maintaining the illusion that it hasn't changed, even though Jerry Garcia is dead, the Vietnam War is ovcr, and Mick Jagger is getting the senior-citizen discount at Denny's.

The Haight today is the sixties packaged and sanitized for retail sale. The street is lined with stores selling vintage clothing, "underground" comics, used records, and incense and crystals; and there are even a few head shops where you can buy tie-dyed shirts and Deadhead souvenirs for the folks back home in Wichita. What little edge there is comes from the tattoo parlors, bondage emporiums, and stores with fetish paraphernalia, but let's face it, even kink has become mainstream these days.

Even so, it's possible to fool yourself into thinking you've hurtled back in time to the summer of 1967, but the illusion is shattered if you wander onto the side streets, where the real estate values of the restored Victorian and Edwardian homes are in the millions, and most of the parking spots are taken by Range Rovers and BMWs. These flower children downloaded their free love from the Internet and got a psychedelic high from bidding on eBay.

The late Allegra Doucet lived on a side street that hadn't been completely gentrified. A few houses and shops remained that looked as if they hadn't been painted since Jefferson Starship was still an Airplane. Doucet's wasn't one of them. Her Victorian house was freshly painted blue with white trim. It had wide bay windows above flower boxes brimming with colorful, blooming roses. A sign in the window said ALLEGRA DOUCET—ASTROLOGER AND SEER. BY APPOINTMENT ONLY, in elegant calligraphy.

When we drove up, the street in front of her house was clogged with police vehicles, a coroner's wagon, and a van from the scientific investigation unit. I didn't bother trying to find a place to park. Monk was the captain now, so I just stopped in the middle of the street, handed the keys for my Jeep Cherokee to a police officer, and told him to make sure nothing happened to the captain's ride.

Monk hurried out of the car while I was talking to

the officer. He hadn't looked at me since I mentioned at the station that I had breasts. I think he preferred to think of me as some kind of asexual creature.

He was met outside Doucet's door by a striking Asian woman in her thirties with sharp features and a piercing gaze that gave her an unsettling intensity. She was dressed entirely in black except for the SFPD badge hanging from her neck, the cap of aluminum foil on her head, and the transistor radio attached to it with duct tape. I could hear the low, static crackle of the local news from the speaker. I didn't think it was taped to her head so she could keep up on current events.

A bespectacled man stood beside her, completely absorbed in whatever he was rapidly text-messaging into his PDA. He looked like he'd fallen out of bed onto the pile of clothes he wore yesterday and decided, what the hell, he'd wear them another day. He wore an untucked, unbuttoned, wrinkled blue oxford over a wrinkled red T-shirt and wrinkled cargo pants. There was something undeniably academic about him. I don't know whether it was the glasses, the rumpled clothes, or just a general sense of studiousness.

"Who are you?" she asked Monk, her voice barely above a whisper.

Monk cocked his head and studied her with scientific curiosity.

"I'm Adrian Monk," he said.

"Prove it," she said.

Monk pulled out his badge and proudly showed it to me, to her, and to the man at her side.

"A badge like that can be bought in Union

Square for spit," she said. "If you really are who you say you are, then you won't object to giving me a swab of your DNA to confirm it."

She reached into the inside pocket of her leather jacket and pulled out a long Q-tip in a sterile package. This action inspired a flurry of excited thumb-typing by the guy beside her.

"You must be Detective Cindy Chow," I said.

She narrowed her eyes at me. "Who do you work for?"

I tipped my head to Monk. "Him. Your boss. The captain of homicide."

"She's my assistant, Natalie Teeger," Monk said.

"Who do you *really* work for?" Chow asked me.

"Nice hat," I said.

"It's crude but it effectively blocks the signal." She smiled. "And that just frustrates the hell out of you and your puppet masters, doesn't it?"

Monk looked incredulously in my general direction, but not exactly at me. He still hadn't forgotten I had breasts. "She's a detective?"

"You're the one who didn't want to read the files," I said.

"What files?" Chow said.

The guy standing next to her couldn't input this stuff into his PDA fast enough.

"Who is your buddy?" I asked.

The man paused in his typing. "Oh, I'm sorry. I should have said something, but I was trying not to influence the natural course of the interaction. I'm Jasper Perry, Cindy's psychiatric nurse."

"You can drop the charade," Chow said. "I know you both work for them."

"Them?" Monk said.

"The extraterrestrials occupying the shadow government," she said, getting a blank look from him. "The ones who designed the CIA's Operation Artichoke program to control the masses with fast food laced with mind-control drugs, subliminal messages in television shows, and transmissions from orbiting satellites to microchips implanted in our brains."

"Oh," Monk said. "Them."

"They wouldn't let me back on the force unless I agreed to let their spy here dope me up and keep me under constant surveillance."

"I'm curious about something," Monk said. "When you got your badge back, did it also come with a gun?"

"Of course," she replied. "Didn't yours?"

"No," Monk said.

"I'm not surprised," Chow said. "Word is that you're nuts."

I turned to Jasper, who was giving his thumbs a workout on his PDA keyboard. "Who are you e-mailing?"

"I'm sending notes to myself."

"About what?"

"Me," Chow said. "Letting his handlers know about everything I think, say, and do."

"Actually, I'm doing my doctoral thesis on the commonality of certain facets of complex, recurring conspiratorial delusions, which form an almost Jungian shared unconscious among paranoid schizophrenics, regardless of language, race, sex, or ethnicity, but that and this is the really surprising thing—incorporates mythological iconography from—"

"Where's the body?" Monk interrupted.

"Inside," Chow said.

Monk went into the house, and we all followed, though Jasper looked a little hurt that we'd so quickly lost interest in the topic of his doctoral thesis, whatever the hell it was.

The front room of Doucet's house was devoted to her business, but there was nothing about the sleek, contemporary decor that was related to astrology. No crystal balls or tarot cards. No beaded curtains or incense. This could easily have been the office of a shrink, a lawyer, or an accountant. There were two leather chairs facing a white wooden desk with a keyboard and a flat-screen monitor on top. The computer screen displayed a circle filled with multicolored numbers, crisscrossing lines, and strange symbols.

Doucet was facedown on the floor, her long black hair fanned out around her head and stuck in the brownish pool of dried blood.

When Officer Curtis said that the homicide victim was an astrologer, I immediately imagined a clichéd old crone with warts, cataracts, and a toothless grin.

But Doucet could have been a fashion model. She had smooth, darkly tanned skin, a slim figure, and was impeccably dressed in a Prada suit with the skirt cut just a bit too short to be professional.

Monk walked around her desk, tilting his head this way and that, holding his hands in front of him as if framing a shot for a movie. His footsteps echoed on the hardwood floor.

Jasper watched Monk in fascination. "What is he doing?"

"His thing," I said.

My gaze was on the Louis Vuitton handbag on a side table. The bag was worth more than my car. Doucet must have been very good at her job. I wondered if the money came from her clients or from using her soothsaying powers to successfully wager on stocks, horses, and the lottery.

"The ME says she was killed sometime last night, stabbed multiple times in the chest and stomach with an ice pick or letter opener," Chow said, standing behind the computer monitor. "One of her clients came by this morning, peeked in the window, and saw her body."

Monk looked at the image on the computer screen. "What is this?"

Chow took out a mirror from her pocket. She reached over the monitor and angled the mirror so she could see the reflection of what was on the screen.

"Why don't you just look at the screen?" I asked her.

"Because I don't want it looking back at me."

I had no idea what she was talking about. Jasper seemed to sense my confusion.

"Her fear is that computers allow the government to spy on us," Jasper whispered to me. "That they log our keystrokes and watch us from cameras hidden in the screens."

"It's a computer-generated, personal astrological

star chart based on how the planets and stars were aligned at the precise time and location of a person's birth," Chow explained to Monk. "The symbols represent zodiac signs, planets, and elements like fire, earth, air, and water. The circle is broken into sections called houses, representing different aspects of your physical, mental, spiritual, and emotional life. She could look at this, figure in the current alignment of the planets, and advance the chart mathematically to predict whether this is a good week to ask your boss for a raise."

"You're very knowledgeable about horoscopes," Monk said. "Do you believe in astrology?"

"Hell, no," she said. "But they do."

"They?" Monk asked.

"Them," she said.

"Oh," Monk said.

"There are probably hundreds of charts just like this one on her hard drive," Chow said. "Every client will have one."

"I'd like to know who those clients are. Maybe one of them had a motive," Monk said. "Do you think you could find out?"

Monk was a deductive genius and had an incredible eye for detail, but I'd never seen him do any digging for facts. He gladly left that grunt work to others.

"I can tell you who they are, who they're sleeping with, how they voted in the last election, and if they pick their noses while they drive their cars."

"People clean their noses while operating heavy machinery?" Monk said incredulously. "Yeah, right."

Monk shot me a look and rolled his eyes. As far as he was concerned, that was the craziest thing Chow had said yet. It was so crazy to him that he forgot he was afraid to look at me.

"I think her murder could be part of something much, much bigger," she said.

"Here it comes," Jasper said.

"Her scrutiny of the alignment of stars and planets on someone's chart led her to accidentally discover the date, time, and location of an alien landing," Chow said. "So they immediately dispatched a local agent to kill her."

"They?" I asked.

"Them," she replied.

But Monk wasn't listening anymore. Something had distracted him. He walked into the center of the room, head at an angle, his hands held up in front of him.

"Do you hear that?" he asked.

"What?" I said.

"A low whine," Monk said. "No, a whistle. A whistling whine."

"I don't hear anything," Chow said.

"Maybe you could if you turned down your radio," Jasper said.

"Oh, you'd like that, wouldn't you?" Chow said accusingly. "You can't wait to get inside my head again."

"Ssshhh," Monk said.

We were all silent. I heard the hum of the computer, the voices from Chow's radio, and a sound that I recognized immediately.

"It's a toilet running," I said.

Monk glared at me. To him, saying the word "toilet" was the same as uttering a particularly ugly profanity.

"Excuse me," I said. "I meant to say it sounds like a bathroom appliance isn't operating properly."

Monk headed down the hall, following the sound. The rest of us dutifully followed.

The bathroom was in the back corner of the first floor, just past the stairs, in what had probably been a closet when the home was originally built. It was narrow and cramped and would have been claustrophobic if not for the small window, which was open, the towel rack below it broken off the wall and lying on the floor in front of the toilet.

There was only room for one person in the bathroom, so Monk went in while we stood in the hall, peering through the doorway.

Monk examined the holes in the wall where the towel rack had once been affixed with screws. "Someone stepped on this and broke it off the wall."

"Looks like you've found how the killer came in," Chow said. "And made his escape after taking a whiz."

Monk grimaced and stepped away from the toilet as if it might spontaneously combust.

"It doesn't make sense," Monk said.

"When you have to go, you have to go," Chow said.

"Perhaps the anxiety, violence, and bloodshed of the killing made him sick and he had to vomit," Jasper said. "It's a common reaction to stress."

"I'll check the toilet for DNA," Chow said, taking out one of her Q-tips. Monk stepped in front of her, blocking her access to the bathroom.

"Are you insane?" Monk said, practically shrieking. "If you open that lid, you could expose us all."

"To what?" she asked.

"God only knows," Monk said. "We'll wait until the house has been evacuated and let the professionals deal with it."

"You want to evacuate the house before lifting the toilet seat lid?" Chow said.

"This is no time for heroics," Monk said.

Jasper's thumbs flew over his PDA keypad. He'd found a new nut to write about.

Monk turned his attention back to the window and the broken towel bar.

"If he broke this on the way in, she would have heard it."

"Maybe he broke it on his way out," Chow said. "She was dead. He could make all the noise he wanted."

"So why was he in such a hurry if the deed was done?" Monk said. "Wouldn't it have made more sense to use the front door, the back door, or one of the larger bedroom windows? This window must have been a tight squeeze."

"He could have been very small," Chow said. "They often are."

"They?" Monk asked.

"Them," Chow replied.

6

Mr. Monk and Madam Frost

"Something isn't right," Monk said as the two of us left Doucet's house.

"Gee, you think?" I said. "What was your first clue? The aluminum foil or the radio taped to her head?"

"I'm talking about the murder. Why weren't there any signs of forced entry?"

"Isn't the window in the bathroom a sign of forced entry?"

"I don't know what it is yet. The only thing I'm certain of is that Allegra Doucet knew her killer."

"Why do you say that?"

"She was standing and facing her killer when he stabbed her," Monk said. "There are no signs of a struggle and no defensive wounds on her body. She didn't know her life was in danger until she'd already lost it."

"I guess this means you haven't solved the case yet," I said.

"I'm having an off day," Monk said.

"I was joking."

"I wasn't," Monk said, his attention shifting to a home across the street. "Maybe she can give us some insight."

I followed his gaze and saw a shabby, faded-purple Victorian house, the dark curtains drawn behind a neon sign that read MADAM FROST—FORTUNE TELLER AND PSYCHIC. TAROT CARDS, PALM READING, ASTROLOGY. The curtains were decorated with half-moons and stars and a couple of yin-and-yang symbols thrown in for good measure.

"Are you going to ask her to look into her crystal ball for you?" I asked.

"Madam Frost might know something about her neighbor and fellow charlatan."

We were heading for her front door when Madam Frost came hobbling around from the back of her house. I knew who she was because, unlike the late Allegra Doucet, Madam Frost looked every bit the part she was playing. She was in her sixties, or perhaps older, draped in a shawl that looked as if it were woven out of spiderwebs, and leaning on a knobby cane seemingly carved from an ancient tree limb. There were rings on every finger of her gnarled hands, and her teeth were as yellowed as the pages of a vintage paperback. Picture Yoda in drag and you've got her.

"Madam Frost?" Monk inquired, though he must have known who she was, too. Who else would dress like that?

"I was wondering when you'd get here," she said in a voice that sounded more like Angela Lansbury than Margaret Hamilton. "I've been expecting you."

"You looked into your crystal ball and saw us coming?" I asked.

"I peeked out my window. It's often a lot more revealing," she replied as she made her way to the front door. "I saw all the police cars in front of my driveway and the medical examiner going into Allegra's house. I figured the police would show up at my door sometime. Come in, please."

She unlocked her front door and beckoned us into her parlor, which, like the woman herself, was everything the sign out front advertised.

The room was lit by several stained-glass lamps that cast a dim glow on the walls, which were lined with sagging bookshelves filled with dusty, ancient books, the spines and jackets covered with strange symbols and unreadable script. The rest of the shelf space was cluttered with mystical ephemera: clay runes, shrunken heads, an Egyptian obelisk, voodoo mojo bones, crystals, Navajo dreamcatchers, unicorns, chakra medicine pouches, chicken feet, Buddhas, chalices and goblets, African fertility idols, scrolls, and a tiny model of the starship *Enterprise.*

She certainly covered all her mystical bases. If an Egyptian Navajo Buddhist Trekkie ever came in for a reading, she was prepared.

There was a round table in the center of the room with a crystal ball, a deck of tarot cards, and a yellow legal pad. She tossed her keys on the table and turned to us.

"So what can I do for you?"

"We're investigating the murder of Allegra Doucet, the astrologer across the street," Monk said, twitching nervously, his eyes panning the room.

"She wasn't an astrologer," Madam Frost said. "She was an actress with a computer. She didn't have the touch."

"She had something," I said. "She made enough money to shop at Prada."

Madam Frost certainly didn't shop there. She must have bought all her clothing at an Addams family garage sale.

"And yet she's dead and I'm alive," Madam Frost said. "Her bank account isn't doing her much good now."

"It doesn't sound like you liked her much." Monk was huffing as if he'd just run up a steep hill. I couldn't figure out what his problem was.

"I've been advising, guiding, and supporting the people in this neighborhood for forty years. Janis Joplin sat at this table. So did Ken Kesey. I dropped acid with Timothy Leary. I read Allan Ginsberg's palm while he read me his poetry," Madam Frost said. "Who was she? A failed actress from LA who showed up here two years ago calling herself an 'astrological counselor' and charging clients two hundred dollars an hour."

"Like a psychiatrist," Monk gasped. His skin was pale. Beads of sweat were forming on his brow.

"It's a comparison Allegra liked to make. But a psychologist has some knowledge, some genuine insight into the human mind. All she had was some off-the-shelf astrology software that could spit out a useless chart in seconds," Madam Frost said, distracted for a moment by Monk's wheezing. "I labor over an ephemeris for days, analyzing the complex movement and subtle influences of the planets and stars, to create a detailed personal chart for my clients."

"Most of whom she was luring away," I said.

"The younger generation was drawn to her," Frost said. "They trust technology, and glory in eroticism. She was an irresistible combination of both. I couldn't compete. The young are bored by books, believe anything done by hand is inferior, and are terrified of aging. But my longtime clients still relied on me for guidance, and the young eventually become old, despite their best efforts to fight it."

It occurred to me that Allegra Doucet was upscaling and reimagining astrology the same way the neighborhood itself, as personified by Madam Frost, was being gentrified and remodeled. Madam Frost and Allegra Doucet were the conflict between the past and future of Haight-Ashbury made human. At least, they were until Allegra Doucet was killed.

Monk started to hyperventilate.

"I can't take it anymore," Monk said, and hurried outside. We went out after him.

He stood on the porch, swallowing air like a drowning man who'd finally reached the surface.

"What's wrong?" I said. "Is there anything I can do for you?"

"You can get her to clean up that mess," Monk said. "Nothing matches. There's no organization. It's anarchy."

"I'm sorry my eclectic decor isn't to your liking," Madame Frost said. "It's a reflection of my years of studying the mystical realms of our existence."

"It's insanity," he said. "How can you live like that?"

"I'm told my home has character, something I find sorely lacking in the world these days."

"Character is highly overrated," Monk said. "Try cleanliness instead. You'll thank me later."

"Is there anything else I can do for you?" Madam Frost said, an edge in her voice. I can't say that I blamed her for being offended. Nobody likes to be told their house is a dump.

"Did Allegra Doucet have any enemies?" Monk asked. "Besides you?"

"Her biggest enemy was herself."

"She didn't stab herself to death," I said.

"It was only a matter of time before someone discovered that the so-called personal chart and analysis they paid her so excessively for was only computer-generated gibberish," Madam Frost said. "She was perpetuating a fraud. People don't appreciate being suckered. The irony is, she could have prevented this. I warned her, but she wouldn't listen to me."

"You knew someone wanted to kill her?" Monk said.

"I did her chart. I knew that whatever happened last night would determine her fate."

"If her murder was in the stars," I said, "what could she have done about it anyway?"

"Astrology is like a weather report; it tells you what conditions you're likely to face in the future.

If the weatherman says it's probably going to rain, you bring an umbrella. If you follow that advice, you won't get wet. But if you choose to ignore it, you will get soaked," Madam Frost said. "She had a choice to make last night, and clearly she made the wrong one. We have free will, and, used wisely, that's more powerful than any force in the heavens."

"The stars and the planets move in a precise pattern of orbits according to the basic laws of physics," Monk said. "Am I right?"

"Yes," Madam Frost said.

"Then as an astrologer, don't you think your belongings should be arranged in a precise pattern as well?"

"Since you seem to have such an obvious appreciation for the alignment of the stars, perhaps you will allow me to do your chart," Madam Frost said. "I can reveal to you what obstacles lie ahead in your investigation as well as your personal life."

"I don't believe in astrology," Monk said.

"What do you believe in?"

Monk thought about that for a long moment.

"Order," he said, and then walked away.

Madam Frost looked at me. "What about you, dear? What do you believe in?"

"Myself," I said.

"Does that work for you?"

"Some days more than others." I said good-bye to Madam Frost, thanked her for her time, and joined Monk in the middle of the street.

"Where to now?" I asked.

"Back to the headquarters," he said. "I was just wondering how we were going to get there."

I turned to my car. Or, at least, where I thought my car would be. It wasn't there. I looked around. It wasn't anywhere. I approached the officer I'd given my keys to. With his square jaw, red cheeks, and flattop buzz cut, his head was like a moss-covered brick. His name tag read, KRUPP, and he was looking at us both with obvious amusement.

"Where is my car?" I demanded.

"You'll have to ask the towing company," Officer Krupp said.

I couldn't believe what I was hearing. "You had my car *towed*?"

"It was parked illegally and was impeding traffic," he said. "Here's your ticket."

Krupp handed me the yellow ticket, which I promptly balled up and threw at his chest. He pretended not to notice, never taking his eyes off my face.

I pointed at Monk. "Do you know who he is?"

"Yeah, I do," Krupp said. "He's the wack-job who is costing me a decent pension."

"He's the wack-job who can fire you right now," I said.

"With a critical shortage of cops on the street?" He smiled, full of smug satisfaction. "I don't think so."

"Fine," I said. "Give me the keys."

He gave me my car keys, but I kept my hand out. "I want the keys to your patrol car."

"That's an official police vehicle," he said. "You're a civilian."

"He's the captain," I said, gesturing to Monk again. "Or maybe you'd like to argue that with the mayor? I happen to have Smitrovich on my speed dial."

I started hunting in my purse for my cell phone, but the officer knew he was beaten. He handed over the keys to his patrol car.

"Thanks," I said, and looked at Monk, who seemed startled. "Let's go, Captain."

We headed for the patrol car.

"You're serious?" Monk said.

"Would you prefer to ride in the backseat of a taxicab that has served a thousand people?" I saw Monk shiver with revulsion. "That's what I thought."

We reached the patrol car and got in. There was a laptop computer, a rifle, and a mike mounted in front of the center console, but otherwise it wasn't so different from any other car. I stuck the key in the ignition and started the car up. The engine roared with a ferocity that made my Jeep Cherokee sound like a golf cart. I had the feeling that if I pressed the accelerator, flames would shoot out of the exhaust.

This was going to be fun.

My cell phone rang. I took it out of my purse and answered it. It was Officer Curtis at headquarters, calling to report that another citizen of the city of San Francisco had met a violent end. She gave me the address of the crime scene, and I told her which patrol car we were in so she could reach us on the radio. I also asked her to track down the towing company that had my car.

Officer Curtis was about to hang up when Frank Porter asked for the phone. He had checked the credit card statements of the Golden Gate Strangler's victims for any running-shoe purchases in the last three months. There weren't any; nor did any of the victims shop at the same stores.

I hung up. The first thing I did was tell Monk what Porter had found out. Monk sulked. Then I told him what Officer Curtis had called about.

"You've got a fresh homicide," I said.

"It's not another Strangler victim, is it?"

I shook my head. "It's a hit-and-run in the Mission District."

He sighed wearily. "That doesn't sound like a particularly difficult case. You interview the witnesses, track down the car that matches the license plate or the description of the vehicle, and then check it for blood or other evidence from the scene."

In other words, solving this case would depend more on grueling legwork than brilliant deductions. Monk didn't like putting in that much effort, not unless it involved removing a stain from something.

"There's a detective on the scene. I'm sure it's not necessary for you to be there," I said, trying hard to sound uninterested. "After all, you're the captain. You've got important administrative work to do."

I admit it, I was manipulating him. I wanted to drive the car. And I wanted to drive it *fast*.

"Do you know how to get to the crime scene?" Monk said.

I nodded and tried to suppress my smile. "Can we use the siren?"

"That what it's there for."

7

Mr. Monk and the Scum on the Street

The godlike power that a simple siren gives you is amazing. Cars moved out of my path, and the streets opened up in front of me. I knew a freedom few drivers in the city will ever experience, unless they happen to be on the street at three a.m. Even so, I wished the crime scene were on the other side of one of San Francisco's notoriously steep hills so I could fly over the rise and land hard, the undercarriage of the car spraying sparks as it shaved the asphalt on the way down.

Unfortunately, the speedometer never topped thirty miles per hour, and there were no hills between us and our destination, an area made up of boxy 1950s-era apartment buildings and struggling small businesses—minimarts, florists, Laundromats, and nail salons—behind aging, neglected storefronts.

There were police cars parked on the street. Several uniformed officers kept a few dozen curious pedestrians on the sidewalk and behind the yellow caution tape that sealed off the intersection, where a body lay covered with a bloodstained white sheet.

But nobody was paying much attention to the dead guy. Everyone was staring at the billowing smoke coming from a building around the corner. I could understand that. A raging fire is a lot more interesting to look at than a covered-up corpse.

Monk sat wide-eyed and pale, molded into the passenger seat as if he'd been pinned by tremendous g-forces. The instant we came to a stop, the ground was rocked by an explosion.

"I think we broke the sound barrier," Monk said in a faraway, dazed voice.

"I barely broke the speed limit," I said.

"Then what was that boom I just heard?"

"It probably has something to do with the fire," I said, motioning to the smoke in the sky.

Monk hesitantly unlatched his seat belt, as if afraid the car might suddenly speed forward of its own volition, and then reached out with a shaking hand to open the car door.

"When I said you could use the siren," he said, "that didn't mean I wanted you to speed."

"What do you think the siren is for?"

"To alert other people to clear the road so that we won't have anyone in our way while we drive slowly and carefully to wherever we are going."

"You're no fun," I said.

"Give me a broom, a dustpan, and a dirty floor," he said, "and I'll show you fun."

He got out and we walked around the corner

together, where we saw the ground floor of a building ablaze. Firefighters were battling the flames that were licking out from the charred remains of a car that had gone through the storefront window. An injured man was being wheeled on a gurney to an ambulance, while paramedics treated a balding, sobbing guy who sat on a bus-stop bench, his shoulder soaked with blood. People were gathered on the sidewalks, watching the pyrotechnics.

Against this backdrop of fire, agony, and pandemonium, a tall figure walked toward us, his arms casually at his sides. He was holding the largest handgun I have ever seen, the sunlight glinting off its smoking silver barrel.

"Who is he?" Monk asked.

I recognized the flinty eyes, the world-weary grimace, and most of all, the destruction in his wake. I was relieved to see he didn't have any grenades clipped to his belt.

"That's Mad Jack Wyatt," I said, "one of your detectives."

"What's he angry about?" Monk asked.

I shrugged.

"You must be the new captain," Wyatt said with a grimace, as if the words were causing him pain.

"I'm Adrian Monk, and this is my assistant, Natalie Teeger."

"An assistant," Wyatt said. "What a nice perk."

"I'm not a perk," I said.

"You look perky to me," Wyatt said.

"How did that car end up in the middle of that store?" I asked, gesturing to the fire.

Wyatt glanced over his shoulder. "Maybe he was

looking for the drive-through window and got confused."

"What got him so confused?" I said.

"Probably the gunshots," Wyatt said.

Monk started to do his thing, walking in a wide circle around us and examining the skid marks on the asphalt. Wyatt watched him warily, as if he might have to draw his gun on him.

"The car was coming from the north and then sped up as it went through the intersection," Monk said, reading the skid marks as if they were a transcript of the events. In a way, I guess they were. "You shot out the front right tire and then, as the car passed, the left rear tire. The driver lost control of the car and careened into the front window of that store."

Wyatt nodded. "Mighty reckless of him."

"Is he the one who ran over the pedestrian?" I asked.

"No," Monk replied before Wyatt could answer. "That's a different set of skid marks." He started to follow those marks back around the corner, where I'd parked the patrol car.

"I still don't get what happened," I said.

Wyatt looked at me. "I arrived on the scene and was beginning my investigation when I recognized that the driver of a passing vehicle was Trinidad Lopez, the leading suspect in a string of ATM holdups."

"So you shot him?" I asked.

"I shot his car," Wyatt said. "If I'd shot him, he'd be leaving in a body bag instead of an ambulance."

I looked over my shoulder to see a man being lifted into the ambulance.

"If that's Lopez, who is that?" I motioned to the tearful, injured man on the bus-stop bench.

"My anger-management counselor."

"You *shot* him?"

"It's just a scratch." Wyatt shoved his weapon into a shoulder holster as long as my thigh. "You shouldn't step in front of me when I'm shooting."

"That's a no-brainer," I said.

"That's what he'd be now if I'd been aiming at him," Wyatt said. "I guess this was his lucky day."

"I'll go tell him to be sure and buy a lottery ticket before he gets home."

I thought I saw a hint of a grin at the edges of Wyatt's grimace. I hoped that didn't mean he was going to shoot me.

Monk came back to us. "What can you tell me about the victim?"

"I don't call a guy who holds up old ladies at ATMs a victim," Wyatt said. "I call him target practice."

"I think Mr. Monk was referring to the victim of the hit-and-run," I said, trying to be helpful.

Wyatt grunted, took a notebook from his back pocket, and referred to the top page.

"The deceased is John Yamada, forty-four, an architect. He lived in the house on the corner and now resides under that white sheet over there," Wyatt said. "He was hit by a car while jaywalking across the street to the market. Nobody got a license number, but the vehicle that struck him has been positively identified by witnesses as a Toyota,

Ford, Honda, Subaru, Pontiac, Hyundai, Chevy, or Kia sedan."

"What do you make of it?" I asked him.

Wyatt shrugged. "Natural selection."

"Excuse me?" I said.

"The moron should have looked both ways before he crossed the street," Wyatt said.

"It wasn't a hit-and-run," Monk said. "It was premeditated murder."

We both looked at Monk. Well, I did, for sure. I think Wyatt, did, too, but he could have been on the lookout for more felons cruising by whom he could shoot.

"The skid marks indicate that the driver was double-parked across the street and floored it when Yamada entered the intersection," Monk said. "The killer was waiting for him."

"You got all that just from some skid marks?" Wyatt said skeptically.

"There's more." Monk led us around the corner to our patrol car. "This was where the car was parked, with a clear view of Yamada's front door. You see this mud?"

"No, I don't," Wyatt said.

I didn't either.

"I'm talking about those big, disgusting globs right in front of your feet." Monk pointed at the ground.

Wyatt and I crouched down and peered at the street. There were some tiny crumbs of mud between the two of us.

"How did he see that?" Wyatt asked me.

"He never misses dirt," I said. "Anywhere. Ever."

"There's more over there." Monk pointed a few feet away. "But none in between those two piles. I believe the dirt was shaken off the car while it was idling."

"So?" Wyatt said.

"It wasn't shaken off anywhere else except those two distinct points, a car length apart, beneath the front and rear license plates. The reason no one saw the license plate numbers was because they were covered with mud."

"A pro would have stolen a set of plates from a car and put them on his ride," Wyatt said. "We're dealing with a civilian making it up as he goes along."

"Maybe someone from Yamada's personal life," Monk said.

"I'll check into it," Wyatt said. "And I'll have the lab analyze the dirt."

"I'm counting on you to clean this up," Monk said.

"With pleasure," Wyatt said.

"Really?" Monk said. "You will?"

"I was born to take scum off the streets."

"So was I," Monk said. "Which cleanser do you prefer?"

Wyatt opened his jacket to show Monk the gigantic gun in his gigantic holster. "Three-fifty-seven Magnum. You?"

"Simple Green," Monk said.

I caught a hint of disappointment in Monk's voice. For a moment he'd thought he'd found a kindred spirit.

My cell phone rang. I reached into my bag and

answered it. Officer Curtis was calling again. I listened carefully, hardly believing what she was saying, and then snapped the phone shut.

"This city is getting way too dangerous," I said.

"That'll change soon enough," Wyatt said. "I'm back in the game, and my gun has bullets."

I looked at Monk. "There's been another murder."

"Three in one day?" Monk said. "If this keeps up, we could become the murder capital of the world."

"If this keeps up," I said, "I'm going to move."

The views from Russian Hill are pretty spectacular. Look to the north and you can see Alcatraz and Marin County. Look to the east and you can see Coit Tower and a sliver of the Bay Bridge. Look to the south and you can see the Financial District high-rises. Look to the west and you've got the Golden Gate. But that evening, the only view anybody was interested in was of the body of Diane Truby at the bottom of a steep residential street, and the bloody grille of the bus that hit her.

She'd been a passenger on that very same bus only a few minutes before. The driver let Diane and several other passengers off at the stop on the top of the hill. A few minutes later the bus was heading downhill when she tumbled off the sidewalk into its path. The bus slammed into her, dragging her corpse to the bottom of the hill before the driver could stop.

An alley bisected the street midway up the hill. That was about where Truby was hit, and that was where Monk and I met Frank Porter and his granddaughter Sparrow, who was leaning against a wall and listening to her iPod, looking so bored that I thought she might throw herself in front of a bus just for the excitement.

Porter sat on a wooden vegetable crate and explained to us what happened, never once referring to his notes.

Diane Truby was a waitress on her way home from work. She rode the same bus every day. She lived with a painter who made most of his living doing caricatures for the tourists who waited in line for the cable car at the Powell-Hyde turnaround.

"I interviewed everybody on the bus," Porter said. "Nobody saw anything except the driver, and his attention was on the street in front of him when she just flew into his path."

Monk listened carefully, then walked out into the street, did an odd little pirouette, and returned to the alley. There was a woman's purse on the sidewalk, circled with white chalk.

"And this is Diane's purse on the sidewalk?"

"Uh-huh," Porter said. "There's sixty bucks in cash in there and a cell phone. I don't think this was a purse snatching gone wrong."

"So she was walking down the hill when someone burst out of this alley and pushed her into the path of that bus," Monk said.

"We're dealing with one pretty sick individual," Porter said. "I remember a case a buddy of mine investigated in New York. Some kids were shoving people in front of subway trains."

"That wasn't a case," Sparrow said. "That was

the episode of *Law and Order* you watched last night."

"They were doing it for thrills," Porter said, ignoring Sparrow's remark. "Sickos like that are the hardest to catch. You never know when or where they are going to strike next."

"That crate you're sitting on," Monk said. "Where did it come from?"

"Right here," Porter said.

"And it was there where you're sitting, tipped upside down like that?"

"I have bad knees," Porter said, sounding defensive and a bit embarrassed.

Monk crouched beside the box and looked toward the street. "This is where the murderer sat, too."

Porter didn't move from the crate. "What makes you say that?"

"From here you're out of sight from the street, but you have a clear view of the houses on the east side of the street near the bottom of the hill."

"What good was that to the killer?" I said. "The victim was walking down from the top of the hill."

"The murderer was looking at the reflection in the mirror," Monk said.

"What mirror?" I said.

"The one a homeowner has mounted on the lamppost outside his garage so he can see the traffic coming down as he backs out."

I crouched beside Monk and followed his gaze. Sure enough, there was a mirror angled in such a way that it reflected the top half of the street. Whoever sat on the crate could see Diane Truby and the bus before they reached the mouth of the alley.

"Does this mean I've got to get up?" Porter said.

"You're sitting on evidence," Monk said. "You've probably already contaminated it."

"Damn," Porter said. "I'm going to need a hand."

Monk didn't make a move to help, which was typical. I sighed, glanced at Sparrow, who also sighed, and the two of us lifted Porter to his feet.

"That's odd," Monk said.

"Wait until you get old and let's see how spry you are," Porter grumbled. "I almost died walking up that hill."

"I'm talking about this." He pointed to a packing slip affixed to the crate with clear tape. "The vegetable crate was delivered this morning to a market two blocks over."

"Does that mean something?" I said. In fact, I asked that question so often around Monk I was tempted to write it on a card so I could just flash it at him when necessary.

"It means the killer brought the crate so he'd have something to sit on." Monk frowned and cocked his head. Something about the crime scene wasn't fitting in the way it should, and it was giving him a kink in his neck. "Why didn't the killer just stand? Or lean against the wall? Or crouch on the ground?"

"Maybe he had arthritis," Porter said. "Or sore feet. Or a bad back. Or, like me, all of the above." Porter caught his breath and shot a worried look at Sparrow. "Oh, my God. Maybe I did it."

"You have an alibi," Sparrow said irritably. "You were at the police station when she was killed."

"I was?" Porter said. "Well, that's a relief."

"And you didn't know her," Sparrow said.

"Are you sure?" Porter asked.

"Yeah," Sparrow said.

"That's good." Porter tipped his head toward me. "Do I know her?"

I wasn't sure whether Porter was serious or having some fun at his granddaughter's expense. I looked into his eyes, hoping to see a glint of mischief. Instead, I saw two rheumy eyeballs looking vacantly into the street. He was serious.

"I'm Natalie Teeger," I said. "Captain Monk's assistant."

Porter nodded, then narrowed his eyes at Monk. "You're the guy who freaked out when Stottlemeyer brought in the doughnut holes. You wanted us to find the doughnuts they came from and put them back."

"They shouldn't have been removed from the doughnuts and sold separately in the first place," Monk said. "It's like selling chicken legs without the rest of the chicken."

"What's wrong with that?" Sparrow said.

"That's how it starts," Monk said. "And the next thing you know, you're selling your mother's jewelry to support your crack habit."

"They're called doughnut holes," I said, "but they aren't actually poked out of the center of doughnuts."

"Yeah, right," Monk said. "If you can fall for

that, then you probably think this was a random thrill killing, too."

"Wasn't it?" I said.

"Diane Truby was the intended target all along."

"How do you know?" That was another question I'd have to write on a card. I figured I'd better start making a list.

"There's nothing thrilling about waiting," Monk said. "The thrill comes from the impulsiveness and potential danger of the act."

I wondered how Monk could possibly know anything about thrills. His idea of being impulsive was to clean a counter with Fantastik instead of Formula 409. And then go back and clean it with Formula 409 after all.

"But this killer brought something to sit on," Monk continued. "He knew it might be a while until the person he was waiting for walked by. And he was willing to wait."

"I'll have some officers canvass the neighborhood and see if anybody saw a guy walking around with an empty vegetable crate," Porter said. "A guy with bad knees, a sore back, and corns on his feet. I'll have them show people my picture, just in case."

"And yet," Monk said, lost in his thoughts, "for a premeditated murder, shoving someone in front of a bus seems strangely impulsive."

"You're contradicting yourself," I said.

"I am," Monk said thoughtfully. "And I'm not."

8

Mr. Monk Plays Make-believe

I talked Monk into coming home with me for dinner but, to be honest, it wasn't because I wanted more of his company or that I thought he might enjoy more of mine. I wanted to take Julie for a ride in the patrol car, and I didn't feel comfortable driving it without a police officer with me.

But I was glad I offered him the invitation, because I don't think he really wanted to be alone. As we drove to my house he sat quietly, staring at his badge. He was obviously troubled.

In all the excitement of rushing from one homicide to another, I'd forgotten that this was Monk's first day back on the force. On top of that, it was also his first time in command, which couldn't have been easy for a guy who barely had control over his own life.

"Big day, wasn't it, Mr. Monk?"

He put the badge back in his jacket pocket and sighed. "I finally got my badge back."

"That's exciting, isn't it?"

"It was while it lasted," Monk said.

"No one has asked you to give it back."

"They will," Monk said. "I haven't accomplished anything."

"It's only your first day," I said. "You've managed to keep the homicide department running efficiently with a skeleton crew of ex-detectives in the midst of a crippling labor shortage. That's a major achievement."

"But I haven't made any progress on the Golden Gate Strangler case."

"How could you? You were occupied with three other murders today."

"And I still have no idea who stabbed the astrologer, or who ran over the architect, or who pushed the waitress in front of a bus."

"You've only been on those cases for a couple of hours."

"I'm such a loser."

"You've barely had a chance to visit the crime scenes, much less do any investigating," I said. "Did you really expect to solve them on the spot?"

"I've done it before."

"Those were flukes," I said.

"Sixty-eight percent of the time isn't a fluke," Monk said. "It's the norm."

"You've kept track?"

That was a dumb question. He counted the lampposts on the street, the ceiling tiles in the police station, the raisins in his Raisin Bran, and probably even the granules of salt in his saltshaker. Of *course* he counted the cases he'd solved and how long it took him to do it.

"This is really going to hurt my stats," Monk said.

"Forget those numbers; look at the big picture," I said. "You've solved every murder you've ever investigated."

"All except one," he said sadly. He was talking about Trudy, of course. His wife. The most important case of all to him.

"You'll solve that one, too," I said. "No matter how long it takes."

"What if I've lost my mojo?"

"You haven't."

"Maybe I should resign and save the mayor the embarrassment of my dismal failure."

"*That's* your strategy for success? Quit the moment the job gets difficult?"

"It could work," Monk said.

"Is that how you got this far, by quitting? No. You did it by relentlessly pushing ahead, battling your anxieties, phobias, and fears until you got what you wanted: your badge. And now that you've got it, you're going to just give up? I'm surprised at you, Mr. Monk."

"You don't understand, Natalie. I've got nothing on these three murders today. All the facts and questions are jumbled together in my head. It's like it's all one case. I can't think."

"You're being too hard on yourself."

"I'm stumped, and these aren't even clever murders," Monk said. "They're mundane. Simple. They don't compare to the impossible murders I've solved."

"Because these are the kinds of murders that Stottlemeyer and Disher handle every day and that you never hear about. They don't call you in for this stuff. The problem is that you're not a consultant anymore. You've got to deal with every homicide that comes along. And what I've learned so far is that most of them aren't committed by rational people who intricately plot every move. They're done on the spur of the moment by irrational people in desperate situations."

"So they should be easier to solve," Monk said.

"Maybe it's the mundane, half-assed nature of these killings that's messing you up," I said. "I think there's no real plotting involved, so you can't get a sense of the thinking and *thinkers* behind the murders."

"You think?" Monk said.

"Besides, you don't have the luxury of devoting your mind to just one case. You had three murders thrown at you today on top of the Golden Gate Strangler killings. Of course you're finding it hard to concentrate."

Monk shook his head. "I don't know how the captain does it."

"You could ask him," I said.

"He won't help me," Monk said.

I shrugged. "Then I guess you'll just have to do what he does when things get tough."

"What's that?"

"Rely on you."

Monk looked at me. "You're suggesting that I rely on myself?"

I nodded.

He groaned. "I'm doomed."

"That's the spirit," I said.

At least he wasn't talking about quitting anymore. I take my little victories where I can find them.

Picking Julie up at her friend Katie's house in a police car was a big hit. Julie made me give her and Katie and Katie's mom a ride around the block with the siren on.

Monk was really nice about it. He endured the squeals of glee from the kids in silence, a handkerchief over his nose and mouth to protect himself from their germs.

I think he was too preoccupied with his own troubles to really make much of a fuss. Besides, there was a big Plexiglas screen between him and the kids in the backseat, so there was little chance of their touching him. He thinks all kids, including my own daughter, are basically no different from the rats who spread the Black Death throughout Europe.

We dropped Katie and her mother back at their place and headed home. Julie bounced excitedly in her seat, thrilled to ride in the back alone.

"Let's pretend I'm a bad guy, a really scary one," she said, holding her hands behind her as if they were handcuffed. "You caught me robbing a bank."

"You wouldn't be in a police car if you robbed a bank," Monk said.

"It doesn't matter, Mr. Monk," I said. "It's pretend."

"Bank robbery is a federal crime," he said. "So we'd also have to pretend that this is an FBI vehicle."

"Okay, fine. We're two FBI agents," I said, then glanced in the rearview mirror at Julie. "Transporting a very dangerous bank robber."

"I also kill people," Julie growled. "And eat them."

"You're a monster," I said, doing my best to sound like a hardened cop, which basically meant lowering my voice and squinting my eyes. "In all my years of law enforcement, I've never met a more terrifying criminal."

"Actually, I don't think we'd be in a car at all," Monk said. "We'd be in a van. An FBI van."

"But we're *in* a real police car. That's the fun part," Julie said. "Why would I want to pretend to be in a boring van?"

"Because you want to pretend accurately," Monk said. "Let's look at the facts. You're a bank robber—that's a federal offense. And you've killed and eaten people. That makes you an extremely violent psychopath. You'd definitely be handcuffed and chained in the back of a van. You might even have a muzzle on."

I glared at Monk. "You're missing the whole point of make-believe."

"I don't think so," Monk said.

"When you're pretending," I said, "you can be anyone, anywhere, doing anything you want. There are no rules."

Monk shook his head. "I believe if you check, you'll see there are some restrictions."

"Check *what*?" I said. "Check *where*?"

But by then it was too late anyway. We'd arrived in front of our place, a cute little Victorian row house in need of a little TLC, which wouldn't come until I got a big R-A-I-S-E.

Julie groaned. "Gee, that was fun."

She opened the door and marched out in a huff. I glanced at Monk.

"Thanks a lot," I said.

"No problem," Monk said, completely missing my sarcasm.

Whatever points I'd gained by taking Julie's friend for a ride in the cop car were lost when Monk ruined the make-believe part on the way home. But I had an idea how to make up for it.

I began by asking Monk to make his famous pancakes for dinner. What makes them famous, at least in the Teeger household, is that his pancakes are perfectly round. Julie watches him, fascinated by his ability to measure the right amount of batter and to pour it into the pan in just the right way to make his circles. The best part for her comes later, when, at his urging, she uses her disinfected geometry compass to confirm the size and absolute roundness of each pancake to the exact degree before they are served.

This was Monk's idea of casual dining. It worked for me, because while they were occupied doing that, I could have a glass of wine, sit in the living room, and unwind.

So that was what we did. Monk made his pancakes, Julie measured them, and I relaxed. Everyone was happy. Monk seemed to forget all about his troubles. I even saw him smile a few times.

As much as Monk likes to complain about children being dangerous and infectious, he enjoys being with them. That's because he shares their wonderment at the world, which I find amazing, considering he's seen so much violence and tragedy in his life.

After dinner, I rewarded Monk for cooking by letting him clean the dishes, and I decided to reward Julie for her great report card by giving her the presents I bought for her yesterday.

"But I don't get my report card until next week," Julie said.

"I have it on good authority that it's going to be terrific," I said as I brought the shopping bags to the table. "Besides, Mr. Monk helped me pick this stuff out for you, so he should get to enjoy seeing you open your gifts, too."

"Mr. Monk helped you shop?" she said warily.

"Yes," I said.

"I already have enough first-aid supplies and disinfectant to open my own hospital," she said. "I really don't need any more."

"You know what they say," Monk said. "You can never have too much disinfectant."

"Who says that?" Julie said.

"The people without enough disinfectant," Monk said. "Shortly before their miserable, drooling deaths."

"We got you clothes and stuff," I said. "What kind of reward would disinfectant be for a great report card?"

"A powerful incentive to excel," Monk said.

Julie sighed with relief. "You had me worried there for a minute."

She reached into the shopping bags and oohed and aahed over the Juicy jacket, the Paul Frank shirts, and the Von Dutch pants, as I knew she would. But when she got to the Nike running shoes, her enthusiasm dimmed.

"What's the matter?" I asked.

"These would have been great shoes for my last report card."

"What's wrong with them for *this* report card?"

"They're the old style," Julie said. "Nike discontinued this line of shoes months ago."

I don't know where my twelve-year-old daughter gets all her inside dope on happenings in the fashion industry, or where she learns phrases like "discontinued this line." While I was amused by her knowledge and vocabulary, I was a little pissed at her attitude.

"That's why they were on sale and why we could afford them," I said.

"And next week they'll be selling them out of trucks at freeway off-ramps."

"Then maybe I should return these and wait to buy them from the truck at an even cheaper price."

"You're missing the point, Mom," Julie said. "If I wear these shoes I'll be out of style."

"God forbid," I said.

"And everyone will know we're poor," she said.

"What they'll know is that you're a savvy shopper. Instead of paying two hundred dollars for the shoes, you got them brand-new for thirty-nine dollars. They should be ashamed of paying so much for the exact same shoes that you were able to get for a lot less simply by being patient and shrewd."

"You have no idea what life is really like," Julie said, stomping her foot in fury.

She'd been stomping her foot when she was angry since she was three years old. I thought it was adorable, and couldn't help smiling whenever she did it, which only infuriated her more.

She stomped her other foot. "Mom! Stop it!"

I turned to Monk for some support on this, knowing how tight he was with his money (my paycheck was certainly proof of that). But Monk had a strange, bemused expression on his face. His mind was somewhere else.

"Mr. Monk?" I said.

He snapped out of it, smiled, and looked at Julie. "How would you like another ride in the police car?"

"Are we going out to get me a different pair of shoes?" Julie said hopefully.

"We're taking you down to police headquarters for interrogation."

"For real?" Julie said.

"For real," Monk said.

"We are?" I asked.

"We are," Monk replied.

"Cool!" Julie said, tossing the Nikes and putting on her new Juicy jacket. Her shoe shame was momentarily forgotten, eclipsed by the irresistible excitement of being a crook.

9

Mr. Monk Improves His Stats

Julie had only been to police headquarters once before, and on that day there had been some sort of big sweep of the Tenderloin by the vice squad. The building had been filled with hookers, drunks, drug addicts, gang members, and murderers. The place smelled like a cross between a men's locker room and the bar where I worked before Monk hired me. And some of the language she heard would have embarrassed Tony Soprano.

She loved it. For her it was like visiting a new attraction at Disneyland, only the performers weren't Mickey Mouse and Buzz Lightyear; they were Georgette the tranny and Julio the pimp. It was scary for her, but in a thrilling, riding-on-a-roller-coaster way: frightening but safe.

It wasn't the kind of environment I wanted to expose my daughter to, but there had been no school that day, I had to work, and I was stuck without someone to take care of her. Besides, there wasn't anyone or anything in that building that wasn't out there, in plain view, every day of the week on the streets of San Francisco, from Union Square to Fisherman's Wharf, from Chinatown to Golden Gate Park. It's that kind of city.

She was going to see it all anyway. And I believe a parent's job is to prepare her children for independence, for survival in the real world; and sheltering them from the uglier aspects doesn't necessarily do them any good. At least at police headquarters, the bad guys were handcuffed and there were plenty of cops around to protect us. There was no real danger. Afterward she grilled me with a lot of tough questions about sex, drugs, and crime, which, for me, made the experience worthwhile. We tackled some big, awkward, important issues that day.

That said, I wasn't thrilled at the idea of taking her back there on a Saturday night, and I hoped Monk had a good reason for the field trip. I didn't have the energy for another one of those major, land-mine-laden discussions with Julie.

The place wasn't the madhouse I expected it to be. There wasn't a perp, skell, or scumbag in sight. With the Blue Flu going on, I guess it was more important for officers to be on the street than at their desks filling out arrest reports.

I was relieved, but Julie was clearly disappointed that she wasn't going to get another peek at the seamier side of life.

We were met by Officer Curtis as we came into the homicide department.

"Your Jeep is parked in the back," she said, handing me the keys. "Officer Krupp and the patrol division would appreciate the return of their black-and-white."

"What about my ticket?" I said.

"It's gone away," she said.

I handed Officer Curtis the keys to the patrol car and introduced her to Julie.

"Mom," Julie protested.

"Oh, excuse me," I said. "This may look like my daughter, Julie, but she's actually a psychopath who eats children. Captain Monk and I have brought her in for a brutal interrogation."

"Then she should be handcuffed." Officer Curtis took out a plastic band from her pocket, looped it around my daughter's wrists, and cinched it closed.

Julie growled. Curtis made a show of putting her hand on her holster.

"Don't make me take you down," Curtis said.

"Try it, cop," Julie said. "And I'll use your bones for soup."

"Comc with me, insane psycho cannibal killer," Monk said, leading her into the squad room, where Frank Porter was putting photos of the Strangler's victims (luckily not the crime scene pictures of their corpses) on a bulletin board covered with the information gathered about their lives. Monk went over to study it.

Sparrow was at a computer, checking her e-mail and eating potato chips.

"I'm surprised you're both still here," I said.

"So am I," Sparrow groaned and glanced at her grandfather. "He won't leave. I think he's afraid that if he does, they won't let him back in tomorrow."

I could understand that. He'd thought he'd lost his badge forever, and now that he had it back again he didn't want to lose it. And yet, he probably knew this reinstatement wasn't going to last and wanted to enjoy every moment of the experience while he could.

"Your piercings are so cool," Julie said, staring at Sparrow's ears. "Did they hurt?"

"It was excruciating," I said. "She was writhing in agony for weeks."

"They didn't hurt as much as piercing my—" Sparrow began, but I interrupted her.

"She doesn't want to hear about piercing your whatever."

"Yes, I do," Julie protested. "Maybe I want to pierce my whatever."

"Believe me, you don't," I said.

"Where's my whatever?" Julie said.

"Julie?" Monk approached. "Could I ask you some questions?"

He brought Julie up to the bulletin board and showed her the pictures of the shoes recovered from the right foot of each victim.

"What can you tell me about these shoes?" Monk said.

"One is a Nike, one is an Adidas, and that's a Puma," she said. "They're all running shoes with air soles."

"Anything else?"

She shrugged. "They're old."

"They look new to me," Monk said.

"They're new but they're old. They are all styles that aren't being made anymore," Julie said. "Whoever wore these shoes were major geeks."

Monk smiled. "You have the makings of a great detective."

"I do?" she said.

Monk nodded. "You've just figured out what the three Golden Gate Strangler victims had in common."

"I did?" Julie said in astonishment.

"What did you say happens to old styles that don't sell at the department stores or at the outlet malls?" Monk asked.

"They're sold out of a truck at a freeway off-ramp," Julie said.

"And those guys don't take checks or credit cards," I said as it dawned on me what Monk was getting at. "It's a cash-only business. I know from experience."

"That's why we couldn't find any running-shoe purchases on the credit card statements of the three victims," Monk said. "Because all the victims paid cash for their shoes from some fly-by-night seller."

"It's not just guys selling shoes out of their trunks," I said. "There are all kinds of closeout, overstock, and remainder outfits that open up in empty storefronts for a few weeks at a time and then go away. They are never in one place for long."

"We need to locate every gypsy shoe seller in San Francisco and show them pictures of the victims," Porter said. "Maybe someone will remember selling shoes to the women."

"Or maybe one of the sellers is the Strangler," Monk said.

"I'll get the information out to patrol and tell them to keep an eye out for anyone selling running shoes on the street," Officer Curtis said.

"I appreciate that," Monk said. "Thank you."

"If this information leads to the arrest of the Golden Gate Strangler," I said, "I think Julie should get some of the reward money."

"You'll have to take that up with the mayor," Monk said.

"Don't worry," I said. "I will."

"What reward?" Julie said.

"Let me put it this way," I said. "If you get it, I promise never to buy shoes on sale for you again."

I took Julie into one of the interrogation rooms and questioned her about her crimes for a while. When I was through with the suspect, Officer Curtis took her down to one of the empty cells, locking her up for ten minutes before cutting her cuffs and setting her free on a technicality. Julie couldn't have been happier.

Monk was pretty happy, too. He finally had a lead to track in the Strangler case. And I was already thinking of ways to spend the city's reward money, which put a smile on my face.

We were on our way out of the building when Officer Curtis ran up to us.

"Captain, there's been a holdup at a minimart near Geary and Van Ness," she said. "They took a couple hundred bucks and shot the proprietor dead."

Monk gave me a look. He wanted to go to the

scene, but there was no way I was taking my daughter there.

"Do you mind staying here with Officer Curtis for a little while?"

"No problem," she said.

"Let's look through some mug books," Officer Curtis said, leading her away. "That's always fun."

At least I knew Julie would be in good hands while I was away. I couldn't ask for a better babysitter than a policewoman with a gun.

The Speed-E-Mart was flanked by an adult video store and a falafel place on the street level of a shabby, four-story office building that was covered with decades of grime. Hand-painted posters in the minimart window advertised cheap beer, cigarettes, and lottery tickets.

The harsh glow from the fluorescent bulbs inside the market spilled out into the street, bathing the police cars, sidewalks and asphalt in a dull yellow light.

A woman stood outside the store, leaning against the wall and nervously smoking a cigarette. She was in her thirties, wearing faded jeans and a red Speed-E-Mart clerk's vest over a long-sleeved white T-shirt. The dark circles under her eyes were as ingrained on her face as the grime on the building.

Standing beside her was a uniformed cop in his fifties, his gut slopping over the edge of his pants and straining the buttons on his shirt. He had his notebook out and was making some notations in it with a stubby pencil. The officer saw us coming and met us at the entrance to the minimart.

"I'm Sergeant Riglin," the officer said. "Are you Captain Monk?"

"Yes, I am," Monk said. "This is my assistant, Natalie Teeger. What happened here tonight, Sergeant?"

"A couple of black guys came in, held up the place. The cashier, who was the owner of the market, emptied the register, and they shot him anyway. The bastards. The name of the deceased is Ramin Touzie, age forty-seven."

Monk tipped his head toward the woman. "Who is she?"

"Lorna Karsch, age thirty-four, works nights here as a clerk." Riglin referred to his notes. "She was in the storeroom when it went down, came out when she heard the shots, and saw two black individuals exiting the premises."

"There's a blue stain on the cuff of her right sleeve," Monk said, adjusting both his sleeves.

"Yeah, so?" Riglin said.

"There isn't one on her left sleeve," Monk said.

"Is that important?" Riglin asked.

It was if I ever wanted to get home tonight. Monk wouldn't be able to concentrate on the case as long as her sleeves didn't match.

"Would you like me to ask her to change her shirt or stain her other sleeve?" I said.

"You've got to be kidding," Riglin said.

"I wish I were," I said.

"It's a beautiful blue," Monk said.

"What is?" I asked.

"The stain," Monk said. "Deep, vibrant, and rich."

"Uh-huh," Riglin said. "Is there anything else, Captain?"

"Who called the police?" Monk asked.

"She did," Riglin said, gesturing to Lorna. "So did the guy who runs the porno shop next door."

"Do we have any security-camera footage of the shooting?"

Riglin shook his head. "The clerk says the VCR broke a couple of days ago. The owner was gonna buy a new one tomorrow."

"Okay," Monk said. "I'd like to look inside. Has anything been moved?"

"No, sir," Riglin said.

Monk and I went into the store. The cashier's counter was to the left of the front door, facing the four cramped aisles of groceries and the refrigerators and freezers that lined the back of the store. The drawer of the cash register was open.

We peered over the counter. Ramin Touzie was crumpled in the tight space between the counter and the wall, a gunshot wound in the center of his chest, his head resting against the side of a plastic trash can. He was wearing a Speed-E-Mart vest over a rugby shirt.

Monk cocked his head, something catching his eye. He walked around the counter, removed a pen from his pocket, and used it to lift out an open box of Ziploc bags from the trash can. Those were the same brand that Monk bought by the case.

He set the box of Ziploc bags down on the counter.

"It's a crime," he said.

"You're talking about the box of Ziploc bags?"

"What else?"

"Oh, I don't know," I said. "How about the dead guy behind the counter?"

"Why would someone open a box of Ziploc bags, take one or two out, and throw the rest of them away?" Monk said. "It's unconscionable."

"Maybe that's why those two guys came in, stole his money, and shot him," I said. "As punishment for wasting Ziploc bags."

"What kind of world are we living in?"

Monk looked into the trash can again and scowled. I followed his gaze. There was an open box of aluminum foil inside, with most of the roll still left.

"It's so wasteful," Monk said.

"I'm going to assume you mean the senseless taking of a human life and not the loss of a couple feet of aluminum foil."

Monk walked to the back of the store and stopped in front of the door that led to the storeroom. There was a handwritten sign on the door that said, *No Public Restrooms.*

He stared at the sign for a long moment, turned around to face the front counter, and nodded to himself.

"What?" I said.

"Now I get it," Monk said.

"Get what?"

"What happened here," he said, and walked out.

I didn't know there was anything mysterious about the robbery, except the identity of the two robbers. Was it possible that somehow Monk had already figured that out?

He walked over to Officer Riglin and Lorna

Karsch, who flicked her cigarette stub onto the sidewalk and ground it under her heel. Monk winced but didn't do anything about it.

"Ms. Karsch? I'm Captain Monk. Could you tell me what you were doing right before you heard the gunshots?"

"I was in the back room, like I told him," she said, gesturing to Officer Riglin. "I was unpacking a box of Doritos. The nacho-cheese ones."

"What were you doing before that?" Monk asked, sniffing the air.

"Unpacking Big Slurp cups and stacking them by the drink machines," she said.

"I see." Monk leaned forward and sniffed her. She would have taken a step back if there weren't a wall behind her. "What did you do after you heard the shots?"

"I opened the door and saw these two big black guys running out of the store. They were both in those puffy jackets, you know, like the rappers wear. And one of the guys was carrying a gun in his hand."

"Then what did you do?"

"I went up to the counter to check on Mr. Touzie and saw all that blood," she said. "I called nine-one-one and sat beside him, holding his hand until the police got here."

"You didn't go anywhere else?"

"I was comforting him," she said. "The man was dying right there in front of me. I wasn't going to leave him alone."

"That's very touching," Monk said. "Did you know you smell like a toilet bowl?"

"What did you just say to me?" Lorna said.

"What did you just say to her?" Riglin said.

"You smell like a toilet bowl," Monk said. "A very clean one, of course, with water the same deep blue as that stain on the damp end of your sleeve."

She looked at her sleeve. "What the hell are you talking about?"

"My favorite toilet bowl cleaner," Monk said. "2000 Flushes with Spring Meadow fragrance. I'd recognize the wonderful scent and beautiful shade of blue anywhere, though judging by the tint, you've got only one hundred fifty-three flushes to go before it needs to be replaced."

Officer Riglin took a step forward and jabbed his finger at Monk's face. "You may outrank me, but if you call her a toilet one more time, I'm going to knock you on your ass. This lady just watched her boss die in front of her."

"Because she shot him," Monk said.

"You're a lunatic," Lorna said.

"You said you were in the storeroom unloading boxes when the robbery happened and that you stayed by your boss's side until the police got here. So when did you stain your sleeve?"

"It was earlier," she said, "when I was cleaning up."

"Which was when?" Monk pressed.

"Before I was unpacking the Doritos," she said.

"You said you were putting out the Big Slurp cups before that," Monk said.

"I was," Lorna said. "And before that I was cleaning the bathroom. What difference does it make?"

"The difference between guilt and innocence," Monk said. "Here's what really happened. There weren't any robbers. You shot your boss, emptied the cash register, and called nine-one-one. You quickly wrapped the gun and the money in aluminum foil, sealed them in Ziploc bags, and hid them in the toilet tank, staining the end of your sleeve in the colored water. If you hadn't left a perfectly good box of Ziploc bags and a full roll of foil in the trash, you might have gotten away with it."

"You don't believe that crazy story," Lorna said to Officer Riglin.

"It's easy enough to check," Officer Riglin said. "I've had to go to the bathroom for the last half hour anyway."

Officer Riglin started toward the store.

"I want a lawyer," she said. "I'm not saying another word."

Officer Riglin turned around, handcuffed Lorna Karsch, and read her her rights.

"I'm sorry about what I said to you, Captain," Officer Riglin said. "I was out of line."

"It's okay," Monk said. "I have that effect on some people."

Officer Riglin led Lorna away.

"That was pretty amazing, Mr. Monk," I said. "You can stop worrying about your mojo. You've still got it."

"God, I hope so," Monk said. "Go back in the store and get some Lysol, a roll of paper towels, and a box of trash bags. I'll stay here and secure the scene."

"What scene?"

Monk pointed to Lorna Karsch's crushed cigarette stub. "It could leave a permanent stain."

10

Mr. Monk and the Secret Rendezvous

Ever since Monk discovered a while back that the kindly old woman I used as a babysitter murdered her husband and buried him in her backyard, day care has been a problem for me.

It took me a while, but I finally found Chelsea, a nineteen-year-old junior college student who took classes in the morning and was free to watch over Julie in the afternoon. She and Julie even did their individual homework together, which was a wonderful motivator for my daughter. If something important came up on weekends, I'd usually be able to draft Chelsea into service then, too.

On Sunday I arranged for Chelsea to take Julie and Katie bike riding in Golden Gate Park, not only freeing me up to work with Monk, but also burning off the "free day" debt I'd incurred only yesterday with Katie's mother.

I picked Monk up at ten a.m. and drove him

down to police headquarters, where Cindy Chow and her psychiatric nurse and Frank Porter and his granddaughter and Jack Wyatt and his anger-management counselor were waiting for us.

Chow was busy dismantling her phone (Why? I don't know), while Jasper Perry took notes on his PDA. She wasn't wearing the aluminum foil or the radio on her head. I figured there was something about the police station that prevented alien beings, secret government agencies, or even Oprah Winfrey from reading her mind.

Porter was wearing the same clothes he had on the day before, and so was Sparrow. So either they'd spent the night on one of the cots in the back room or they were trying to cut down on their loads of laundry.

Wyatt leaned back in his chair with his feet up on his desk, trying his best to ignore his anger-management counselor, whom I recognized from the scene of the hit-and-run. The counselor's arm was in a sling, and his eyes were kind of glazed over, probably from the painkillers.

As I looked at the assembled detectives, it suddenly occurred to me that every one of them had their own personal assistant (or enabler, counselor, or watchdog, depending on your point of view). All of us sidekicks should get together and talk shop, I thought. We could share war stories about our long hours, lack of benefits, and miserable salaries. We could even form our own union, the International Association of Detectives' Sidekicks, to address our concerns.

What would all the brilliant, eccentric detectives

out there do if their beleaguered costars decide to stage our own Blue Flu?

Monk faced his squad of detectives, Officer Curtis, and all of us underpaid, underappreciated, and, in at least one case, bullet-ridden sidekicks. Monk cleared his throat and shifted his weight between his feet.

"Good morning," he said. "Since there has been a lull in the killings, I think we should take this opportunity to clean up the squad room, straighten the pictures on the walls, align the furniture in rows, organize our desks, sort our paper clips by size, and equalize our pencils."

"Equalize our pencils?" Wyatt said.

"He wants you to make sure they're all sharpened and the same length," I said.

Monk smiled approvingly at me, presumably pleased by my appreciation of his worldview.

"Oh." Wyatt took all his pencils in his hand, broke them in half, and dumped them in the trash. "Done."

"Try to control your anger," his counselor mumbled.

"I did, Arnie," Wyatt said to him. "If I was angry, I would have shot the pencils."

Arnie swallowed hard. I was wondered if Arnie had been shot by accident. I was sure Arnie wondered the same thing.

"What day is it?" Porter asked.

"Sunday," Sparrow said.

"That's good to know," Porter said. "What year?"

"Two thousand seven," Sparrow said.

"No, really," Porter said. "What year?"

"Two thousand seven," Sparrow said.

"That's not possible," Porter said. "I'll be dead by then, and there will be Holiday Inns on the moon."

"Have you swept the room for bugs?" Chow asked.

"No," Monk said.

"Then it's a good thing I did," she said, taking a device that looked like Mr. Spock's tricorder out of her purse and setting it on her desk. "We're clear. But you never know when a drone might pass overhead."

"What's that?" Sparrow said.

"Robotic surveillance craft employed by the government to pick up transmissions of all kinds, including brain waves," Chow said. "It operates with sophisticated software designed to search for specific words or thoughts and then lock onto the sender, logging everything for later examination."

Jasper nearly dislocated his thumbs trying to type all that on his tiny PDA keypad.

"Any new developments in your homicide investigations?" Monk asked the detectives.

"John Yamada, the roadkill from yesterday, was going through an ugly divorce," Wyatt said. "His estranged wife, who still happens to be the beneficiary of his one-million-dollar life insurance policy, reported her car stolen two days ago. When we locate her car, I'm betting we'll find some of her husband in the tire treads."

"I'd like to talk to her," Monk said.

"I found out Allegra Doucet had a rich client, a

guy named Max Collins, who made all his investments based on her astrological advice," Chow said. "He isn't so rich anymore. He's lost millions, thanks to her."

"Sounds like a strong motive for murder," Monk said. "I'll follow up on that."

"I'm still checking her other clients and digging into her past," Chow said. "It wouldn't surprise me if she was somehow involved with Project Subzero."

"What's that?" Monk said.

"The government's secret mind-control program," Jasper said. "They track psychics from birth and enlist them for thought surveillance activities."

"If it's such a secret," I said, "how do you know about it?"

"He's part of it," Chow said. "He's strip-mining your brain right now."

"I think that's what happened to me," Frank Porter said. "I have these little memory lapses, like part of my mind has been wiped."

"It has," Chow said. "It's common knowledge now that Alzheimer's is a side effect of thought surveillance. They were probably digging into your head the whole time you were investigating the county supervisor's murder in 1998."

"I don't remember that," Porter said.

"I'm not surprised," Chow said.

"But I remember that Diane Truby, the gal hit by the bus, had a customer at her restaurant who was stalking her," Porter said. "She even got a restraining order against him after he sent her a bouquet of roses and a vial of his blood. He showed up at her restaurant yesterday morning and screamed in front of witnesses that if he couldn't have her, nobody could."

"He could be the guy," Monk said. "I'll talk to him."

"We've got a list of about twenty-five itinerant sellers of running shoes," Officer Curtis said. "Should we start showing them photos of the Strangler's victims?"

"No," Monk said. "I want to be there."

"Could I talk to you for a moment, Mr. Monk?" I asked. "In private?"

He nodded and we went into Stottlemeyer's office. I closed the door behind us.

"You just said you wanted to interview Max Collins yourself and John Yamada's wife and Diane Truby's stalker."

Monk nodded. "They're all strong suspects."

"And you want to go around the city yourself and show all those shoe salesmen the pictures of the Strangler's victims," I said.

"One of the salespeople could be the Strangler."

I motioned to the detectives in the squad room. "What are they going to be doing while you're investigating all those cases?"

"Cleaning up the office, organizing their desks, sorting their paper clips," Monk said. "Preventing the San Francisco Police Department from slipping into anarchy."

"And what about any new homicides that come in?" I said. "Are you going to handle those yourself, too?"

"Of course," Monk said.

"While you're continuing to work on the Strangler killings and the Doucet, Yamada, and Truby murders."

"How else am I supposed to solve them?"

"Who said that you, personally, have to solve each murder that's committed in San Francisco?"

"That's why I'm here," Monk said. "Isn't it?"

"Mr. Monk, you can't do it all. You're just one man. There aren't enough hours in the day."

"I'll just have to solve them faster."

"Remember how you felt yesterday? It's only going to get worse," I said. "You're going to exhaust yourself, and then these cases will never get solved."

"But I don't know how to do it any other way," Monk said.

"You'd better find one," I said.

Monk frowned and paced and frowned some more. Finally he stopped and looked at me.

"We need a consultant," Monk said.

On TV cop shows, people are always having secret meetings in empty warehouses, in deserted parking garages, or in abandoned amusement parks.

There aren't a lot of empty warehouses in San Francisco, at least not that I know of. Most of the parking structures in this city are packed with cars and people, but even if they weren't, Monk's wife was killed in one, so that wasn't an option. And with real estate so valuable, the closest thing we had left to an abandoned amusement park was the ruins of the Sutro Baths.

So that's where we found ourselves, on a windswept gravel parking lot above the weedy swamps and the wave-splashed footings that once supported six hundred tons of iron girders and one hundred thousand square feet of rainbow-colored stained glass over six saltwater swimming pools, one freshwater pool, a museum, and art galleries.

Stottlemeyer was waiting for us, sitting on the hood of his car, smoking a cigar and watching an elderly park ranger show some overweight, middle-aged tourists a creased scrapbook full of pictures of the Sutro Baths, built in 1896, and the adjacent Cliff House, a five-story, wooden, faux French château erected at the same time and perched improbably over the churning sea.

The Cliff House crumbled in flames a decade later and was subsequently rebuilt on a smaller, much less ambitious scale (and remodeled many, many times over the ensuing decades). But the baths survived until 1967, though by then it had become a forgotten, decaying skating rink, relentlessly hammered by time and tide. It finally burned down, too, while being demolished for a resort that was never built.

It's not much of a story, is it?

But the park service treats the place as if the submerged foundations and scattered chunks of exposed concrete are the ruins of some Mayan temple, when, in fact, it's got no more historical significance than the remains of a Howard Johnson.

It was chilly and gray, and the air was thick with sea mist. The seals were barking on the jagged rocks offshore, and seagulls cawed overhead.

"What are we doing here, Captain?" Monk asked Stottlemeyer.

"You tell me, Monk," he said. "You asked for this little rendezvous."

"I mean, why did we have to meet way out here?" Monk said. "Surely there was someplace closer that doesn't overlook rocks bleached with seagull guano."

"Because I don't want to be seen with you. If just one cop spots us together, I'm finished in the department. No one will ever trust me again."

"But everyone knows we're friends," Monk said.

"We shouldn't be," Stottlemeyer said. "Not anymore. Friends don't betray each other."

"I didn't betray you."

"You're sitting at my desk," Stottlemeyer said.

"I'm sitting in an interrogation room."

"It doesn't matter where the hell you're actually sitting, Monk. You're the captain of homicide."

"*Acting* captain," Monk said.

"The two most important things in my life were my wife and my job. Now I've got neither one. I think you know exactly what that's like."

Monk blinked hard. Stottlemeyer might as well have slapped him.

"I'm sorry," Monk said. "This was a very bad idea."

He lowered his head, hunched his shoulders, and started slouching his way back to my car. My heart broke for both men. I looked at Stottlemeyer's face. What I saw wasn't anger. It was pain.

"Wait," Stottlemeyer said. Monk turned back to face him. "What I'm trying to tell you is that I know how you feel, maybe more now than I ever did before, and why you had to take the badge when Smitrovich offered it to you."

"You do?" Monk said.

"I'm not saying what you did was right, or that I appreciate your screwing over every cop in the department, but I understand why you did it."

"So, you'll help me?"

"You mean will I work against my own best interests and those of my fellow cops?"

"I mean, will you help me catch a serial killer before he takes any more lives, and stop three murderers from getting away with their crimes?"

"It's more complicated than that."

"Not to me," Monk said.

"That's one of your big problems right there." Stottlemeyer scowled and ground his cigar out on his hood. "Okay, tell me your troubles."

Monk told him.

Stottlemeyer rubbed his unshaven chin and took a deep breath, letting it out slowly. "Let me tell you about Randy Disher—"

"I don't think he can help us," Monk interrupted.

"Let me finish," Stottlemeyer said. "You think Randy is enthusiastic and hardworking, but you don't respect him much as a detective."

"I never said that," Monk said.

But that's what he must have thought. I did. Don't get me wrong; I like Disher. He's a friendly guy, but I often wondered how he ever made it to lieutenant.

"Randy is a people person. He's likable, nonthreatening, and courteous. People naturally open up to him, even the ones who should be on their guard," Stottlemeyer said. "They tell him things they wouldn't tell anybody else, things that they sure as hell wouldn't tell me, and they don't even realize they're doing it. That's his gift."

"Does he solve any cases?" I asked.

Stottlemeyer narrowed his eyes at me. "Do you think I'd keep him around, that he'd be my right-hand man, if he didn't? He's got an excellent clearance and conviction rate."

"I didn't know," I said.

"Why should you? You're not a cop, and the cases he solves aren't unusual, high-profile, or particularly colorful. But, by God, he closes them."

"What does Lieutenant Disher's work have to do with me and my problems?" Monk asked.

"Frank Porter is the most dogged investigator I know. If the facts are out there, he will find them. Cindy Chow can untangle a conspiracy better than anybody because she sees them everywhere. She finds connections between people, places, and events that anybody else would miss. Mad Jack Wyatt is a force of nature on the streets, relentless, fearless, and unstoppable. He won't let go of a case once he's on it. And you, Monk, are a deductive genius, but I'm just guessing. The truth is, I don't know how the hell you do what you do."

"I appreciate the compliment," Monk said. "But I'm missing your point."

"For a genius, it's amazing how often you can be a complete idiot."

"*That's* your point?" Monk said.

"I don't investigate every murder myself. I delegate. I keep an eye on things, and I offer advice, but mostly I match cases to the unique talents of my individual detectives," Stottlemeyer said. "You have a team of skilled detectives. Use them. Save yourself for what you do best and let the others do the rest."

"What if they miss something?"

"Then they miss something. Maybe you'll catch it later; maybe you won't. You've got to live with that."

"I don't know if I can," Monk said.

"Then you aren't ready to be captain."

"Is that what you think?" Monk said. "That I'm not qualified to do this?"

Stottlemeyer looked out at the sea. "I can't answer that."

"Can't or won't?"

I glared at Monk. It was bad enough that he'd already asked Stottlemeyer to choose between his friendship to him and his loyalty to the police force. It seemed to me that Stottlemeyer made the choice and didn't much like himself for what he'd picked. Now Monk was making things worse by pressing his friend even further.

"The truth is, Monk, that I don't care whether you are or not," Stottlemeyer said. "The best thing that could happen to me and every cop in this city is for you to fail miserably. So I'll give you one guess what I'm rooting for."

I didn't have to guess, and if Monk was smart, he didn't either. I headed for my car, hoping Monk would take the hint and keep his mouth shut.

"Thank you for your help," Monk said.

"Don't ask for it again, because you won't get it," Stottlemeyer said, his back to him. "You're on your own until this flu bug passes."

"Then I hope everyone gets well very soon," Monk said, and then got into my car.

On the drive back downtown, Monk called headquarters and asked Porter to oversee the sweep of gypsy shoe sellers, assigned Wyatt to search for the stolen car belonging to John Yamada's ex-wife, and asked Chow to find Diane Truby's stalker and bring him in for questioning. Monk decided to handle interviewing Max Collins, the investor who lost millions of dollars following Allegra Doucet's bad astrological advice.

"Why did you pick the astrologer case for yourself?" I asked.

"Following the shoe lead requires legwork and manpower; they don't need me for that," Monk said. "It's clear what happened to Yamada and Truby. We just don't know who the killers are or why they committed the crimes. Those answers will come through investigation and perseverance. But Allegra Doucet's murder is a complete mystery to me. All I know is that she was stabbed, but nothing else about the crime scene makes sense."

"You're hoping you'll meet Max Collins and get one of your aha moments."

"That would be nice," Monk said.

"And you're okay letting Porter, Chow, and Wyatt run with the other cases in the meantime."

"No. The only thing stopping me from curling into a fetal position and sobbing is my seat belt."

"But you're following Stottlemeyer's advice anyway," I said.

"He's good at this," Monk said.

"You ought to tell him that sometime," I said.

"He knows," Monk said.

I don't know why men can't tell anyone, even their closest friends and loved ones, what they feel. Do they just assume that everybody around them is psychic? Or do they think that admitting any feelings, even something positive like love or admiration, somehow makes them weak?

"But has he heard it from you?" I asked him.

"He doesn't want to hear it from me. Not anymore."

"Only until this is over," I said.

Monk shook his head. "That depends on how it ends."

11

Mr. Monk and the Masterpiece

The Greenwald Gallery was filled with what I assumed were astronomically expensive paintings and sculptures. Otherwise it wouldn't have been in Union Square, wouldn't have been open by appointment only, and wouldn't have been protected by armed security guards inside and outside the doors.

We were greeted by a tall, thin, sharply dressed British woman. The cut of her suit at the shoulders, waist, and hips was almost razor-edged. Even her features were sharp. Anyone who got close to her ran the risk of slicing their throat on her pointy cheekbones, her angular chin, or the tip of her surgically refined nose, which she held up high as if to keep it above our foul stench.

"I'm Prudence Greenwald, owner of the gallery. Mr. Collins is expecting you, Detectives. He's in the back," she said with a refined British accent.

"Follow me, and please do not touch any of the artwork."

Her accent was fake, something she picked up to go with her surgical makeover.

Okay, I don't really know if that's true, but that's what I wanted to believe. I didn't bother telling her that I wasn't a detective and that Monk was acting captain of homicide. I liked her mistakenly thinking I was an authority figure.

"Do you have any of those paintings of dogs playing poker?" I said. "We simply adore them."

"Not presently," she said.

"How about portraits of Elvis?"

She sneered at me. "I'm afraid not."

"Then I guess we'll just be browsing today," I said.

We found Max Collins admiring a tangle of iron strands that resembled an enormous hairball coughed up by a cat. The sculpture was displayed on a white pedestal under a pinpoint halogen.

Collins wore his impeccably tailored suit as if he were modeling it for himself, but I looked around and couldn't see his reflection anywhere. He must have been imagining how good he looked. He was in his mid-thirties, with teeth so white and skin so golden that George Hamilton probably sent him fan letters.

"Thank you for meeting me here, Captain," Collins said, offering his hand to Monk, who shook it, then motioned to me for a wipe. "I couldn't miss this appointment. These pieces just came in from a private collector who is selling some items to raise cash for another endeavor. His loss is my gain."

"I understand you've had a few losses of your own lately," Monk said, wiping his hands. "Thanks to Allegra Doucet's investment advice."

"Let's just say I'm focusing my investing interests these days on works of art."

"You've given up on astrological advice?" I asked, taking the wipe and putting it in a Ziploc bag, which I then stuffed in my purse.

"I still read my horoscope in the *Chronicle*; I've just stopped relying on the stars to guide my investing."

"And this exquisite sculpture would be a particularly good investment," Prudence said. "It's one of Lofficier's finest works. It's called *Existence.*"

Monk looked away, repulsed.

"You don't like it?" Collins said.

"It doesn't have a shape," Monk said. "It isn't even symmetrical. It's wobbly and uneven."

"That's its beauty," Prudence said. "It depicts the circle of life and, within it, the eternal struggle between the spiritual and the physical, between politics and art."

"But it's not a circle," Monk said. "It's a mishmash."

"What you're seeing is the complexity of the piece," Prudence said.

"What I'm seeing is the mish," he said. "And the mash."

"I take it you're not a fan of abstract art," Collins said to Monk.

"I like things that are neat and clean," Monk said. "How did you get involved with Allegra Doucet?"

"Interesting segue," Collins said. "I'd been hearing about her for a while. She advised some heavy hitters in the business community on investing, using astrology and their personal charts as her guides. I heard they had some success."

"So you sought her out," Monk said.

"Not really. I grew up in the Haight. My mom still lives there. I was visiting my mom one day, passed Allegra's place, and finally decided, 'What the hell?' Allegra and I connected immediately. She did my chart. It was uncanny how accurate it turned out to be. So I kept going back for more advice."

"Even though you were losing money?" I said.

"Did I mention she was great in bed?" Collins smiled at me and then strode over to a painting that was an explosion of colors expressed in brush-strokes, splashes, and dribbles of paint.

It looked to me as if someone had hung the canvas on the wall, threw balloons filled with paint at it, then ran his brush across it a few times before pouring some more paint over it all from a can.

Monk shielded his eyes from the painting. "So what went wrong?"

"I lost three million. I couldn't believe the stars suddenly went so bad. So I hired a PI to do a little digging. He discovered that Allegra was being paid by the companies I invested in to steer rich people their way. Astrology had nothing to do with her advice. So I broke it off with her."

I was surprised he was having this conversation with us in front of Prudence, but she appeared not to be paying any attention, nor to feel the least bit awkward, though she was obviously hearing every word. She was adept at remaining present but unobtrusive at the same time.

"That's it?" I said. "You simply broke it off?"

"I also recommended that she leave San Francisco while she still had use of her legs."

"Did you have a key to Allegra's house?" Monk found a place to stand so he wouldn't have to look at the painting while facing Collins.

"As a matter of fact, I did," Collins said, moving so that once again, Monk would have to see the painting if he looked at him.

"Where were you two nights ago?" Monk said, moving to Collins's side and glancing at him out of the corner of his eye.

"Visiting my mother, who lives around the corner from Allegra's house." Collins took a step back, so Monk had to turn to look at him and, again, catch a glimpse of the painting. "Not only did I have a motive to kill Allegra, I also had the means and opportunity."

"I'm surprised you're being so candid," Monk said, squinting to blur his view. "Would you like to confess while you're at it?"

"I figure the more open and honest I am with you, the more likely you are to scratch me off your list of suspects."

"It could simply be a ploy," Monk said. "Like all the moving around you're doing so I have to look at that painting."

Collins feigned surprise. "Oh, excuse me. I had no idea. You don't like the painting?"

"It's a mess," Monk said.

"This is a classic Wallengren, one of his earliest explorations of abstract expressionism." Prudence regarded the painting with reverence. "It's called *Laura,* a portrait of his mistress. As you can see, he was deeply influenced by Pollock and de Kooning."

"Definitely," Collins said, nodding.

"The emotion here is raw, almost animalistic," Prudence said, "yet tempered with sensuality and, dare I say it, whimsy. You feel its power instinctively rather than emotionally or intellectually."

"A blank canvas would be more pleasant to look at," Monk said. "The painting doesn't look anything like a woman."

"Abstract art doesn't depict objects," Prudence said in a patronizing tone. "It captures their nature, their ambiguities, their feeling, their essence."

"How much is it?" Collins asked.

"Seven hundred thousand dollars," Prudence said.

"I'll take it," Collins said.

"You don't want to buy it," Monk said. "It's not art."

"I'm curious," Collins said. "Is there anything here that you would deem a work of art?"

Monk let his gaze roam the gallery until he found something pleasing.

"This is a masterpiece," he said.

He led us over to a pedestal, where a spray bottle of Windex gleamed under a pinpoint halogen.

"Its red-white-and-blue color scheme evokes freedom, democracy, and peace, underscoring our patriotic duty to keep surfaces germ-free," Monk said. "The graceful, flowing lines of the bottle and the deep, vivid blue of the liquid represent nature, purity, and the spiritual deliverance that can come only from clean living. It's beautiful."

"It's a bottle of window cleaner," Prudence said. "It wasn't on display. I was cleaning the windows and left the bottle there. It's worthless."

I didn't like this lady, and I was tired of her superior attitude. She was no better than me, and I had to let her know it.

"A box of Brillo soap pads is just a disposable consumer product in colorful packaging. But when Andy Warhol made exact plywood replicas of the Brillo boxes and stacked them in a gallery, they became art," I said. "Like the Windex bottle, the bold use of red, white, and blue on the Brillo soap-pad box ties patriotism, virtue, and independence with the act of keeping aluminum clean, while the squareness of the box itself evokes order, balance, and harmony.

"Warhol used the ordinary nature of his subject to ask: Why is a representation of something art and yet that which it depicts is not? And, in doing so, he completely undermined the prevailing philosophy of art. I submit that by putting it on a pedestal under a spotlight in a gallery you have made it art by virtue of its context. The question is: Is it art regardless of the context? I think Mr. Monk has proven that the answer is yes."

They all stared at me for a long moment in silence. I may look working-class, but that doesn't mean I don't have an education. I enjoyed their astonishment and tried not to appear smug.

Collins picked up the bottle of Windex and offered it to Monk.

"It's yours," he said, "with our compliments."

Monk took a step back, holding his hands up in front of him.

"Do you really think I could walk out of here with that and no one would notice? It's a bribe."

"It's Windex," Collins said.

"What you're doing is the desperate act of a guilty man, and it's tantamount to a confession."

"I didn't kill Allegra Doucet," Collins said.

"They why are you trying to bribe me?" Monk said. "You must have done something wrong. I'll find out what it is. You can be sure of that."

On that note Monk walked out, shielding his eyes the whole way from the painful images of abstract expressionism.

We walked back to my car, which was parked a few blocks north on Sutter. The sidewalk was crowded with people. Monk's hands were shoved deep into his coat pockets, and his head was hung low as he tried hard not to brush against anyone. His efforts to avoid all contact with passersby turned his walk into something resembling interpretative dance. He weaved, twirled, and contorted. I was tempted to put a hat on the sidewalk and collect donations for his street performance.

"It's one thing not to like a work of art," I said. "But don't you think that covering your eyes was going a little overboard?"

"I was protecting myself."

"From a painting?"

"You don't know what it's like for me to have to look at something that awful."

"How is it you can casually examine a bloody,

mutilated corpse but you're repulsed by a creative splatter of color and paint on a canvas?"

"The longer I look at something so messy, so disorganized, so *wrong*, the stronger and more irresistible my compulsion becomes."

"The compulsion to do what?"

"To fix it," Monk said.

"How could you fix a painting? How would you bring order to something intentionally abstract?"

"I don't know, and that's what I'm afraid of. I have no idea what I might do."

"Surely you could control yourself," I said. He looked at me. "Never mind, I take it back."

"With an unsolved murder, I'm driven by the same compulsion to fix the problem. But I know how to do it," Monk said. "I assemble the evidence into a clear picture of what occurred, and then I make sure that the murderer is punished for his crimes."

"Do you think Collins killed Allegra Doucet?"

"By his own admission, he had means, motive, and opportunity," Monk said. "The fact that he had a key and was Doucet's lover would explain how he got in the house, why she was facing her killer, and why she didn't know that she was in danger until it was too late."

"What about the open bathroom window and the broken towel bar?"

"Collins could have staged the whole thing to make it appear that there was an intruder when there wasn't one."

"You'd think if he was planning to murder Allegra Doucet he would have come up with a better alibi for himself."

"You'd think," Monk said.

"Then again, maybe that's what he wants us to think," I said. "Perhaps he has a lousy alibi on purpose so he'll appear less guilty."

"Perhaps," Monk said.

"So which is it?"

Monk shrugged. "I don't know yet. But I was very impressed by the speech you made in the gallery."

I smiled. I may have even blushed. It was the first time Monk had ever told me he'd been impressed by anything I'd said or done.

"Really?" I said, fishing for more compliments.

"I can't stop thinking about it."

"You mean the thorny, philosophical question of what constitutes art?"

"I mean the box of Brillo soap pads," Monk said. "It sounds incredible. Where can I see it?"

My cell phone rang. Officer Curtis was calling to report that the city of San Francisco had one less taxpaying citizen.

We were on our way to a homicide, so the victim of the crime was beyond help, but I still felt a sense of urgency. That's not to say I was speeding, though I was certainly driving aggressively.

If we kept at this cop thing for much longer, I was going to ask for a magnetized red bubble light, like Kojak had, so that I could reach up and put it on the top of my car when it was time to press the pedal to the floor.

But my pedal wasn't pressed anywhere near the floor, so I was surprised when I saw a cop car zooming up in my rearview mirror, his lights flashing.

"What does he want?" I said.

Monk looked over his shoulder. "Maybe he's our escort."

"I doubt it," I said.

I kept driving for a block or two anyway, until the cop gave me gave a short squawk of his siren, signaling me to pull over.

I parked in a red zone, the only open space on the street, and rolled down my window. Monk gave me a scolding look.

"Now you've done it," Monk said.

"I haven't done anything," I said.

"The police don't pull you over for nothing," Monk said.

"They do if you're driving the guy who accepted the mayor's offer to lead the homicide division during a Blue Flu."

"I don't understand what you mean," Monk said.

"They knew we were on our way to the crime scene and that we'd probably be taking this route," I said. "This was a trap. I wouldn't be surprised if every patrol car in the city is on alert to ticket me for something."

"Someone has a persecution complex," Monk said.

"They towed my car from a crime scene," I said.

"You were parked illegally, weren't you?"

"You're missing the point," I said.

"You need to start reading the signs before you park," he said.

The officer strode up to my window. He was an

Asian man in his mid-thirties. His name tag said Officer Nakamura.

"Driver's license and registration please," he said.

I handed him my license. While he looked at it, I reached across Monk, opened the glove box, and took out my registration.

"You're in some hurry, Ms. Teeger," Officer Nakamura said.

"This is Captain Monk of homicide, as you already know." I gave the officer the registration slip. "I'm his driver. We're on our way to a crime scene on official police business."

Monk held up his badge.

"That's no excuse for speeding in a residential zone," Officer Nakamura said. "You are a civilian in a civilian vehicle. You have to obey the traffic laws."

"That's what I keep telling her," Monk said.

"Thank you for your support," I said to Monk, then turned back to the officer. "I wasn't speeding."

"I'm afraid that's not an accurate statement," Officer Nakamura said. "I clocked you on radar going twenty-eight miles per hour."

"Good God, woman, what were you thinking?" Monk exclaimed.

"This is a twenty-five-mile-per-hour zone, Mr. Monk. I was going *three miles* over the speed limit."

"So you admit you were speeding?" Officer Nakamura said with a grin.

"You can't be serious," I said.

"I'm dead serious, Ms. Teeger. These intersections are full of women with baby carriages, senior citizens, and children," Officer Nakamura said, barely able to keep himself from laughing. "It's not a drag strip."

"A drag strip?" I said. "What is this, 1957?"

"How could you be so reckless?" Monk admonished me. "Don't you place any value on human life?"

"C'mon, Mr. Monk, can't you see what's happening here? This has nothing to do with whether or not I drove a mere three miles over the speed limit; it's all about you," I said. "This is blatant harassment."

"You're also parked in a red zone," Officer Nakamura said. "That's a parking violation."

"See," I said to Monk. "*Now* do you get it?"

"You're a scofflaw," Monk said.

"Please remain here while I write up your tickets," Officer Nakamura said, returning to his car.

"God bless you, Officer," Monk said.

I glanced in my rearview mirror and saw Nakamura laughing to himself. The jerk.

"You should be grateful he's going so easy on you," Monk said.

"Easy on me? I can't believe you," I said, nearly screaming in exasperation. "The tickets he's writing for these bogus violations will probably cost me hundreds of dollars!"

"Don't look at me," Monk said. "I'm not the speed demon."

"You're a police captain," I said.

"Are you saying I should arrest you myself?"

"You should tell him to what he should do with those tickets."

"I will," Monk said.

"You *will*?"

The officer returned and handed me the tickets, my license, and my registration slip. "You should drive more attentively in the future, Ms. Teeger, for your own safety and the good of the community."

I looked at Monk. "Don't you have something to say to the officer?"

Monk cleared his throat. "I'm the captain of homicide; are you aware of that?"

"Yes, sir, I am."

"Good, then listen very carefully. Here's what I want you to do with those tickets." Monk leaned across me and looked the officer in the eye. "Make copies and mail them to her in case she loses the originals."

"I'll do that," Officer Nakamura said, a little bewildered, and walked away.

"Thanks a lot," I said to Monk.

"I'm just looking out for your best interests."

"How, exactly?" I said.

"If you lose them and fail to pay the fine, they could issue a warrant for your arrest," Monk said. "Then who would drive me?"

12

Mr. Monk Goes to Another Crime Scene

The Richmond District was once a foggy wasteland where the city buried its dead. Now it's become a multicultural, multiethnic neighborhood of dim-sum restaurants and Italian bakeries, French bistros and Russian tearooms. Turn-of-the-century Edwardian homes stand shoulder-to-shoulder with Victorian row houses and stucco apartment blocks. It's a quirky place, on the cusp of becoming *très* chic and *très* unaffordable. The city's only Church of Satan is in the neighborhood, but you won't find that mentioned by many real estate agents or highlighted in any of the tourist guides.

Scott Eggers's corpse was in the alley behind his pastel-colored house on Tenth Avenue. There was a white plastic grocery bag over his head and cinched around his neck.

Eggers wore a tank top and shorts. He had the sculpted muscles of a man who worked out with weights rather than the natural physique of someone who got buff from his labors.

The body was between a shiny Lexus convertible and a bunch of trash cans, which were making it difficult for Monk to concentrate on the task at hand.

Monk stood a few feet away from the body and kept his eye on the cans as if they might suddenly pounce and gobble him up.

A woman in an unflattering white jumpsuit, emblazoned with the letters SID across the back in big yellow letters, crouched over the body, her long red hair tied in a ponytail and stuffed under her collar so she wouldn't contaminate the crime scene. She was in her late thirties and freckle-faced. She introduced herself to us as Terri Quinn.

"Here's what I think happened—" she began, but stopped midsentence when Monk held up his hand.

"There's a set of keys under the car, and the back of the victim's head is matted with blood," Monk said. "So it's clear he was on his way to his car, taking his keys out to disable the alarm, when he was struck from behind. He fell facedown. The killer grabbed a grocery bag from the trash, pinned the victim down, and suffocated him."

"How do you know the bag came from the trash as opposed to the killer bringing it with him?" Terri asked.

Monk pointed to the store logo on the bag. "We passed that grocery store on Clement Street on our way over, so I'm assuming that's where the victim shops and that his garbage can is full of those bags."

"You're good," Terri said.

"I'm sorry," Monk said. "Usually I'm better than that."

It was a remark that would have come off as arrogant if he didn't deliver it with such genuine disappointment in himself.

Terri gave me a questioning look. I didn't know how to convey the answer with an expression, not that I even had an answer to give her.

"Mr. Eggers was struck with a blunt object, like a pipe or crowbar. Whatever it was, we haven't recovered it," Terri said. "There's a bruise on the victim's back, presumably from where he was pinned down by the killer's knee, and there are plenty more of those grocery bags in the trash."

"What a horrible way to die," I said.

"It could have been worse," Terri said. "He could have been conscious when it happened. He basically died in his sleep, and it was all over in less than five minutes. Mr. Eggers never knew what hit him."

"Or *who* hit him," Monk said. "It was all done behind his back."

"Makes sense to me," Terri said. "This guy was strong. I wouldn't want to take him on in a fair fight, and I've got a black belt."

"What is this car worth?" Monk said.

I shrugged. "I'd guess close to a hundred thousand dollars."

"I wonder why the killer didn't take it," Monk

said. "It would have been easy. The keys are right there on the ground."

"Maybe the car has LoJack and the killer was afraid the police would activate it and pinpoint his location," I said.

"The killer didn't take Eggers's wallet, either," Terri said. "There's two hundred dollars in cash and several credit cards in it."

Monk frowned, rolled his shoulders, and fiddled idly with the top button of his collar, as if his clothes were itchy or didn't fit right. But it wasn't his clothes that were irritating him; it was the facts of the case.

"How long has he been dead?" Monk asked.

"I'm guessing about an hour. His body was still warm when we got here. His lover came back from a run in the Presidio, found the body, and called it in. That's him, with the baseball cap." She motioned to a man in front of the crowd that had gathered on the other side of the yellow caution tape. The man was dressed in a bright blue running suit, and there were tears running down his rough, unshaven cheeks. "His name is Hank Criswell."

"Thank you, Terri," Monk said.

"It's what they pay me for, sir," she said with a smile. A flirty smile. I almost did a double take. Monk missed the implications of her smile, of course. He is an incredibly observant man except when it comes to the subtleties of human behavior.

If I thought Monk was open to the idea of dating, I would have pointed out to him what he'd missed. But he was still in love with his late wife and, as far as I could tell, wasn't the least bit interested in pursuing a romance. I wondered what it was about Monk that attracted her to him.

He walked up to the police line and casually flipped open his badge for Hank Criswell to see. Monk enjoyed it so much, he flipped his badge case twice more to the uniformed cop.

"I'm Adrian Monk. I'm investigating the homicide of Mr. Eggers. I'm sorry for your loss."

"There's nothing to investigate. Go arrest Merle Smetter," Criswell said, wiping the tears off his cheeks with the palms of his hands. "He killed Scott."

"How do you know?" Monk said.

I would have asked who Merle Smetter was first, but I wasn't the detective.

"Smetter put a redwood deck and a hot tub on his roof without getting any of the necessary permits. He parties up there all the time. The noise from that is bad enough, but the pool equipment is right outside our bedroom window, whining and gurgling day and night," Criswell said. "So we filed a complaint against him with the city, and they're making him tear everything out."

"It seems like a minor dispute between neighbors," Monk said. "Not something that would lead to murder."

"People kill each other for pocket change. It's costing Smetter a hundred and sixty thousand dollars to remove everything and restore the roof to its original condition, and he blames us for it," Criswell said. "It could cost him more if we win the lawsuit."

"You're suing him?" I said. "What for?"

"We're artists, graphic designers. The noise is causing us to lose sleep, which affects our creativity and our business. So we're demanding one-point-five million for lost income and intentional infliction of emotional distress," Criswell said. "But that amount is going to go way, way up now. I am suffering *extreme* emotional distress."

More tears spilled from Criswell's bloodshot eyes, and he was racked with fresh sobs.

"Where can I find Mr. Smetter?" Monk asked.

Criswell sniffled and pointed an accusing finger at a man who would stand out in any crowd.

Smetter looked like a cross between a munchkin and a ferret. He was a bald, beer-bellied man with tufts of body hair poking out from underneath his collar, and a waxed mustache that curled at the ends.

He was also barely five feet tall.

The only way Merle Smetter could have attacked Scott Eggers from behind was if he launched himself at him from a pogo stick.

Monk and I shared a look. He didn't seem convinced, either.

"Thank you for your help, Mr. Criswell," Monk said. "I'd like to have an officer take your statement, if you're feeling up to it."

"You're not arresting Smetter?"

"Not just yet," Monk said.

We walked over to one of the officers. As we got closer, I recognized him as Officer Milner, the guy who loaned Monk the binoculars at McKinley Park. He smiled warmly when he saw us.

"I didn't know your beat extended across the entire city," I said.

"With this flu bug going around, the department is spread pretty thin," Officer Milner said. "So I'm going wherever they need me."

"Officer, could you get statements from Hank Criswell, Merle Smetter, and any other neighbors with homes that overlook this alley?" Monk asked.

"Sure thing," Officer Milner said enthusiastically.

"You don't mind helping Mr. Monk out?"

"It's my job, isn't it?"

"I was thinking with the flu and all, you might have a problem with our being here."

Officer Milner shrugged. "We've all got to make a living. Look at me—I'm taking all the overtime I can get."

"Then perhaps you could also round up some other officers and look for anyone who could verify that Hank Criswell was actually jogging in the park at the time of the murder," Monk said.

"Will do, Captain," Officer Milner said. "How's the Strangler case coming? Has the mayor's reward brought in a lot of leads?"

"Nobody has come forward yet," Monk said.

"Someone will," Officer Milner said. "There are people who'd finger their own kid for two hundred and fifty thousand dollars."

Millner took out his notebook and walked over to Criswell. I watched him go. He was a good-looking guy.

"You think Criswell killed his lover and then pretended to discover the body?" I asked Monk.

Monk shook his head. "I'm just being thorough. Criswell wouldn't have attacked Eggers in broad daylight in the alley behind their home. There's too much of a chance he'd be seen and recognized."

"So what's your theory?"

"I don't have one," Monk said. "Nothing about this homicide is right."

"There's a right way to kill someone?"

"If this was a robbery, why go to the trouble of suffocating him when he was already unconscious and defenseless? And why wasn't anything taken?" Monk said. "If this was a premeditated murder, why attack him in broad daylight? If the killer intended to suffocate him from the outset, why not bring a bag rather than digging through the trash for one?"

Monk shuddered at the thought of it.

"It looks as if the killer improvised the whole thing in a hurry," Monk said. "No attempt was made to make this seem like anything except what it is."

"Which is what?"

"A homicide that isn't right," Monk said.

13

Mr. Monk Goes to Headquarters

Monk stood in the doorway to the homicide squad room in stunned silence. I was pretty astonished myself.

Porter, Chow, and Wyatt, their assistants, and Officer Curtis were at their desks, either talking on the phone, using their computers, or sorting through papers, and were only gradually becoming aware of our arrival. But seeing them all hard at work wasn't what was so amazing.

It was the squad room itself. In our absence it had been transformed into a showroom for the principles of balance and order.

All the desks were lined up in rows and spaced apart so evenly, it looked as though someone had actually measured the distance between them to the centimeter.

The telephones, lamps, legal pads, computer monitors, keyboards, pencil holders, and other desktop items were each in the same spot on every desk, as if they'd been permanently glued in place.

Every pencil cup contained exactly four pencils of equal length, four pens (two black and two blue), two pairs of scissors, and two rulers.

Every poster, photograph, map, and bulletin board on the walls was centered, straightened, spaced evenly apart, and arranged by size, shape, and color. Even the papers, photos, and notes on the individual bulletin boards were aligned by size, shape, and color.

The place had been thoroughly Monked.

The only corner of the squad room that remained untouched was Captain Stottlemeyer's office, which, by comparison, looked as if it had been ransacked.

By the time Monk had taken it all in, everyone in the office had set their work aside and turned to face him. He was so moved by what he'd seen that he could barely summon the breath to speak.

To be honest, I had tears in my eyes. I was happy for Monk and genuinely touched by what these strangers had done to show their appreciation and respect for him.

"Thank you," he said, his voice trembling with emotion. "I can't tell you how much this means to me. I won't let you down."

He wanted to say more, but couldn't find the words. He simply smiled, nodded a few times, and retreated to the interrogation room that he was using as his office.

Wyatt grimaced. "What the hell was he talking about?"

"He's obviously nuttier than a can of cashews," Chow replied.

"He sure is," Porter agreed. "Whoever he is."

I was confused. I went over to the coffeemaker, where Jasper, Sparrow, and Arnie had congregated. I guess that made that corner of the room the assistants' lounge.

I met Jasper's gaze and gestured to the detectives. "How did they ever manage to pitch in and do all of this?"

"They didn't," Jasper said. "Sparrow and I did it."

"Why?" I asked.

"It's obvious that Monk suffers from obsessive-compulsive disorder."

"You mean he's a freak," Sparrow said.

"He's already under an unusual amount of stress," Jasper continued, ignoring Sparrow's remark. "A disorderly environment would be crippling for him. The more comfortable he is in his surroundings, the more likely it is that he'll perform at the peak of his abilities."

All true. But that begged a cynical question.

"Please don't take this the wrong way," I said. "But what difference does it make to you if Mr. Monk succeeds or not?"

"I care about people. Otherwise I wouldn't be in the mental health field. But I suppose you could also say it's selfish interest in my patient," Jasper said. "I've never seen Cindy so happy or her paranoia so subdued."

"That's subdued?" I said, glancing at her.

Chow was heading toward a file cabinet, dodging

and weaving and using a circuitous route so she wouldn't be seen by the computer monitors that she passed along the way.

"She left the house without a radio taped to her head," Jasper said. "That's a big step."

"Most people have got those cellular phone thingies stuck to their ears," Sparrow said. "I don't see a big difference between them and her."

Jasper smiled appreciatively. "That's true, Sparrow. I wish more people had your enlightened, relative view toward mental health."

I looked at Sparrow. "I'm surprised you helped Jasper with his little scheme."

"Jasper's got a nice butt," she said matter-of-factly. Jasper blushed. "I'll do a lot for someone with a nice butt. Besides, Grandpa really needed this. It reminds him who he is again so I don't have to all the time. It may be his last chance to be himself, and know it, before he goes completely mad-cow."

"Monk is the only thing holding this group together," Jasper said. "None of them will say it, but they're pinning their hopes for redemption on him."

"Son of a bitch!" Wyatt yelled to no one in particular. "Who glued my pencil cup to my desk?"

Jasper shrank back behind me and Sparrow. There's bravery for you: hide behind the girls.

Wyatt leaned back in his chair, brought up his boot, and kicked the plastic pencil cup until he shattered it, leaving only the base stuck to the desktop. Satisfied, he returned to his work.

"That's progress," Arnie said to us. "The old Mad Jack would have shot it."

"Is there anything that man won't shoot?" I asked.

"His mother," Arnie said. "Well, not lately, anyway."

Monk returned to the squad room. He seemed relaxed for the first time since he got his badge back. He went up to Porter's desk. "Where are we with the questioning of fly-by-night dealers of discontinued and overstock running shoes?"

Porter glanced at his notes. "I've got reports back from seventeen interviews conducted by officers in the field. No merchants have recognized any of the women in the photos yet, but I've logged the names, addresses, and other vital stats of each person the officers talked to in case we have to go back to them later."

Monk nodded. "Keep up the good work."

"I'm not leaving my desk until we crack this case wide-open," Porter declared.

"He's not kidding," Sparrow said to me. "I hope you've got showers in this building."

Monk moved down to Cindy Chow's desk. "Any luck finding Diane Truby's stalker?"

"He's in the wind, but he's got relatives in Sacramento, so I've alerted the cops up there and the Chippies along the way to be on the lookout."

"Chippies?"

"The CHP," Chow said. "The California Highway Patrol. Where have you been?"

"Away," Monk said.

"State or private institution?"

"My apartment," Monk said. "It's reasonably private."

"Uh-huh," Chow said, nodding as if there were some double meaning to what Monk was saying and she understood it. But there wasn't any other meaning. At least, I *think* there wasn't.

"I've made some important discoveries about Allegra Doucet," Chow said, pausing for a moment to add significance to what she was about to say. "Shortly before she moved from LA to San Francisco, she spent a few months with 'friends' in Albuquerque."

Monk shrugged. "Does that mean something?"

Chow looked flabbergasted. "It's *huge*. The headquarters of the Omega Agency, the secret order of humans and extraterrestrials who pull the strings of every world government, is located underneath Kirtland Air Force base in Albuquerque. That's where the ETs, mostly grays and greens, live and conduct their mind-control experiments, including Project Subzero, which is basically an illegal, unauthorized offshoot of Operation Grillflame."

"That last part is real," Jasper whispered to me while Chow kept rambling on.

"The gray and green space aliens?" I replied.

"Operation Grillflame," Jasper said. "The CIA spent twenty million on a secret program to use psychics to read the minds of enemy agents, change the orbit of spy satellites, and detect plutonium in North Korea. It was an outgrowth of MK-Ultra, the CIA's mind-control division, that was funded in 1953 with six percent of the agency's operating budget until it was finally shut down in 1972."

I stared at him.

"Honest," he said. "They're the ones who put LSD on the streets and accidentally created the 1960s."

I stared at him.

"It's true," he said. "You can check it out yourself."

Jasper scared me. He was a mental health professional. If some of Chow's paranoia could rub off on him, what did that say about what was going to happen to me after hanging around with Monk? How long would it be before I was measuring the ice cubes in my freezer to make sure they were perfectly square?

Talking to Jasper, and getting lost for a minute in my private little nightmare, I missed a lot of what Chow had to say, but I can probably summarize the gist of it simply enough: Extraterrestrials are scrambling our brains, probing our bodily orifices, and controlling the world with the help of nefarious government agencies.

"What about Max Collins?" Monk asked. "Do you know anything about him?"

"That's where it gets really interesting," Chow said. "He made his fortune developing advanced software for radar systems," she said. "One of his biggest customers is the United States government. Connect the dots."

"What dots?" Monk said.

"Albuquerque. Radar software. Kirtland Air

Force base. Astrology. Extraterrestrials. Project Subzero. Roswell. Murder. Do I need to draw you a picture?"

"Would you, please? I think that would be very helpful." Monk moved on down to Wyatt's desk and froze when he saw the missing pencil cup. "Your pencil holder is missing."

"I busted three chop shops, but there's no signs of Yamada's wife's car," Wyatt said. "It's probably been stripped into parts by now that are already on their way to Mexico, China, and South America. This time next week, her front seats will be in a taxi in Manila."

"All the other desks have pencil holders," Monk said. "Yours doesn't."

"I've got the tech geeks in the lab trying to match the tread marks from the intersection with marks on the floor of her garage," Wyatt said. "I'm also checking her whereabouts at the time of the murder. She says she was at her boyfriend's place, and he backs her up on it, but I'm sure he'd lie for a percentage of Yamada's lifc insurancc moncy. I'll break him, if I have to do it with my bare hands."

"We need to get you something for your pencils." Monk turned to Officer Curtis, who was standing off to one side, awaiting orders. "It's imperative you get him a pencil holder, one that matches the others."

She nodded and made a note of it on her pad. "Pencil cup. Imperative. Got it."

"Excuse me," someone said.

We all turned to see a gangly man in his thirties standing in the doorway, after being escorted in by a police officer. The stranger was thin, with a long neck, long arms, and a narrow face. He jittered like he had a live current running through his bony body, and pulled nervously on a tuft of hair on his chin.

"Who's in charge around here?"

Monk stepped forward. "I think that's me."

"Get ready to cut me a very big check," the man said. "I can give you the Golden Gate Strangler."

14

Mr. Monk Leads the Charge

Monk hustled the man into an interrogation room. I went with them, even though I wasn't a cop and hadn't been invited. I'm pretty sure that Dr. Watson would have gone with Holmes in the same situation.

"I'm Captain Adrian Monk. Who are you?"

"Bcrtrum Grubcr."

"You can start by unbuttoning your shirt, Mr. Gruber," Monk said.

"I didn't come here for a physical."

"You skipped a buttonhole," Monk said. "Your entire shirt is misaligned."

"So what?"

"You're in a police station. It's our job to enforce law and order," Monk said. "You, sir, are out of order."

"Mr. Monk," I said, "this man says he has information that could lead to the arrest of the Golden Gate Strangler."

"That's what I've got," Gruber said.

"I'm supposed to trust a man who is drunk and disorderly?" Monk said.

"I'm not drunk," Gruber said.

"Then why are you so disorderly?"

Gruber grudgingly unbuttoned his shirt. Monk turned his back to the man and motioned to me do the same.

"I'm not bashful," Gruber said.

"You should be," Monk said.

"What do you know about the Strangler?" I said with my back to Gruber.

"There's this community garden next to McKinley Park. I went out there early Saturday morning to water my strawberries. I was crouching down, you know, to water them, when I saw this guy come out of the dog park, but he didn't have no dog. He didn't see me. The weird thing is, he was clutching this running shoe to his chest like it was made of gold or something."

A shoe.

My heart skipped a beat. If Monk knew my heart did that, he would have demanded that it beat one more time to make up for it.

Monk turned around and so did I.

"Your shirt is still misbuttoned," Monk said.

Gruber looked down at himself. "No, it's not."

It was. Monk glanced imploringly at me.

"You don't seriously want me to button his shirt for him," I said.

"Show some compassion for your fellow man," Monk said.

"Yeah," Gruber said. "Show me."

I knew Monk wasn't going to be able to concentrate with the misbuttoned shirt. I had to take one for the team. I sighed and unbuttoned Gruber's shirt, exposing his scrawny, sunken chest. He grinned at me.

"Nice, huh?" Gruber said. "I work out."

"I'd better get a big raise," I said to Monk, but his back was already turned.

"Tell us more about this man you saw," Monk said.

"He was a fat white guy in his mid-thirties or early forties. He was medium height with greasy brown hair and big, round cheeks, like he had a couple of tennis balls in his mouth."

I buttoned the shirt up as fast as I could. "I'm done."

"If you find yourself dreaming about this moment, give me a call," Gruber said. "We can go sailing on my yacht."

"You've got a yacht?" I asked.

"I will soon." He winked. "It's on the top of my list of things to buy with my two hundred and fifty Gs."

"You haven't given us anything we can use," Monk said.

"I'm not done yet," Gruber said. "The guy wipes his shoe against the edge of the curb to get some dog crap off of it, then gets into his car, an oxidized blue 1999 Ford Taurus with a broken left rear taillight and a dent on the bumper. You want the plates?"

"You remember his license plate number?" Monk said incredulously.

"Just the last letter and the numbers 'cause they match my mom's birthday," Gruber said. "M-five-six-seven. Like May fifth, 1967."

"Stay here," Monk said to him. "The room has a nice mirror. You might want to practice buttoning your shirt while we're gone."

As soon as we were out of the room, Monk went straight to Officer Curtis, who, like everyone else, was waiting in the squad room to hear whatever news he had.

"I need you to run a plate right away," Monk said. "The last part is M-five-six-seven."

"With just a partial plate," she said, "you're going to get hundreds of hits."

"I only want those that are registered to a Ford Taurus," Monk said.

Officer Curtis sat down at a computer and typed in the information.

"What do you think of his story?" I said.

"He knew about the left shoe. That information wasn't released to the public. He also said the man was coming out of the dog park. The specific location where the body was found wasn't released, either."

"So this is a good lead."

"I don't trust him," Monk said.

"You're just saying that because his shirt was misbuttoned."

"You won't find a better indicator of a man's character," Monk said. "So I wasn't surprised when he lied."

"What did he lie about?"

"What he was doing in the park that morning," Monk said.

"How do you know?" There I was, asking that question again. I should print the question on a T-shirt, along with a few others I frequently repeated, and wear it at work every day like a uniform.

"He said he was checking on his strawberries."

"There's an open garden there," I said. "People can grow whatever they want."

"But it's too soon to plant strawberries. The optimum time is between November first and tenth to catch the winter chill; otherwise you'll get very few, if any, berries."

"It could be that he's just a lousy farmer," I said. "I wouldn't know when the right time to plant strawberries is, either."

Officer Curtis spoke up. "I've got one hit for a 1999 Ford Taurus off that partial plate, sir. It's here in San Francisco and is registered to Charlie Herrin."

"I know that name," Porter said.

"You do?" Monk said.

"I think it's mine," Porter said.

"It's not yours," Sparrow said. "Your name is George Clooney."

"Then there's another reason I know that name." Porter sorted through the loose papers on his desk. "Ah. Here it is. Charlie Herrin. He sells overstock shoes at a flea market in the Mission District."

My heart skipped another beat. If this continued, I'd have to schedule an appointment with a cardiologist.

Charlie Herrin had to be the killer. Otherwise all these facts coming together the way they did would have qualified as one of the biggest coincidences in the history of coincidences.

The only downside was that Bertrum Gruber was going to get $250,000 for his tip. I admit it: I was envious and resentful. Monk solved eighteen or twenty murders a year and got a paltry consulting fee, from which I drew my pathetic salary. But some jerk came in with a license plate number and got a quarter of a million dollars. It would take Monk years of servitude to the city to make that much.

Wyatt rose from his seat and leaned over Officer Curtis's shoulder. "You got a residential address on Herrin?"

Officer Curtis nodded. "It's coming out of the printer now."

Wyatt marched over to the printer and snatched the sheet out. "He lives in a dive in the Mission District. We've got to take it down with a full tactical assault ASAP."

"Couldn't we just knock on his door and see if he's home?" Monk said. "That's how I usually do it."

"We're talking about a psycho. If a couple uniforms interviewed him about the dead women today, he knows it's only a matter of time before we're on his ass," Wyatt said. "He's either getting ready to bolt or preparing to hunker down and fight it out."

"He's right," Jasper said. "Psychologically speaking, of course."

"I'm sure the police showing up at his place of

business made him very angry," Arnie said. "But having them show up at his home, violating his personal space, will make him livid."

Monk motioned me over to a corner and whispered, "What do I do?"

"I hate to say it, but Wyatt is probably right," I said. "If anybody here should lead a tactical assault, it's him. Just make sure you're wearing Kevlar from head to toe."

"Do I really have to be there?" Monk whined.

"You're the captain," I said.

The tactical assault team met in the parking lot of a Safeway supermarket around the corner from the building where Charlie Herrin lived.

Monk stood in his Kevlar vest while the thirty other officers double-checked their weapons and communications gear. He looked uncomfortable in his vest and awkward in his surroundings, as if he were the only straight man in a gay bar (like that would ever happen to him). He couldn't stop fiddling with his headset and adjusting the microphone in front of his mouth, which probably took his mind off of how out of place he felt.

Wyatt, however, was entirely in his element. His Kevlar vest fit him so well, I wondered if he'd had his tailored. He spread a blueprint of Herrin's building out on the hood of a car and confidently gave orders to the officers while Monk stood to one side, still adjusting his headset until it was balanced just right.

When Wyatt finished his briefing, everybody synchronized their watches and moved into position. He glanced disapprovingly at Monk.

"Are you carrying a weapon?" Wyatt asked.

Monk reached into his pocket and pulled out half a dozen packets of disinfectant wipes.

"They kill germs on contact," Monk said.

Wyatt grimaced with disgust. "Remain behind me and take cover when the shooting starts."

Monk nodded. "And when should I begin cowering?"

"You never cower," Wyatt said.

"I'm pretty sure that I do," Monk said. "I thought it might help if I warmed up by cowering now so I'm fully cowered when it counts."

Wyatt just shook his head and walked away. Arnie intercepted him.

"Remember those breathing exercises I taught you," Arnie said. "Try to stay calm and focused."

"I'm always calm and focused when I have a gun in my hand," Wyatt said.

"Don't let your anger drive you," Arnie said. "Drive your anger. Steer it to the garage and park it."

Wyatt gave him a steely look. Arnie wilted and shuffled away.

Since Arnie and I were civilians, they wouldn't us go along on the raid. I was thankful for that. Instead we got to watch the entire operation unfold from the comfort of the mobile command center, a retrofitted Winnebego with TV monitors that played live feeds from the microcameras mounted in the SWAT guys' helmets.

Before I tell you what happened, keep in mind that I wasn't actually there. This account comes from what I saw on those "cop cams" in the command center and what I learned later from Monk, so if I sound omniscient here, you'll know why.

The cops swarmed the building from several different entrances. They moved with choreographed precision, with the exception of Monk, who was like a dancer in a chorus who couldn't stay in step. Wyatt kept yanking him back into formation.

The cops cleared out the first-floor tenants before going upstairs to Herrin's apartment. The corridor was narrow and badly lit, with stained carpet and peeling paint.

Wyatt and the officers hugged the walls. Monk did his best not to brush against the walls or step on the stains on the floor, which made him look as if he were playing hopscotch down the corridor.

The officers flanked Herrin's door, their weapons trained dead center. Wyatt stepped up, raised his foot, and with one mighty kick smashed the door open.

He dived low into the room, rolled, and came up in a firing stance, the officers rushing in behind him, their guns aimed at a giant poster of a smiling Jessica Simpson in short-shorts and a halter top. At her feet, on a tiny table, was a pile of left-foot running shoes.

The officers swarmed into the empty apartment, throwing open doors to make sure nobody was hiding in the bathroom or bedroom. When Wyatt yanked open the closet door, a ladder fell out and he nearly shot it.

Monk came in behind the officers and quickly went to the shoes.

"Get these back to headquarters right away," he said to the nearest officer.

Several cops dutifully followed Monk's command and bagged the shoes.

"Stand down," Wyatt said to his men, and holstered his weapon. "It looks like we're too late."

Monk began to wander around the tiny living room, examining the thrift-shop furniture, shoe catalogs, and podiatry journals. He stopped beside the coffee table and crouched to examine a fine white powder on the surface.

He frowned, looked up at the ceiling, and saw a crack opening up like a zipper. And just when he began to register what the crack and the powder meant, the ceiling split open, raining plaster, wood, insulation, and one very fat man right on top of Monk.

I screamed, startling everyone in the mobile command center, which wasn't wise. When cops are startled, their immediate reflex is to draw their weapons. Within an instant, I had three guns aimed at me. I immediately forgot about Monk and began worrying about my own safety.

"Sorry," I mumbled sheepishly.

The flustered cops holstered their weapons, and we all turned our attention back to the screens.

"Relax," Arnie said to me. "This is what Wyatt does best."

Charlie Herrin had scrambled to his feet, lifting Monk up in front of him. He had one arm across

Monk's chest and held a gun to Monk's head with his other hand.

Every officer in the tiny apartment spun around and aimed their weapons at Herrin and Monk.

"Drop your guns or I'll blow his head off," Herrin rasped, coughing on the plaster dust, which covered him and Monk.

"You heard the man; lower your weapons," Wyatt stepped out in front of the others and pointed his massive gun directly at Monk's stomach. "With the price of bullets, we need to economize."

The cops followed Wyatt's command.

Monk tried to wipe the dust off himself, but stopped when Herrin jammed the gun in his ear.

"Stop squirming," Herrin said to Monk, then shifted his attention to Wyatt. "Put your gun down, too."

Wyatt shook his head. "Here's what's going to happen, punk. I'm gonna shoot your hostage."

Monk's eyes widened. "Okay, that's one idea. Let's set that one aside for a moment and see if the three of us can put our heads together and come up with something else."

"The bullet will go clean through him," Wyatt said to Herrin, "and lodge deep in that oversize belly of yours."

"I'll shoot," Herrin said. "I'll splatter his brains all over the room."

"You'll spasm, piss yourself, and lose control of your bowels," Wyatt said. "But you won't shoot."

"Hey, I have an idea. How about everybody puts down their guns and we settle this with an arm-wrestling competition?" Monk said. "It'll be fun and won't leave a mess."

"You'll both live and I'll only be out one bullet," Wyatt continued, ignoring Monk's suggestion. "As opposed to shooting off your kneecaps and putting a bullet in your skull when you let go of your hostage. That's three bullets, which is pricey for a guy on my salary."

"He's wearing Kevlar," Herrin said, squeezing Monk tight against him. "I'm protected."

"My gun is loaded with cop-killer bullets," Wyatt said. "They're armor-piercing."

"Those are illegal."

"You gonna arrest me, punk?" Wyatt said. "These bullets can cut through that Kevlar like it was toilet tissue. While you're squirming in agony in a puddle of your own excrement, I'll convince you to confess."

"I'd really like this to be an excrement-free hostage situation," Monk said. "What if we let Charlie go, count to ten, and *then* chase after him? I think that would work for everyone."

"So what do you say, punk?" Wyatt cocked the trigger of his gun. "Ready to have some fun?"

"This is great progress," Arnie said to me, nodding with approval.

"It is?" I said incredulously. "Wyatt is talking about resolving the situation by shooting Mr. Monk in the stomach!"

"Isn't that wonderful?"

"Somehow I don't see it that way."

"The old Wyatt would have shot him already and not wasted his time talking about it first." Arnie smiled, pleased. "This is a meaningful step forward for him."

I had no doubt at all that Wyatt would really shoot. I'm sure that Monk had no doubt, either. And, apparently, neither did Charlie Herrin. The killer dropped his gun, stepped back from Monk, and raised his hands.

Two of the SWAT guys immediately tackled him, pinned him to the ground, and cuffed him. While that was going on, Wyatt holstered his gun and approached Monk, who was frantically slapping his clothes, stomping his feet, and shaking himself to get the dust off.

Wyatt shook his head at Herrin, disappointed. "Spoilsport."

"The old 'shoot the hostage' ploy," Monk said, brushing himself off. "It's amazing that people still fall for that one."

"I don't ploy. I *always* shoot the hostage," Wyatt said. "Until today, that is. I must be getting soft."

"No one in his right mind would do that," Monk said.

"It helps to be a little crazy. That's what gives me an edge over everyone else," Wyatt said. "You, of all people, should understand that."

He winked at Monk, flashed a cynical grin, and strode out the door.

15

Mr. Monk and the Press Conference

Charlie Herrin was in a holding cell asserting his right to remain silent. Wyatt felt he could convince Herrin to be more talkative, but Monk wisely chose not to take the detective up on his offer.

The crime lab quickly confirmed that the missing shoes belonging to the three murdered women were among those in Herrin's collection. They also found red gravel from the McKinley Park track, as well as forensic evidence relating to the other two killings, in Herrin's Ford Taurus, inextricably linking him to the murders.

Although the police recovered dozens of left running shoes in Herrin's apartment, Monk didn't think that they were souvenirs of other killings Herrin had committed. Monk believed Herrin had been stealing shoes from women for years and only recently escalated to murder. Even so, Monk asked Frank Porter to start investigating Herrin's past and to contact other law enforcement agencies in any cities where Herrin had lived before.

Regardless of what that investigation turned up, one thing was certain: The Golden Gate Strangler case was closed.

Within minutes of Herrin's arrest, Mayor Smitrovich called Monk in the squad room to congratulate him and arrange for a press conference that night to announce the news to the public.

"How did the mayor find out so fast?" I asked Monk. Before he could answer, Cindy Chow spoke up.

"He has spies everywhere," she said.

I hated to say it, but she was probably right. What other explanation was there?

But if the mayor was spying on us, I couldn't help wondering who else might be watching us and eavesdropping on our conversations. I tried not to think about that too much, or things could spiral out of control, and before I knew it, I'd be using aluminum foil to wrap my head instead of for leftovers.

Jasper was eager to interview Charlie Herrin and delve into the killer's bizarre left-foot fetish, but Monk wouldn't allow it. The DA was taking over the case and bringing in his own psychiatric expert.

"I could probably have written a kick-ass landmark thesis on that guy," Jasper lamented.

"What happened to your notion of an almost Jungian shared unconscious among paranoid schizophrenics?" I asked.

"What do you think is going to have more impact? A study of paranoid schizophrenics," Jasper said, "or the forensic psychiatric analysis of a psychopathic killer with a foot fetish who kills women and collects left-foot running shoes? Which would *you* rather read?"

Jasper had a point.

Monk spent the next few hours in his office writing down his remarks for the press conference on index cards. He practiced in front of me, reading directly from his cards.

After introducing himself, he thanked each of his detectives by name for their dedication and hard work. He wrapped up by urging the city to mend its relations with the police force, giving the officers the respect, benefits, and compensation they deserved for their tireless service to the community.

"That's a terrific speech, Mr. Monk," I said. "But aren't you going to thank Bertrum Gruber for coming forward with the vital lead?"

"No."

"I don't like him either, but you can't deny that without him, there wouldn't have been an arrest today."

"He cheated," Monk said.

"Isn't Charlie Herrin the Strangler?"

"He is," Monk said.

"And wasn't it the license plate number that Gruber gave you that pointed to Herrin out of all the possible suspects?"

"It was," Monk said.

"Do you think Gruber had something to do with the murders?"

"No," Monk said.

"So where's the cheating?"

I really hated defending Gruber, but I had to give the guy credit for going to the police with what he saw.

"Gruber is lying," Monk said.

"You're not talking about those strawberries again, are you?"

"Gruber is in his thirties. He said he remembered the last part of the license plate, M-five-six-seven, because it matched his mother's birthday, May fifth, 1967. That would mean she was ten years old when she gave birth to him."

Okay, Monk had a point. For whatever reason, Gruber wasn't being entirely honest about how he got his facts. Even so, there was no denying the end result of his actions.

"What difference does it make how Gruber got the license plate numbers? Herrin is the killer, and he's off the street," I said. "And all those pairs of running shoes are being reunited. The balance of the universe has been restored."

"Except for one thing," Monk said. "He cheated."

"So what's that knock out-of-whack?"

"Me," Monk said.

The press conference was held that night in the opulent City Hall rotunda on the broad landing of the grand marble staircase, which was surrounded by ornate columns of Colorado limestone topped by sculptures of acanthus leaves and decorative scrolls.

The rotunda was dramatically lit to highlight the elegant balconies, add dramatic impact to the Greek mythological figures carved on the walls, and make the elaborate designs on the pink Tennessee-marble floors gleam.

Mayor Barry Smitrovich stood behind the podium, flanked by Bertrum Gruber on one side and Monk on the other. Gruber wore a brand-new, off-the-rack suit and tugged nervously on his goatee. Monk sorted through the notes on his index cards.

I stood behind Monk along with a couple of the mayor's aides, who held a giant reproduction of the $250,000 check made out to Bertrum Gruber, the creep.

There were only a half dozen reporters, two still photographers, and four cameramen in attendance. But it wasn't the number of people who showed up that mattered anymore; it was the number who were tuning in to the live broadcasts, podcasts, and webcasts that counted. If only one person had shown up with a video camera, a laptop, and a broadband connection, he could still potentially reach millions of viewers around the world.

Mayor Smitrovich stepped up to the podium and smiled into the audience, playing to the unseen multitudes instead of the handful who were actually there.

"I'm pleased to announce that an arrest has been made in the Golden Gate Strangler killings, and that the women of this great city can once again feel safe on our streets," Smitrovich said. "The capture of this individual is the direct result of law enforcement officers and the community working together toward a common goal."

"What can you tell us about the suspect?" one of the reporters yelled out.

"His name is Charlie Herrin, and that's all I'm prepared to say about him at this time," Smitrovich said. "But what I can tell you is that he would still be at large if it weren't for a witness coming to the police and sharing crucial information. And for that act of bravery, it's my great pleasure to present the two-hundred-and-fifty-thousand-dollar reward to Bertrum Gruber."

The mayor motioned Gruber forward, and the two aides presented him with the prop check.

"It is my honor to give you this check for two hundred and fifty thousand dollars as a reward for your vigilance, courage, and selflessness." Smitrovich shook Gruber's hand.

If the mayor went on much longer, I was going to need a barf bag.

"I was just doing my duty as a citizen and a San Franciscan," Gruber said. "I would have done it for nothing."

"So you'll be donating this money back to the city?" the mayor joked.

"I don't think so, Barry," Gruber said.

That got a big laugh from the crowd, loud enough that no one but those standing right next to Smitrovich heard him say to Gruber, without a trace of humor, "It's Mr. Mayor to you."

They posed together for another moment, hands clasped in a long handshake in front of the cardboard check, and then the mayor went up to the podium again.

Gruber winked at me. I looked away. Did he really think I was going to fall at his feet simply because he was $250,000 richer?

"While it was Mr. Gruber's tip that ultimately led to the arrest, the information he provided would have been useless if not for the facts previously gathered by Captain Adrian Monk," the mayor said. "I personally appointed him only forty-eight hours ago to head an investigation that had stalled in the hands of those detectives who've walked off the job and are demanding more benefits. To those detectives, currently engaged in an illegal walkout, I say: For shame. To Captain Monk I say: Thank you, not only for capturing this heinous felon but, in so doing, proving that the SFPD can be a leaner, more efficient department."

The mayor and his staff applauded, but Monk barely looked up from his index cards. I whispered into his ear.

"You have to say something in defense of Captain Sottlemeyer. You can't let the mayor use you like this, Mr. Monk."

"Don't worry," Monk said. "I'm on it."

The mayor waved Monk up to the podium and they shook hands.

"Thank you, Mr. Mayor," Monk said, then signaled to me for a wipe. I gave him one, stood there while he cleaned his hands, then took the used wipe from him and stepped back.

"Do you have a few words you'd like to say?" the mayor asked.

"Yes, I do," Monk said.

The mayor moved aside, and Monk took his place.

Monk cleared his throat, set his index cards on the podium, and carefully adjusted the microphone.

And adjusted it some more. And more after that.

Seconds ticked by like hours.

Monk adjusted the microphone up.

The cameramen set down the cameras and waited.

Monk adjusted the microphone a bit to the left.

The mayor tapped his foot impatiently.

Monk adjusted the microphone ever so slightly to the right.

Bertrum Gruber leered at me.

Monk adjusted the microphone down.

My gaze drifted to the east wall and a detailed carving of a naked Father Time, an hourglass in his hand. He was flanked by the naked Past and the naked Future. I wondered why none of them could find a few minutes to put on some clothes.

Finally Monk got the microphone in perfect position and tapped it. The sound drew everyone's attention back to him.

The cameramen picked up their cameras again.

The mayor sighed with relief.

"I'm Adrian Monk," Monk began, laying his hands on either side of the podium.

It wobbled.

"I'm Adrian Monk," he repeated, and gently rocked the podium to see which end was uneven.

It was the right front corner.

"Everyone remain calm," Monk said. "I have everything under control."

He slowly folded his top index card, and the passage of time as we knew it came to a grinding halt.

I looked back up at Father Time, half expecting

him to use this opportunity, his first in an eternity, to run out to Nordstrom for some underwear.

Once the card was perfectly folded, Monk bent down, tipped the podium, and placed the index card under the front right corner. He stood up and rocked the podium to make sure it was even.

It was.

He straightened up and leaned into the microphone again. "I'm Adrian Monk, and I—"

Monk stopped and looked at the second index card. He seemed lost. I knew what had happened: He'd folded up the first index card before he'd finished reading what was on it. He'd lost his place.

The mayor had broken into a sweat. I had no idea there were so many veins in a person's forehead until I saw them all bulging on Smitrovich.

Gruber had shifted his lascivious gaze from me to one of the female reporters, who, in a fit of devastating boredom, seemed to be enjoying the attention.

Monk put the second card back on the stack, evened the stack out, then bent down in front of the podium, pulled out the folded card, and slowly unfolded it, reading aloud what was on it:

". . . and I would like to take a moment to thank the detectives who. . ."

He folded the card again, leaned down, and put it back under the front corner. While he was doing that, the mayor cracked. I think he might even have let out a desperate little squeal.

Smitrovich rushed up to the podium and snatched the microphone.

"Thank you, Captain," the mayor said. "We don't want to hold you up any longer from the fine work you're doing."

Monk stepped back into place beside me.

The mayor talked for a few more minutes, but I was still coming out of my Monk-induced coma and missed most of it. When the mayor finished, he and Gruber were besieged by reporters, allowing Monk and me to slip out unnoticed.

We were outside, walking against a bone-chilling wind to the parking area for official vehicles, when Monk spoke up.

"I think I made my point," Monk said to me.

"All you said was your name."

"The whole time the mayor was talking, the podium was uneven," Monk said. "He looked like a buffoon. But I stepped up and confidently fixed the podium. I think that sent a powerful message to the populace."

"I'm sure it did, Mr. Monk."

We approached the guard shack outside the parking lot. Thc policc officer inside the shack had the press conference playing on his little TV, and he glared at us both as we passed.

"How is the mayor ever going to live down the embarrassment?" Monk said.

"It may cost him reelection," I said.

"He won't get my vote," Monk said. "If he can't balance a podium, how can he expect to lead a city?"

Before we even reached my car, I could see that something was very wrong. My car was slouching in its parking space on three slashed tires.

Monk was mortified. I was furious.

"How could this happen in a parking lot that's under twenty-four-hour police protection?" he said.

"I guess there were some people who didn't receive your powerful message."

I glanced at the cop at the parking lot entrance. He sneered at me and ducked back into his shack.

Monk crouched beside the car and examined the one tire that remained unscathed.

"Do you have a pocket-knife?" Monk asked.

"No."

"Maybe you could ask the police officer if he has one," Monk said.

"Of course he does," I said. "He's probably the one who did this."

"Could you ask if we could borrow it?"

"Mr. Monk, I am not going to ask the man who slashed my tires if I could borrow the knife he used to do it," I said. "Why do you want a knife?"

"They missed a tire," Monk said.

"You'd slash a perfectly good tire just so it matches?"

"A car has four tires," he said. "They only slashed three."

"I don't care," I said.

"Be a sport," Monk pleaded.

"No," I said firmly.

Monk rolled his shoulders. "Look at this tire. The treads are almost smooth. If you get three new tires, they won't match this one."

"I'll live," I said.

"Maybe not," Monk said. "With treads this thin, the tire could blow at any moment. Think of your safety. Think of Julie's. You really need four new tires with the same amount of tread."

He had me there. I threw my keys at Monk.

He dodged them. "You could poke out someone's eye that way."

"Really?" I said, scrounging in my purse for my cell phone.

He picked up my keys and used one of them to depress the pin in the tire's valve stem and release the air.

I called AAA and asked for a tow truck. Monk sighed contentedly as he deflated my tire and the car slumped evenly to the ground.

"You'll thank me later," he said.

"I'll *bill* you later," I said.

16

Mr. Monk and the Conspiracy Theory

The tow truck took my car to a full-service gas station, where I had four overpriced tires installed. I made Monk pay for it. He didn't argue too much with me, because I convinced him that he wasn't buying the tires; he was paying for the rare privilege of helping the technician balance them and place the proper counterweights on the rims.

I drove Monk home. Stottlemeyer was parked in front of Monk's building on Pine Street, sitting in his Crown Vic, smoking a cigar.

Here's something odd I've noticed about cops: They drive around all day in black-and-white and unmarked Crown Victorias, the standard vehicle used by law enforcement agencies nationwide. So you'd think that when they bought their own cars, they'd want something entirely different, something less big, boxy, and official. But no. They don't feel comfortable in "civilian" cars. They want to be cops at home, too. Which may be why divorce rates among cops are so high. Perhaps if they ditched their Crown Vics they would be less likely to be ditched themselves.

Monk got out. I rolled down my window and smiled at Stottlemeyer.

"Aren't you afraid of being seen with Monk?"

"I figured it was worth the risk," Stottlemeyer said, tossing his cigar stub. Monk leaned down and picked it up.

"You littered," Monk said.

Stottlemeyer snatched it back from him. "Thanks, Officer Friendly."

"Are you mad at me for arresting the Golden Gate Strangler?" Monk asked.

"No, Monk, I'm not. That was a good thing. But did you have to participate in the press conference?"

"The mayor asked me to."

"You could have said no," Stottlemeyer said.

"He's my boss," Monk said.

"He's using you to undermine our negotiating position and turn public opinion against us. It's one thing for you to be working for him. I could almost justify that to other cops, at least those who know you. But when you stand there while he tears us down, that's a betrayal."

"Did you notice the podium was unbalanced?"

"Yes, I did."

Monk grinned. "He stood in front of millions of people with a wobbly podium. It was political suicide. When it was my turn to go up, I could have let it stand the way it was."

"No, you couldn't," Stottlemeyer said.

"But I fixed it. I delivered a devastating blow. It was a deft political move that has left him crippled. He's vulnerable now. You can take him."

Stottlemeyer took a deep breath and let it out slowly. There was no way he was going to make Monk see things any differently. "I'm asking you, as a personal favor, not to publicly align yourself with the mayor or the police commissioner. If you're going to continue working for the department during this labor action, do it in the background. Keep a low profile."

"Okay, but I think that's like asking a star quarterback not to . . . to . . ." Monk struggled to finish the thought, which wasn't easy, since he knew nothing about football. "To quarter his back."

"We'll take that chance," Stottlemeyer said.

Monk nodded, said good night to us both, and went into his house. Stottlemeyer turned to me.

"I expected more from you, Natalie."

"What is that supposed to mean?" I asked.

"Your job is to watch out for him."

"I am," I said, feeling my face flush with anger. "I'm watching my employer and my friend enjoy his dream come true. He's got his badge back."

"But at what price?" Stottlemeyer said.

"That's not my problem," I said, but I knew that wasn't true. I had four new tires that proved it. Stottlemeyer didn't need to know that, though.

"Sometimes we have to put our dreams aside for the good of others."

Spare me, I thought.

"I think Mr. Monk has sacrificed enough in his

life already," I said. "All he has left are his dreams. If you ask him to sacrifice those, what else does he have?"

"Life isn't always fair," he said.

"Fine," I said. "You take the hit this time and grouse about how unfair life is, not Mr. Monk. Get off his back."

Stottlemeyer regarded me as if I'd just sprouted a second nose. After a long moment he nodded his head. "I was wrong about you, Natalie. You *are* watching out for him."

I let him have the last word, especially since I came out on top. I put the car in gear and drove off. That doesn't mean things were good between us. I was still pissed off.

How dared he pull that "life isn't always fair" crap, especially when it came to Monk or me. He'd touched a raw nerve with a branding iron.

I knew Stottlemeyer was going through a rough patch and feeling sorry for himself, but he'd crossed the line with that remark. Everybody wanted something from Monk lately without caring whether it was good for him or not.

They could all shove it, as far as I was concerned. It was time someone looked out for Monk's interests. By default, that someone was me.

I was so angry and hungry and tired that I didn't notice the cop car behind me until he squawked his siren once and flashed his lights.

Cursing to myself, I pulled over and gripped my steering wheel so tightly my knuckles turned white. I had had as much as I could stand of this crap from those petulant children in uniform. A female officer walked up to my window. She looked like she wrestled alligators for a hobby and then ate them raw afterward.

I wasn't intimidated.

Okay, I was, but I wasn't going to let her see it.

I rolled my window down. Her name tag identified her as Officer Paola Gomez.

"Do you know why I pulled you over?" Officer Gomez asked.

"To harass me over Adrian Monk's decision to step in as interim captain of homicide, and frankly, I don't want to hear it. Ticket me, tow me, slash my tires again if you want to; I don't care. Because it isn't going to change a thing. Mr. Monk is going to keep solving murders, because that's what he does. In fact, he probably does it better than anybody else on earth. I know you've got money troubles. I know you're worried about your health care and your retirement. But that's no excuse for how you're treating him and me. You're all so upset that you've forgotten what wearing that badge means. Well, he hasn't. He's a sweet man who doesn't want to hurt anyone. He's just doing his job. You should all be ashamed of yourselves."

Officer Gomez glared at me. "Are you done now?"

I nodded. "So is this when you tell me I ran a red light, made an illegal U-turn, and drove the wrong way on a one-way street?"

"Your trunk is open," Officer Gomez said. "If you hit a bump, all that stuff you've got back there is going to fall into the street. I thought you might want to close it before you drove any farther."

That was when I realized the interior light was on, indicating a door was ajar. I looked up into my rearview mirror and saw that, sure enough, my hatchback wasn't closed. All of Julie's soccer equipment was in the way-back, along with my folding chair, a case of Monk's bottled water, a case of Wet Ones, and a five-year-old edition of the Thomas Bros. San Francisco map.

Once again that night I felt my face flushing. But this time it was from embarrassment.

"Oh," I said. "Thanks."

"Have a nice night," Officer Gomez said, and walked back to her car.

On Monday morning I overslept. I must have swatted the alarm off when it rang at six forty-five. When I awoke, I stepped into the shower for about one minute, just long enough to get wet, and hurriedly got dressed. I didn't even have time for a cup of coffee. I made Julie her lunch and hustled her out of the house.

I dropped Julic off at school, picked up Monk, and got him into the office by nine a.m. But we still didn't beat Frank Porter. He was already settled in at his desk when we walked in. I was relieved to see he was wearing a fresh set of clothes.

I don't know how long Porter had been there, but he'd managed to put all the information on the four open murder cases up on the board that had previously been covered with stuff relating to the Golden Gate Strangler case.

Allegra Doucet, John Yamada, Diane Truby, and Scott Eggers each had their own column of vital stats topped with a color photo of each of them taken before their grisly deaths.

Considering Porter's questionable grasp on details, I wasn't sure how much Monk should trust the stuff on the board, but I kept my concerns to myself.

Sparrow was sitting with her head on a desk, sound asleep and still plugged into her iPod. Her mouth was open, and drool was spilling out onto the desk blotter. It wasn't a pretty sight, which was why Monk took a napkin from his pocket, unfolded it, and draped it over her face.

If I didn't get a big jolt of caffeine and sugar I was going to end up just like Sparrow, so I left Monk standing in front of the board and ran out to get some coffee and doughnuts from the Winchell's across the street. Another week on the policeman's diet and I was afraid I'd be using my butt for shelf space.

I came back upstairs with my coffee and a dozen doughnuts. I didn't buy any doughnut holes, of course, and I ate the evidence that I'd bought a baker's dozen (the thirteenth doughnut) so Monk wouldn't wig out.

Monk had pulled up a chair in front of the board and was staring at it in rapt attention, as if he were watching his favorite TV show (which, at the time, was an infomercial for the Wonder Wiper, an appliance you could use to clean floors, ceilings, windows, and cabinets, and even to power-wash your car. Monk never got tired of watching the toothy, insincere host demonstrate the product to the awestruck, paid members of the studio audience. Monk owned four of the Wonder Wipers and had given me two for Christmas). Porter was sitting next to him, dozing in his chair and snoring loudly.

Cindy Chow, Mad Jack Wyatt, and their two assistants, Jasper and Arnie, had arrived in my brief absence. Chow was walking around the room, waving some kind of electronic device, undoubtedly sweeping the place for bugs. Wyatt sat at his desk, dismantling his gun and cleaning it with little brushes, rags, and oils.

Sparrow was talking with Jasper over at the coffeemaker. Her whole body was inclined toward him, and they both maintained smiles and eye contact for way too long. The coffee wasn't brewing, but romance certainly was. I guess it was inevitable after Sparrow's cute-butt comment. Arnie was making coffee, oblivious to the mating ritual taking place next to him.

"To the fetishist, the shoe represents different parts of the female anatomy," Jasper told Sparrow. "But I believe that Charlie Herrin was interested more in the *smell* of the shoes than what they represented. His victims were all running and sweating. He was a pheromone junkie, and suffered from violent kleptophilia, the need to steal fetish objects for sexual excitement."

"Like if you were to steal my bra," Sparrow said with mock coyness.

"It looks to me like someone already has," he said.

"Oh, my," Sparrow said. "Should I report the crime?"

Jasper grinned. "There's no hurry."

Yuck. Psychobabble as seduction. Maybe there was a thesis in that.

"The murders have more to do with Herrin's hatred and fear of women than anything else," Arnie said, offering his unwelcome opinion. "He can't relate to women, so he kills them and replaces them with a nonthreatening, representational object of femininity instead: their shoes. But why the left shoe and not the right? That's the real mystery."

Jasper and Sparrow both glared at him, upset at his intrusion into their little flirt-fest. I decided to save Arnie.

"Doughnuts, anyone?" I said.

Porter woke up instantly and practically flung himself out of his seat. If his heart ever fails, instead of using defibrillator paddles on him, someone should just wave a Krispy Kreme glazed doughnut under his nose.

I set the box of doughnuts down on the table and opened it up.

Everybody came over and grabbed a doughnut except Monk. He didn't like eating anything sticky, covered with sugar, or with holes.

Monk cocked his head, looking at the board from various angles, as if that might change what he was seeing. Maybe it did. I don't know.

I walked over to him. "What are you doing?"

"These murders are troubling me," Monk said.

"Of course they are. They're unsolved."

He turned his back to the board, bent over, and looked at it between his legs, seeing it upside down.

"It's something else," he said.

"And you think looking at the facts out of the

corner of your eye and upside down will reveal what's wrong."

"They say it helps to look at things from a new perspective."

"I think they mean it figuratively," I said. "Not literally."

"Let's go over the facts again," Monk said.

We did.

Everyone gathered around, and we rehashed every detail of the four unsolved murders. I won't bore you by going over *everything* again, but here's a little refresher.

Allegra Doucet was working on an astrological chart when she was stabbed in the chest, presumably by someone she knew, who either came in or left through the bathroom window. She was bilking her wealthy clients, like Max Collins, by advising them to invest according to "the stars" in companies that paid her kickbacks. Max had a key to her place and was in the neighborhood the night she was killed. Means, motive, opportunity. I'm told that's a big deal when it comes to a murder investigation or when you're playing a game of Clue.

Architect John Yamada was walking across the street when someone ran him over and sped away. It was no accident. The driver was waiting for him to step into the intersection. At the time, Yamada was in the midst of an ugly split with his wife, whose car was stolen a few days before the murder. What a coincidence.

Waitress Diana Truby was walking home when someone pushed her in front of a bus. That same day, the drooling stalker who'd been terrorizing her for weeks suddenly disappeared. Interesting timing, huh?

At least we had suspects in those three cases. Scott Eggers's murder was a dead end so far. He was attacked from behind, clobbered on the head, and suffocated in an alley for no apparent reason—unless his neighbor did it for ratting him out to the city for installing a rooftop hot tub that wasn't up to code.

"Yamada, Truby, and Eggers were all taken by surprise and never had a chance to defend themselves," Monk said.

"It figures," Wyatt said. "Most killers are cowards."

"But Allegra Doucet was face-to-face with her killer," Monk said.

"What's the point of comparing the killings?" Wyatt asked. "They're all different cases with nothing in common."

"They're all unsolved," Monk said.

"Three of them are forty-four," Porter said.

It was a strange non sequitur. I would have ignored it, but Monk didn't.

"Excuse me?" Monk said.

"Everyone but the astrologer was forty-four years old," Porter said. "That's something in common."

Monk rose from his chair, stood in front of the board, and leaned so close to the papers taped to it that his nose was almost touching them.

"Frank," Monk said, "you're a genius."

"He is?" Sparrow said.

"Who is Frank?" Porter asked.

"Not only were they all forty-four," Monk said. "All three of them were born on the same day—February twentieth, 1962."

So there was *another* serial killer running around San Francisco. What wonderful news. And not even twenty-four hours had passed since the Golden Gate Strangler was apprehended.

The San Francisco Chamber of Commerce and the Tourist Bureau might as well close up for good. Who would want to live in or visit a city with so many psychopaths prowling the streets? I was about ready to call a real estate agent myself. We wouldn't have to move far. Berkeley, maybe.

"That's it!" Chow shouted. "All the pieces of the conspiracy are falling into place. The four killings are all connected."

"You mean the *three*," Monk said. "Allegra Doucet was twenty-seven, and she wasn't born on February twentieth."

"She's the center of the whole conspiracy," Chow said.

"Here we go," Jasper mumbled.

"On February twentieth, 1962, astronaut John Glenn made history by becoming the first person to orbit the Earth. That same day these three people were born. Allegra Doucet was an astrologer, perhaps even an escapee of Project Subzero," Chow said, her words tumbling out in an excited rush. "Remember how I said her murder might have been a result of her stumbling on the date, time, and location of an alien landing? That date was February twentieth, 1962. John Glenn's orbit was a distraction from the real, historic, interstellar event. Are you with me so far?"

Monk, Jasper, and Sparrow nodded. Arnie, Porter, Wyatt, and I shook our heads.

"Remember how I said Doucet spent time in New Mexico, where the extraterrestrials have their underground base and conduct their mind-control experiments? Okay, this is where things get interesting. Like thousands of women, I've been abducted and impregnated by aliens."

"Maybe you'll start getting more dates here on Earth now that there isn't a radio taped to your head," Wyatt said. "But I doubt it."

"Open your eyes to what's going on, Jack. The Omega Agency is desperate to create alien/humanoid offspring capable of surviving here *and* on their home planet," Chow said. "I think Yamada, Truby, and Eggers were three of the offspring of their crude, initial experiments in crossbreeding, which began on February twentieth, 1962. Doucet found out, and all four of them had to be eliminated."

Chow sat back down in her chair, quite pleased with herself.

"Of course, this means agents are being dispatched at this very moment to kill us," she said. "We know too much."

"Just give them the Vulcan neck pinch when they walk through the door," Wyatt said.

Monk looked at her for a long moment, and I looked at him. I knew what the spark in his eye and the smile tugging at the corner of his lips meant. But I didn't believe what I was seeing.

"Cindy," Monk said. "You're a genius."

I stepped in front of Monk. "Look me in the eye and tell me that you honestly think she's right."

"She's solved the murders of John Yamada, Diane Truby, and Scott Eggers," Monk said.

I knew he was going to say that. It was all over his face.

"You've lost your mind, Monk," Sparrow said, then elbowed Jasper in the side. "You'd better give him one of your cards."

"Detective Chow is right," Monk said. "All four murders *are* connected. Allegra Doucet is at the center of it, and February twentieth, 1962, is the key."

"You really think Yamada, Truby, and Eggers were extraterrestrial test-tube babies, that Allegra Doucet was killed by the men in black, and we're all next on the hit list?" Wyatt asked.

"I didn't say that," Monk said.

Now I was sure Monk was losing it. "Mr. Monk, you just said Cindy Chow solved the murders."

"I did," Monk said.

"I'm lost," I said.

"Me, too," Frank Porter said. "Could someone please show me how to get back to my desk?"

"I don't know why Allegra Doucet was killed or who did it," Monk said. "But I know why the other three were murdered, and if we don't move fast, more people will die."

17

Mr. Monk Cleans Up the Mess

Of course, Monk didn't tell us why someone killed three people born on the same day, or why other lives might be at stake. That would make life far too easy.

Monk has this incredibly irritating habit of making big, dramatic announcements like that and then keeping all the details to himself until he can find the missing piece that confirms what he already knows.

So why doesn't he just keep his mouth shut until he's got that obscure fact or crucial evidence?

I think it's because he enjoys seeing us all look at him in slack-jawed amazement, and he gets a thrill out of keeping us in suspense.

The only thing he enjoys more than that is the summation, the moment when he can tell us exactly who committed the crime and how it was done. But the thrill he gets from that doesn't come from showing off and proving how much smarter he is than everybody around him. It's the satisfaction of knowing with absolute certainty that he's cleaned up an ugly mess.

At Monk's insistence, he and I went out to Allegra Doucet's house. Chow and Jasper followed us in her black Suburban with a dozen antennae on top and windows tinted so dark, she must have relied on radar to drive her car.

Doucet's place was exactly as we left it, except for the tape across the front door and the official notice designating the place as a sealed crime scene.

We broke the tape and went inside. Monk went directly to Allegra's desk, carefully avoiding the big bloodstain on the floor, and asked Chow to turn on the computer.

"Can you call up the astrological chart that was on this screen when she died?" Monk said.

"Sure." Chow sat down in front of the computer and started clicking and typing. Monk wandered off to the rear of the house.

"Aren't you afraid of being seen by *them*?" I was referring, of course, to the computer monitor and the cameras hidden inside.

"I dismantled the monitor the last time we were here," she said. "It was clean. The black-ops agents must have removed the cameras before they left."

"How do you know they haven't been back since then and reinstalled them?"

Chow froze, and Jasper glared at me. I know he was pissed at me for provoking her paranoia, but I couldn't resist. Sometimes I enjoy a little mischief.

She shrugged off her hesitation and resumed her typing.

"With what we've discovered, we're dead already," Chow said. "There's no place on earth we can hide now."

Monk returned wearing a flowery apron and yellow dish gloves and carrying a bucket of soapy water. He crouched beside the bloodstain, took a sponge out of the bucket, and began scrubbing.

There was a time when I might have questioned what Monk was doing. I might have pointed out to him that it wasn't his house or his responsibility to clean up the mess. I might have mentioned that simply scrubbing the stain was insufficient, even if any obvious signs of it were gone, and that eventually someone would hire professional crime scene cleaners to remove all traces of the blood and bodily fluids that had seeped into the floors.

But Monk knew all that, and I've learned the futility of arguing with him about cleaning up anything that has spilled anywhere he happens to be.

This was a double treat for him: He got to clean up two messes at once—the stain *and* the murder that caused it. Monk was practically whistling with happiness.

I was surprised, though, that Jasper hadn't whipped out his PDA to take more notes about Monk's obsessive-compulsive behavior. I guess Charlie Herrin was occupying Jasper's professional interest now.

"Here's the chart," Chow said.

Monk didn't bother getting up or even looking at the screen. He continued scrubbing.

"I can't read an astrology chart," he said, "but I'm certain it's for someone born on February twentieth, 1962."

"It is," Chow said, astounded. "How did you know?"

I'm glad she asked that instead of me. If I ever print up those T-shirts with the questions on it, I'll give her one.

"Because whoever it was written for witnessed her murder," Monk said.

"Isn't his name on the chart?" I asked.

Chow shook her head. "Doucet plugged in the date and the software spit out the chart. She hadn't saved it yet when she was killed. I saved it and gave it a file name."

"Wait a sec," Jasper said. "How does any of this prove there was a witness?"

"The proof was right in front of us the very first time we walked in here," Monk said as he worked. "Here's what happened."

And as Monk explained it all, I could almost see the scene playing out in front of me, the ghostly images of the people involved moving through the room, all of them faceless except for Doucet herself.

Allegra Doucet was meeting with a client, preparing his astrological chart, when he excused himself and went to the bathroom. A few moments later the killer came in. It was someone Doucet knew and didn't feel threatened by. She rose to face him and was stabbed. Taken totally by surprise, she had no real opportunity to defend herself.

Her client flushed the toilet, started to open the

door to the bathroom, and saw Doucet being murdered. He fled out of the bathroom window, breaking the towel rack in the process.

The killer never got a good look at the witness. All the killer had to go on was the birth date on the astrological chart.

"So now Allegra Doucet's murderer is killing anybody born on February twentieth, 1962," Monk said, and stood up to admire his work. The bloodstain was gone. "That also explains the seemingly improvised nature of the killings. The murderer had no time to prepare. He was in a hurry. All he cared about was accomplishing the murders, and didn't give any thought to covering up his crimes."

"There must be tens of thousands of people who were born on that date," Jasper said. "How is the killer narrowing it down? How did he pick Yamada, Truby, and Eggers out of everybody?"

"I don't know," Monk said, and carried the bucket of dirty water back into the kitchen.

"It's obvious," Chow said. "They are only targeting those people who were part of the alien crossbreeding program, and are tracking them through computer chips implanted in their skulls at birth."

Monk came back into the room. He was no longer wearing his apron and gloves. I turned to him and asked him the question that was puzzling me about all of this.

"If what you say is true, why hasn't the witness come forward and reported what he or she saw to the police?"

"Perhaps the witness was among the three

people who have already been killed," Monk said. "But there's no way the murderer can be entirely sure, so he has to keep on killing."

"The witness was one of the children of the alien crossbreeding program," Chow said. "It's the only explanation that makes sense."

If that sounded logical to her, I couldn't imagine what would qualify in her mind as a really crazy idea.

"Let's suppose, just for the sake of argument, that the killer isn't tracking his victims using computer chips or lists of alien offspring," I said.

"You're wasting your time," she said.

"Humor me," I said. "What other way is there of narrowing down the field of possible victims so you can save the next person on the list from being killed?"

Monk sighed heavily. "I wish I knew."

Chow tapped the screen. "I'll analyze this chart. It could be the key that will unlock the entire alien conspiracy on Earth."

Or she could just ask the aliens next time she was abducted.

My cell phone rang. It was Officer Curtis again. Before she spoke, I knew by now what she was going to say. A murder had been committed somewhere in the city, and they needed Monk to come down and look at the corpse.

I was right.

But what she said next was a shock. The victim was a cop. And it was someone Monk and I knew.

* * *

To the east of Potrero Hill, the derelict Bethlehem Steel warehouses, foundries, machine shops, and welding sheds rot away on Pier 70, their windows broken, their bricks weathered, and their rusted, corrugated metal siding peeling off like flakes of dry skin.

Officer Kent Milner's body was sprawled on the concrete floor in front of his black-and-white police cruiser, which was parked inside the cavernous remains of a brick-walled machine shop. The ceilings were high and gabled like a church, light spilling in from a thousand broken windows and skylights. Birds flew among the exposed rafters overhead.

There seemed to be far more uniformed police officers around than were necessary to secure the scene, but their attendance was understandable. One of their own had been killed.

Monk clipped his badge to his jacket as we walked in, just in case anyone was unaware of his new status as a captain in the homicide division. The crowd of officers and SID techs parted to let us through, revealing Captain Stottlemeyer in front of us, crouching over Milner's body, and Lieutenant Disher standing behind him, taking notes.

The captain quickly glanced up at us, acknowledged our presence with a barely perceptible nod, then returned his attention to the victim.

Monk crouched across from Stottlemeyer, the corpse on the concrete floor between them. There was a bullet hole in the center of Milner's forehead and a look of wide-eyed surprise frozen on his face.

I turned away. It was hard enough for me to see

the dead bodies of strangers. But seeing the corpse of someone I knew, even someone who was barely an acquaintance, was too much.

But I looked back, and the longer I stared at the corpse, the less it resembled Officer Milner. This wasn't the Officer Milner I spoke to yesterday; it was a wax likeness with glass eyes and a hole in his head.

And, for a moment, I felt what must be the cold, professional detachment that Monk, Stottlemeyer, and Disher have toward death.

I didn't know whether to be proud of it or feel sorry for myself.

"Captain?" Monk said. "What are you doing here?"

"My job," he said.

"What about your flu?"

"An officer is down, Monk," he said. "That trumps everything."

"How did you find out about this?" Monk asked.

"I've sort of been monitoring the police band while I've been sick," Stottlemeyer said a bit sheepishly, like he expected to get some flak about it. He didn't get any from us.

"I know him." Monk tipped his head toward the body.

"Officer Kent Milner. Potrero Hill was his beat," Stottlemeyer said. "He was at the park, securing the scene. He loaned you some binoculars."

"We saw him again yesterday in the marina at the scene of another homicide," I said. "He told us he was working all over town and trying to accumulate some overtime."

"He was married with two kids," Disher said, not looking up from his notes. "Ages four and six."

Monk pointed to Milner's gun belt. "He didn't draw his gun. The holster isn't even unsnapped. He wasn't expecting trouble."

"These docks are patrolled by private security," Stottlemeyer said. "There was no reason for him to be down here, unless he saw something suspicious or was rousting some vagrants. But he would have called that in to dispatch. Since he didn't call in or tell anybody he was going to be here, I'm thinking he was meeting an informant. Either his snitch shot him or he was set up."

"I bet the shooter tossed the gun into the bay afterward," Disher said, still conspicuously not looking at either Monk or me. "It might be worth having some divers spend a few hours checking out the water off these docks."

"Good idea," Stottlemeyer said, nodding his approval. "Get the dive crew out here."

"Milner was a young patrol officer." Monk stood and wandered over to the police car. "Wouldn't it be unusual for him to be meeting with informants?"

Stottlemeyer shrugged. "Maybe he was a better cop than anybody thought. Maybe he got a line on something big and stupidly tried to pursue it himself instead of alerting his commanding officer."

"Maybe he saw whatever it was as his ticket to a gold shield," Disher said.

"That's a lot of maybes." Monk opened the driver's-side door of the police car. There were travel brochures and car magazines on the passenger seat.

"Chasing the maybes. That's what detective work is all about, for most of us anyway," Stottlemeyer said. "Whatever Milner's story is, we'll find out. We're working this twenty-four/seven until the shooter is either behind bars or on a slab in the morgue."

I was getting annoyed by Disher's refusing to look at us, so I stepped in front of him and leaned my head over his notebook. "Is something bothering you, Randy?"

"You're consorting with the enemy," Disher said.

"I haven't consorted with anyone in so long, I may need lessons before I can do it again."

"Monk sold us out for filthy lucre," Disher said.

"First off, Mr. Monk wouldn't touch anything filthy," I said. "Second, what *lucre*?"

"The badge." Disher snorted. "Isn't that the ultimate irony? He betrayed it to get it."

Consorting? Lucre? Irony? Hmmm.

I narrowed my eyes at Disher. "Have you been taking an English class of some kind?"

Disher blinked hard, stunned. "How did you know?"

My God, I made a deduction. And was Monk there to witness it? No. He was busy peering into Milner's cruiser. Stottlemeyer milled around behind him, pretending he wasn't looking over Monk's shoulder.

"Just a hunch," I said.

I sounded like a thousand TV cops. Nobody but TV crime solvers ever say, "Just a hunch," so I savored the opportunity to use it in proper sleuthing context.

"Since I had some time on my hands, I thought I'd finally get started on that novel I've got in me," Disher said. "So I signed up for a university extension class taught by Ian Ludlow, the Tolstoy of the mean streets."

"I didn't know you had a novel in you," I said.

"I have all kinds of stuff in me," Disher said. "I'm filled with complexity."

Monk sat down in Milner's cruiser, picked up a copy of *Motor Trend* magazine off the passenger seat, and began flipping through it.

Stottlemeyer dropped any pretense of doing anything but waiting to see what Monk came up with.

Disher watched Stottlemeyer for direction and, getting none, simply followed his lead. He waited, too.

"For the record, 'Golden Gate Strangler' was a lousy name for Charlie Herrin," Disher said to me. " 'The Foot Fiend' was much better and more alliterative."

"Did the Tolstoy of the mean streets tell you that?" I asked.

"He's very attuned to the savage heart of the urban wilderness," Disher said. "Like me."

"This is odd," Monk said. "Officer Milner marked down the corner on an article about German luxury cars."

"I know you find marking down corners offensive," Stottlemeyer said, "but lots of people do that when they want to save their spot or read an article later."

"But he couldn't afford to buy a BMW." Monk unfolded the corner and smoothed the page out. "He was also reading Hawaii travel brochures and a magazine of new home listings in Marin County."

"So he liked to dream," Stottlemeyer said. "I've got a magazine on Caribbean cruises in my bathroom. I like to picture myself on one of those ships, sipping a tropical drink. I've been doing that a lot lately."

"Officer Milner was behaving like a man with money to spend," Monk said. "I find that unusual for someone at the lowest pay grade in the department and who was risking the scorn of his fellow officers by working overtime during a labor dispute."

"Are you saying that you think he was on the take?" Stottlemeyer said.

"I'm saying something just doesn't fit," Monk said.

I rolled my shoulders, preceding Monk's rolling of his shoulders by a second. I'm not sure whether I did it because my shoulders were stiff or because I was unconsciously mimicking what I knew he was about to do.

I caught myself before I tipped my head from side to side in tandem with Monk, too, but not before Stottlemeyer noticed what I was doing.

"We'll check out his bank account," Stottlemeyer said. "But I don't think we're going to find anything unusual."

"Okay." Monk got out of the car and motioned to me for a wipe. I gave him one, and he cleaned his hands. "I guess I'll go home now. Give me a call if you need anything."

"You can't go home," Stottlemeyer said. "Your shift isn't over."

"But you're back," Monk said.

"You're still a captain," Stottlemeyer said.

"I *am*?"

"Until the mayor says otherwise," Stottlemeyer said. "You've got four open homicide cases to close, and a squad of detectives waiting for your instructions. Since I was the first on the scene here, I'd like to take this one while you stick with the others."

"That's up to you, Captain," Monk said. "You're the boss."

"You're a captain, too, Monk. We have equal rank. You don't work for me. I'm asking you this as a colleague."

"That is so wrong," Disher muttered.

"No, Randy, it's not," Stottlemeyer said pointedly. "It's the way it is. So, Monk, what'll it be?"

"Whatever you want, Captain."

"Thanks, Captain," Stottlemeyer said.

"My pleasure, Captain."

"Can we please stop calling each other captain now?"

"Sure," Monk said. "Captain."

18

Mr. Monk and the Helpful Horoscope

The astrological chart from Allegra Doucet's computer was tacked to the board in the squad room along with all the other information on the four murders.

Cindy Chow and Sparrow were talking to each other in front of the board while Porter, Wyatt, Jasper, and Arnie sat around, waiting for something to happen. I think that something was us.

Everybody turned our way as we walked in. Wyatt got up.

"Word is that a cop was killed," Wyatt said. "Put me on the street and I'll hunt down the bastard who did it."

"We aren't handling the investigation," Monk said.

"It's a homicide," Wyatt said. "You're the captain. Who else is gonna handle it? Parking enforcement?"

"Captain Stottlemeyer is back on duty," Monk said.

"Of course he is, only hours after we exposed the alien conspiracy," Chow said. "Coincidence? I think not. The cover-up is already beginning. Our 'accidental' and 'natural' deaths will follow shortly. There will be no trace left of us or our work here."

"It was fun while it lasted," Wyatt said. "Where do we turn in our badges?"

"You don't," Monk said. "Captain Stottlemeyer is handling the Milner homicide, and we're continuing with these."

"We are?" Chow said incredulously.

"We are," Monk said.

"You're very clever," Chow said to the nearest computer monitor. "Plots within plots. Machinations within machinations. Boxes within boxes. I wonder what your endgame is?"

"Who is she talking to?" Porter asked Jasper.

"Them," Jasper said.

"Oh." Porter looked at his computer and waved at the screen. "Hey, how's it going?"

Monk stepped up to the board and squinted at the astrological chart. I don't know what made him think that squinting would suddenly give him the ability to make sense of what was in front of him, but I gave it a try, too. It didn't make the mishmash any clearer to me.

The chart looked like a wheel. There was a narrow band around the outer ring filled with numbers, which were written as degrees, and dozens of symbols, none of which I recognized. It could have been Sanskrit, for all I knew. The inner ring was divided like a pizza into twelve slices, each of which was also filled with numbers and symbols. In the center of it all was another circle filled with multicolored intersecting lines that gave me a frightening flashback to high school geometry and Mr. Ross, the math teacher who continues to have a starring role in many of my nightmares.

"What were you able to learn about the witness from his astrological chart?" Monk asked Chow.

"Everything important about him except his name, address, and phone number," Sparrow said. "Mercury is in Aquarius, and Venus is in Pisces, so you're looking for someone who is charming and creative, but also probably secretive, greedy, and really full of himself. Uranus is in Leo, so this is a guy who likes his freedom, bucks authority, and has very litle self-discipline. I'd be worried about this Neptune in Scorpio; it means he's capable of extreme violence."

Monk turned to her, surprised. "You know about astrology, too?"

"My name is Sparrow," she said. "What do you think?"

Monk stared at her blankly. He had no idea what she meant.

"What kind of parent names their kid Sparrow?" she said.

He still didn't get it. She sighed, imbuing it with so much hopeless frustration, it was a wonder she could breathe at all.

"My parents are very New Age and consider themselves plugged into the cycles of nature," she said. "And those cycles are all tied to the movement of the Earth around the sun, the most profound cycle of all."

One of Sparrow's parents was Frank Porter's child. I had a hard time imagining one of his kids being that liberal and earthy. It must have been an act of rebellion against Frank that his kid never outgrew.

One of these days Julie was going to start acting out against me, just like I did against my parents. I couldn't help wondering what form her rebellion would take. I figured I still had a couple of years left to prepare myself for it.

"So how does this chart help us locate the killer's next victim?" Monk asked.

"It's a map," Sparrow said. "If you know how to read it."

"The longitude and latitude on the chart indicates that Allegra's unknown client was born in San Francisco," Chow said. "These things here, around the outside of the chart, are 'transits,' which represent the daily motion of the planets. The transits are calculated based on where the subject lives now."

"San Francisco," Monk said.

I could see that glimmer in his eye. Chow hadn't even finished her explanation, but I knew that the clues were all starting to fall into place in his mind.

"That's right," Chow said. "The transits indicate he lives in San Francisco. The solar return chart is pinned on his *next* birthday, which has the same transits, so that implies that he's planning on sticking around here until then. Or at least, he was until he saw Allegra Doucet stabbed to death."

Now it made sense, even to someone like me with no detective skills whatsoever.

"So that's how the killer narrowed the field of possible witnesses," I said. "He knows whoever was in Allegra Doucet's bathroom the night of the murder was born in San Francisco on February twentieth, 1962, and is still living in the city. But how could he get a list of people who fit that description?"

"It's in the public record," Porter said. "All you'd have to do is cross-reference names gleaned from San Francisco birth certificates issued on February twentieth, 1962, with current data available from the Department of Motor Vehicles, the county tax rolls, voter registration lists, that kind of thing."

"How hard would that be?" Monk said.

"Any twelve-year-old with an Internet connection could do it," Arnie said. "I know a very hostile teenager who used that information to steal his teachers' identities, get credit cards in their names, and go on a shopping spree."

"Could you create the same list the killer has?" Monk asked Porter.

"Just give me a couple of hours," he said. "But it might go faster if we could get that hostile kid to help me out."

"No problem." Arnie reached for the phone with his good hand. "I'll pull my son out of school. He'll jump at the opportunity to get near a computer keyboard again. He's been insufferable ever since the judge banned him from any computer with an Internet connection. But I'm sure the judge would understand and grant him an exception. This is for a good cause."

Monk turned to Wyatt. "After Frank gets that list together, I'd like you and Detective Chow to start contacting the people on it until you find Allegra Doucet's client."

"Assuming he or she isn't already in the morgue," Wyatt said.

"Shouldn't you put them all under police protection?" I asked.

Monk shook his head. "Telling them to stay inside for the next hour or two and not open the door to any strangers should be all the protection they need."

I smiled. Without coming right out and saying it, Monk had just revealed that he'd solved the mystery. He knew who the killer was.

"You think simply locking their doors is going to keep them safe?" Wyatt said.

That was the wrong question. Wyatt should have asked why Monk felt they needed to stay inside for just the next couple of hours.

"Only if the murderer is waiting for them outside their home or office right now," Monk said. "But we'll find out soon enough."

"How?" Chow asked.

I grabbed my purse and jacket. "Because we're heading out to arrest the killer right now. Isn't that right, Mr. Monk?"

"That's the plan," Monk said.

It sounded like a very good plan to me.

Max Collins was leaving Madam Frost's house as we pulled up alongside his silver Maserati Quattroporte, which is a much sexier and much more expensive description than "Italian four-door sedan." He was dressed in an Armani suit that probably came standard with the car. Or maybe it was the other way around.

I double-parked in the street. Monk and I got out of the car. I assumed that Officer Curtis and her partner, in the black-and-white police *quattroporte* behind us, wouldn't have my car ticketed and towed this time.

"Captain Monk, what an unexpected surprise," Collins said.

"Didn't Madam Frost tell you we were coming?" Monk asked.

"Did she know?" Collins said.

"If she didn't," Monk said, "she's not very good at seeing the future, is she?"

"Unfortunately, astrology isn't that precise. But Madam Frost did say some exciting things were in store for me."

"I thought you were giving up on astrology," I said.

"Only as an investment guide, as I told you before," Collins said. "But I find it helpful in other areas of my life. Madam Frost has been advising me and my family for years."

"Until Allegra Doucet came along," Monk said.

"Madam Frost is like a beloved aunt; Allegra was more like a Playboy Playmate." Collins shrugged. "She seduced me away. So, is that why you're here, to ask me more questions about Allegra?"

"We're here to arrest her murderer," Monk said.

"Should I be calling my lawyer?"

"Perhaps you should ask Madam Frost that question," Monk said.

As if on cue, Madam Frost stepped out of her house and hobbled toward us, leaning heavily on her thick, knobby cane, which looked old enough to have belonged to Merlin himself. Her skin was withered, and her hair was gray, but her eyes blazed with startling intensity. In that moment I believed that not only could she peer into the future, but straight into my soul.

"Do you know why they're here, Madam Frost?" Collins said.

Madam Frost nodded sagely. That was a skill I didn't possess. I couldn't nod sagely if my life depended on it. If I tried, I'd just look like I'd eaten something very sour.

"I foresaw this moment days ago," she said.

"Was that before you killed Allegra Doucet?" Monk said. "Or was it after you murdered John Yamada, Diane Truby, and Scott Eggers?"

Max stared at Monk in disbelief. "You think Madam Frost killed Allegra *and* three other people?"

"I know she did," Monk said. "There's no doubt about it."

"He's never wrong about this stuff," I said, though I was pretty surprised by his statement, too.

"You can't be serious," Collins said. "Madam Frost is a frail woman in her sixties. Allegra was a young woman in top physical condition. Do you really think Madam Frost could have taken her?"

"You're underestimating Madam Frost, which was Allegra Doucet's fatal mistake," Monk said.

Madam Frost didn't say a word; she just stared at Monk with those penetrating eyes. Monk looked right back at her unflinchingly. When he's solved a case and is confronting the killer, Monk never wavers. It's the one time he seems to be completely at ease with himself and the world around him. He's in his zone.

"Allegra was a fraud who stole all of Madam Frost's clients and was driving her out of business," Monk continued. "Madam Frost couldn't compete with Allegra, so she killed her. Here's what happened. . . ."

And Monk laid it out, taking great pleasure in the telling. He didn't have to give the performance; he could simply have arrested Madam Frost and saved it all for the district attorney. But where was the fun in that? This was the moment he lived for in every investigation.

Monk told us that Madam Frost walked in the front door of Allegra's house on Friday night, probably on some friendly pretense. When Allegra rose from her chair, Madam Frost stabbed her in the chest and kept on stabbing. Allegra never had the chance to fight back. She was dead before she hit the floor.

That was when Madam Frost heard the toilet flush and realized that there was someone else in the house. By the time she got to the bathroom, whoever it was had escaped out the window. Madam Frost was too old and frail to chase after him to his car, so she examined the astrological chart on Allegra's computer screen to get the clues she'd need to hunt the witness down.

"Madam Frost isn't quite as averse to computers as she would like us to believe," Monk said. "She used the Internet to compile a list of possible witnesses based on the information she learned from the chart."

Monk explained that she was in a hurry to kill them before the witness, whoever he was, had a chance to go to the police. That was why all three killings looked improvised—because they were. And like Allegra Doucet, they were all attacked by surprise or from behind. She couldn't take the risk that one of them might resist, because she wasn't physically capable of subduing them.

"When we came to see you Saturday morning, you were walking up to your house," Monk said. "You had to park your car, the one you'd just used to run over John Yamada, on a side street, because the police were blocking your driveway."

"Let's open up your garage and take a look at your car," I said. "I bet the front end is smashed."

"A lot of people my age have dented cars," Madam Frost said. "Unfortunately, I'm not as good a driver as I used to be. A few weeks ago I hit a lamppost."

"Lampposts don't bleed," I said. "Yamada's blood and other trace evidence will be on your car—even if you've had it washed since the murder."

I had no idea if that was true. All of my forensic knowledge came from watching reruns of *CSI*, but I said it with the confidence that comes from complete ignorance, and she didn't jump to contradict me. So I got cocky.

"And they found mud that dripped off your car at the crime scene," I said. "The lab should have no trouble tracing it to this neighborhood."

Again, another big guess on my part, but I was having too much fun to care. I had never played detective before; I never would have dared with Captain Stottlemeyer and Disher and all those crime scene techs around. But since it was just Monk and two uniformed officers this time, I figured I could indulge myself a little.

"This is insane," Collins said. "Look at her. Does she really look like a mass murderer to you?"

"What are they supposed to look like?" I asked, though I actually agreed with him. She didn't strike me as a very scary figure.

"Well, for one thing, they don't have bad knees and shuffle around on canes," Collins replied.

"That's why Madam Frost grabbed an empty vegetable crate from a grocery store on her way to kill Diane Truby," Monk said, shifting his gaze back to Madam Frost. "You needed something to sit on while you waited for your victim to stroll by."

"You're not making any sense," Collins said.

I could see how Monk's comments might seem like gibberish to Collins, but he was making a lot of sense to me. I felt the satisfying mental snap of an obscure clue falling into place. I realized that was what Monk must feel, only a thousand times stronger, when he solved a case.

Monk had been very puzzled by the crate. I remembered him wondering why the killer had bothered bringing it along. Frank Porter had suggested that maybe the killer, like himself, had sore feet or a bad back. Neither Monk nor Porter realized it at the time, but Porter was right.

"You pushed Diane in front of a speeding bus and then crept away in the pandemonium," Monk said. "But you left the crate behind. That was a mistake."

"I wonder if you left a fingerprint on it somewhere," I said, just to give her something else to worry about.

"You also waited for Scott Eggers in an alley," Monk said. "You hit him from behind and then smothered him with a bag you took out of the trash."

"I'm guessing you whacked him with that cane," I said.

"So am I," Monk said. That was a big relief because it really *was* a wild guess on my part.

"How hard do you think it would be for the crime lab to find a speck of Eggers's blood on that cane, Mr. Monk?"

"Not hard at all," Monk replied, meeting Madam Frost's eye, the intensity of her gaze diminishing like a flashlight running out of batteries. She was caught, and she knew it.

"All their accusations are ridiculous," Collins assured Madam Frost. "I'll line you up with a top criminal defense attorney, but even a bad lawyer could tear this flimsy case apart."

"I don't think so," Madam Frost said.

"Don't worry," Collins said. "These two are full of crap."

"The evidence is overwhelming, even without a witness," Madam Frost said. "I killed them all, just like they said."

Collins looked at Madam Frost as if she'd suddenly transformed into a werewolf. His jaw dropped, his eyes widened, and I think maybe his hair even stood on end, but I can't be entirely sure. Let's just say he was shocked and leave it at that.

"I'm not a cop, Mr. Monk," I said, "but I think this would probably be a good time to read Madam Frost her rights."

"Can I?" Monk said.

"You're the captain," I said.

Monk took a little card out of his pocket, cleared his throat, and read aloud from it. He told Madam Frost she had the right to remain silent, have an attorney present before questioning, and all that good stuff. He enjoyed it so much, he offered to read it a second time just to be sure Madam Frost was clear on her rights.

"I know my rights, thank you," Madam Frost said.

Monk had waited a long time for the opportunity to read someone their rights and wanted to savor it. It think it reinforced for him that he was really a cop again.

"That section about the lawyer can be confusing," Monk said. "We should probably go over that part again."

"I waive my rights," she said. "There's no point reading them to me again. I killed Allegra Doucet and the others."

Monk glanced at Max Collins. "Would you like to hear them?"

"Am I being arrested for something?" Collins asked.

"No," Monk said. "But everyone should know their rights under the law."

"I'll pass," Collins said.

Disappointed, Monk slipped the card back into his pocket.

I still had one more question for Madam Frost about her killing spree that Monk hadn't answered.

"You killed Allegra Doucet on Friday night," I said. "When no witnesses came forward on Saturday after you ran over Yamada and pushed Truby in front of a bus, why did you keep killing? Why didn't you assume you'd killed the right person or that the witness was going to keep quiet?"

"I was following the stars," she said glumly. "They told me I was going to get caught. I was trying to change my fate."

The stars had been right. And Max Collins got the excitement that they said was in store for him. I decided there might be some truth to astrology after all. I'd have to start reading my horoscope more closely.

19

Mr. Monk Goes to Dinner

To celebrate Monk's clearing his remaining open homicide cases, I invited him out to dinner with Julie and me. That meant, of course, that we had to stop by his apartment on the way to pick up a set of dishes and silverware that he could bring with him to the restaurant in a special padded picnic basket.

We went to Mario & Maria's, or M&M's, as Julie calls it, a family-owned restaurant on Twenty-fourth Street within walking distance from my house in Noe Valley, a neighborhood that has a real small-town feel. We'd brought Monk with us to M&M's a few times before, so they were used to clearing their dishes off the table and watching him lay out his own.

Monk ordered exactly ten perfect squares of ravioli with meat sauce, while Julie and I shared a cheese pizza, which he insisted on cutting for us into eight equal slices using a compass and ruler he brought along for the occasion. We would have preferred to order a pepperoni pizza, but it would have been a hassle with Monk there. He would have demanded that each piece of pizza have an equal number of pepperoni slices and that they be aligned in a symmetrical pattern over the entire pie.

While we ate, Julie talked about her day at school, her squabbles with friends, and the activities she had planned for the rest of the week. It was your typical mundane, domestic chatter, but Monk seemed to revel in it. And so did Julie, who often complained to me about how strange Monk was and yet always seemed eager for his attention when he was around.

Monk even put a slice of lemon in his Sierra Springs water, which, for him, was like having a martini. It's a good thing he didn't have to drive.

After dinner Monk went back to the kitchen to wash his dishes with the rubber gloves, scouring pad, soap, and sponge he'd brought specifically for the task. Julie gladly tagged along with him. She even helped him wash dishes, a chore that she considered to be cruel and unusual punishment at home.

The restaurant owners didn't mind Monk's weird behavior because he made up for it by doing *all* the other dishes along with his own, and he happily cleaned their appliances, too. In fact, Mario & Maria's was one of the few restaurants in San Francisco where Monk was still welcome—as long as he was with me.

"That's a classy place," Monk said as we were

walking back to my house. "You don't find many restaurants with perfectly square raviolis."

"There aren't many people who'd actually measure them," I said.

"Only the true gourmets," Monk said.

"You're a gourmet?" Julie asked.

"I have the dining tape measure and compass, don't I?" Monk said. "It was nice to have a chance to relax over a good meal. I really needed to unwind."

I couldn't imagine anyone else who would consider going out to dinner, washing all the dishes, and cleaning the kitchen afterward relaxing. Most people go to restaurants as an escape from things like cleaning pots and pans, but I wasn't going to argue with him.

"Thank you for inviting me," Monk said.

"It was our pleasure," I said.

"The last few days have been very stressful," Monk said. "But I think this could be a turning point for me."

"I hope so, Mr. Monk," I said.

"I couldn't have done it without you," he said.

"You don't need me to solve murders."

"I need you for everything else," Monk said. "Without you, I'd be lost."

"When you don't need Mom's help anymore," Julie asked, "will you still come see us?"

"I'll always need help," Monk said.

"But if you're a homicide detective again, you'll have lots of cops around all day who can help you," Julie said. "What will you need Mom for?"

She had a point. I'd been so caught up in Monk's

hectic new life over the last few days, I hadn't thought about the long-term implications of his getting his badge back. I doubted they would tolerate a civilian hanging around with Monk all day. But at the moment I was less concerned about my job security than I was by Julie's question and what it revealed about her feelings.

Since her father was killed in Kosovo, Monk had been the only man who was always in her life. And mine. He was someone she could rely on. If nothing else, Monk was consistent. Obsessively so. Kids like routine; it gives them a sense of security. That goes double—make that *triple*—for Monk. He gave her a sense of security, and, along the way, she'd become emotionally attached to him.

The truth was, so had I.

Not so long ago, all three of us lost someone to a violent death. We were all adrift until we found Monk and he found us. What we had now wasn't love, but it was something close, something worth holding on to.

Now I was as interested in Monk's answer to the question as Julie was.

Monk tilted his head from side to side and adjusted his collar, which didn't need adjusting.

"I'll need you and your mom in my life no matter what I'm doing," he said. "I'm helpless. But you aren't."

"What do you mean?" Julie asked.

"I'm a high-maintenance individual, like a supermodel," Monk said. "People get tired of me. My father. Sharona. The list goes on."

"I'll never get tired of you, Mr. Monk," she said, looping her arm around his, "if you promise never to get tired of me."

"Deal," he said.

I looped my arm around his, too.

"Deal," I said, and gave him a little kiss on the cheek.

He didn't like it, but at least he was smart enough not to ask for a wipe.

I drove Monk home. Julie was asleep by the time I got back. I was exhausted and expected to fall into a deep slumber within seconds of laying my head on my pillow. But that didn't happen.

I couldn't stop thinking about our little after-dinner conversation. What *would* I do if Monk didn't need me anymore?

Although the pay was terrible, the hours were insane, and the benefits were nonexistent, I'd become very comfortable in the job, which I fell into by accident rather than design.

In some ways I envied Monk. He had direction in his life. He knew who he was, what his talents were, and what he was put on this earth to do. He'd known since he was a kid. Monk was born to be a detective. And he's brilliant at it.

I wasn't sure what I was born to do, what I was good at, or where my life was going.

I assumed there had to be other people out there as aimless as I was, but I still felt like the only one who wasn't born with preinstalled software.

I've never had a natural affinity toward one profession or another. I've never had any obvious artistic or physical abilities. I'm jealous every time I meet someone who has known all her life that she wanted to be this or that.

I've tried to imagine what it's like growing up with the certainty that you've got a natural talent for painting, or singing, or arguing, or pitching a baseball. I've wondered what it's like growing up with a burning desire to be something in particular, like a veterinarian or an astronaut, lawyer or chef, gardener or engineer. It must be great. (I wanted to be one of Charlie's Angels for a while, but I don't think that really counts. I also wanted to be a rock star, but mostly for the wardrobe and the adulation.)

A lot of people find their direction in college, finally discovering in a class or an internship what it is that they want to do or be. Or they find out after a job or two once they graduate. Sometimes their calling finds them.

I mean, nobody grows up dreaming of selling car insurance, but there are people who do it and are very successful at it. They find out only once they are in the car insurance world that, hey, this really is who I am and what I was born to do and I'm darn good at it.

I was still waiting for that moment of realization.

My husband, Mitch, always knew he wanted to fly. He wasn't happy with his feet on the ground for very long. He had to be in the air. But it wasn't enough for him just to fly; there had to be a purpose behind it greater than simply carrying tourists or packages from one city to another. He also had an overwhelming need to serve his country. I admired him for his passion for flight and his dedication to the military, but I only pretended to understand it, because I'd never felt that kind of calling myself.

I'd sort of bounced around through life, from one odd job to another. I'd even bounced into marriage and motherhood without really consciously planning it or desiring it.

Working for Monk had been the most interesting and fullfilling job I'd ever had—and the most aggravating, time-consuming, frustrating, and financially uncertain, too. But I stumbled into the position the same way I stumbled into everything else in my life.

Was being the assistant to a great detective my calling?

I didn't know.

Maybe there was another dysfunctional detective I could help. But what were my professional qualifications? Would Monk, Stottlemeyer, and Dr. Kroger give me letters of recommendation? If so, what would they say?

And even if they did back me up for a career as a detective enabler, I had a hard time seeing myself with Frank Porter, Cindy Chow, Mad Jack Wyatt, or some other sleuth with issues.

My relationship with Monk was unique. There was something about his temperament, his gentle soul, and our shared pain that made us a good match.

I just had to hope I'd stumble into something else, hopefully something that paid enormous amounts of money. So I worried and I fantasized into the wee hours before finally, mercifully, drifting off into a troubled sleep.

20

Mr. Monk and the Dust Bunny

On Tuesdays, Monk has his regular appointment with Dr. Kroger, his psychiatrist. The shrink makes me nervous. I'm afraid he's analyzing everything I say, my body language, and even the dilation of my pupils to determine how screwed up I really am.

He's also way too relaxed all the time. It's unnatural. I'm sure that I could walk into Dr. Kroger's office with a hatchet in my chest and a monkey on my head and it wouldn't startle him. In fact, I'm tempted do it just to see what would happen.

Dr. Kroger greeted us as we walked into his immaculate waiting room. I don't know whether it was so clean because disorder would irritate his patients like Monk, or if the doctor had a touch of OCD himself.

"Congratulations, Adrian," Dr. Kroger said.

"On what?" Monk said.

"Your reinstatement to the force and your promotion to captain, of course. I'm very happy for you."

"You saw me on TV?"

"I did."

"Then you know it was a moment of high political drama that ranks up there with the Kennedy-Nixon debates," Monk said.

"It was certainly memorable," Dr. Kroger said, ushering Monk into his office. "Make yourself comfortable, Adrian; I'll be right in."

The doctor closed the door behind him and looked at me.

"How is he doing?" Dr. Kroger asked.

"Isn't that a question you should be asking him?"

"There's a difference between his perception of the situation and yours."

"He's doing fine," I said. "He's giddy."

"How's he handling his additional responsibilities?"

"There's a steep learning curve," I said. "But he's solved every homicide that's come his way."

Dr. Kroger nodded sagely. I wondered if he and Madam Frost practiced that expression in the mirror to get it right or if it naturally came from a deep awareness of one's own depth of knowledge that I simply didn't have yet.

"Has he exhibited any performance anxiety?"

"Don't all men have performance anxiety?"

Dr. Kroger smiled, but it seemed forced. For a guy who was so relaxed, he didn't have much of a sense of humor.

"Nobody from the department asked me if I

thought he was ready to be reinstated," Dr. Kroger said.

"Are you feeling left out?"

That was a shrinky sort of question, and I wasn't surprised when he dodged it. But he did surprise me with his next comment.

"Nobody asked me about Frank, Cindy, or Jack, either," Dr. Kroger said.

"They're your patients, too?"

"They were all initially referred to me by the department," Dr. Kroger said. "Under normal circumstances, I don't think they'd be back at work without a positive report from me and an interview with a review board."

"These aren't normal circumstances," I said.

"But things will go back to normal, Ms. Teeger. The police and the city are back at the negotiating table. I can't help worrying about what will happen to Adrian and the others when this labor dispute is resolved."

"They've proven themselves," I said. "The fair thing to do would be to let them stay where they are."

"Life is seldom fair," Dr. Kroger said. "Politics even less so."

And on that hopeful note he stepped into his office and I settled down with the latest issue of *Cosmo*. But I found it hard to concentrate on "The Ten Bedroom Secrets That Will Drive Your Man Insane," and it wasn't because I didn't have a man to try them on.

I could feel the tension in the homicide squad

room the instant we walked in. Many of the "sick" detectives had returned to work to investigate the cop killing and were congregating on one side of the room, glaring nastily at Wyatt, Chow, and Porter on the other.

Stottlemeyer was in his office, buried in paperwork, ignoring the animosity on display outside his door.

Jasper, Arnie, and Sparrow stood in the demilitarized zone around the coffee machine.

Disher took a seat at his desk and tried to move the pencil cup closer. It wouldn't budge.

"Who glued my pencil cup to my desk?" Disher demanded. "Is this someone's idea of a joke?"

Jasper drew up the collar of his coat and tried to become invisible as other cops around the room began to discover that their blotters, phones, and other desktop items were also glued in place.

Monk's team all gathered around Porter's desk.

"Frank gave us a list of fifteen possible witnesses to Allegra's murder," Wyatt reported. "We found our guy on the third door we knocked on. His name is Tono Busok."

"Why didn't he come forward?" Monk asked.

"He sells bootleg movies," Wyatt said. "There was a bank of about fifty DVD burners in his apartment. He was afraid if he went to the police, his bootlegging operation would be exposed and we'd arrest him for pirating *Basic Instinct 2.*"

"And for that petty crime he'd let a murderer go free?" Monk said. "What kind of person is he?"

"Did I mention his apartment is in his mother's

basement?" Wyatt said. "All I had to do was threaten to turn him over to the FBI and he cracked. He gave me a detailed statement about what he saw at Allegra Doucet's house. The murder went down exactly the way you said it did."

"Not exactly," Chow said, and turned to Monk. "Didn't Madam Frost tell you the first time you met her that she knew all the key figures behind the Summer of Love?"

"She said she dropped acid with Timothy Leary and hung out with Janis Joplin," I said.

"Cool," Jasper said.

"It's obvious what really happened here," Chow said. "Madam Frost was an MK-Ultra operative in the 1960s. She supplied LSD to the youth culture, turning them into lab rats for MK-Ultra's mind-control experiments. It's no coincidence that Allegra Doucet moved across the street from her. Allegra knew who and what Madam Frost was. And when Allegra uncovered too much about the alien conspiracy, the Omega Agency ordered Madam Frost to eliminate her and the crossbred humans."

"So you think everybody on the list of people born in San Francisco on February twentieth, 1962, is an alien test-tube baby?" Sparrow said.

"Some are," Chow said. "Some aren't. We'll see who is still alive a year from now."

"What about us?" Porter asked. "Don't we have to be silenced, too?"

Chow shook her head. "Not anymore. Monk has inadvertently helped them pull off the perfect cover-up. Everyone believes Madam Frost's story because it 'makes sense.' No one will look any deeper. It's another win for the space alien shadow government."

"Whew," Wyatt said. "It's sure nice to know I won't have to keep looking over my shoulder for ET."

Monk asked them to write up their reports on the homicide cases and went to see Captain Stottlemeyer. He poked his head into the office.

"How is it going, Captain?" Monk asked.

"Not so good, Monk," Stottlemeyer said. "I hear you closed four homicides last night."

"It was a lucky break," Monk said. "What have you learned about Officer Milner?"

"Squat," Stottlemeyer said.

Monk squatted. Stottlemeyer rose from behind his desk and looked down at him.

"What the hell are you doing, Monk?"

"Squatting," Monk said.

"It's an expression," Stottlemeyer said. "It means zilch, zero, *nada*."

"I'm pretty sure it means sitting on your heels," Monk said. "Like so."

Disher came in, carrying a file. "What are you doing?"

"The captain wants us to squat," Monk said.

Disher squatted beside him. "Why? Did he lose one of his contacts?"

"Get up," Stottlemeyer said. "Both of you."

They did.

"You have dust bunnies under your desk," Monk said. "Were you aware of that?"

"No, I was not," Stottlemeyer said, sitting down in his desk chair.

"If you squat right here"—Monk squatted again—"you can see them."

"Then don't squat," Stottlemeyer said.

"But I'll still know they're there," Monk said. "And so will you."

"I can live with it," Stottlemeyer said, glancing into the squad room. "Get up, Monk."

"I'm going to go get a broom and a dustpan," Monk said, starting to go. "You'll thank me later."

"No," Stottlemeyer said firmly, stopping Monk. "You can't go get a broom and sweep my office."

"Why not?" Monk asked.

"Because you're a captain now, and it will send the wrong message to the rank and file." Stottlemeyer motioned to the detectives outside, who were making a show of not paying attention to what was happening in the office but who clearly were.

"That dust bunnies are bad?" Monk said.

"That you are subservient to me," Stottlemeyer said. "We've got the same rank."

"The men would lose all respect for your authority," Disher said.

"Exactly," Stottlemeyer said. "Randy, go get me a broom and a dustpan."

"But, sir," Disher said, "it will send the wrong message to the men."

"What's that?" Stottlemeyer asked.

Disher lowered his voice. "That I am subservient to you."

"You are, Lieutenant," Stottlemeyer said.

"Can't the dust bunnies wait?" Disher said, almost pleading.

"They are called bunnies for a reason," Monk said gravely. "They multiply. Soon you will have hordes of dust bunnies swarming the building. And then things get ugly. Very, very ugly. It's not something you want to see. Trust me on this."

Stottlemeyer sighed. "Monk can't think with dust bunnies under my desk, Randy. And I need him to think right now."

"Yes, sir." Disher dropped his file on Stottlemeyer's desk and marched out in a huff.

"What do you need me to think about?" Monk said.

I saw Disher approach another detective and give him some orders—like getting him a broom and a dustpan.

"The Officer Milner shooting. I went to see his wife," Stottlemeyer said. "They live in a tiny little apartment in San Mateo. She drives an eight-year-old Nissan. If they've got money, they're hiding it well. My kid has more change in his piggy bank than they've got in their checking account. She has no idea what Milner was up to besides working as hard as he could to support his family."

I saw the detective Disher talked to march up to an officer and give her some orders. I had a pretty good idea what he was telling her to do.

"Did he have any enemies?" Monk bent down, keeping an eye on the bunnies in case they made a break for it. "Maybe someone he arrested seeking revenge?"

"He was a rookie." Stottlemeyer picked up a sheet of paper and handed it to Monk. "Here's his arrest sheet. And that's all it is, one sheet. Look for yourself. It's nothing but routine traffic violations, some drunk-and-disorderlies, a few nickel-and-dime drug busts. We're talking overnighters in a holding cell, tops. Nothing that anybody would kill over."

I saw the officer return with a broom and dustpan and bring them to the detective, who brought them to Disher, and Disher brought them into the office. I was so busy watching the little power play unfold that I almost missed Monk subtly straightening his back. It was a tell. Monk was onto something.

Stottlemeyer noticed it, too. "What?"

"It says here that eight months ago Officer Milner arrested Bertrum Gruber making a drug buy at that park on Potrero Hill."

"So what?" Stottlemeyer said.

Monk looked up from the paper and saw Disher. "They're right there, near the foot of the desk."

Disher, irritated, shoved the broom under the desk.

"Be careful," Monk said. "One wrong move and they'll scatter, and it's game over, pal."

"Monk," Stottlemeyer said, trying hard to keep the anger from his voice. "Could we please concentrate on what's important?"

"I couldn't agree more." Monk snatched the broom and dustpan from Disher. "Stand back. This is a very delicate procedure. I need room to maneuver."

Monk crouched, eased the broom under the desk, and swept the dust bunnies into the dustpan as if he were dealing with nitroglycerin. Sweat broke out on his brow. He chewed on his lower lip. The whole thing must have taken five minutes.

Stottlemeyer leaned back in his chair and massaged his temples.

Once Monk had the dust bunnies in the dustpan, he lifted it up slowly, keeping it even, careful not to tip it. He made his way gingerly to the trash can, eased the dustpan over it, and tipped it until the dust bunnies dropped inside. Mission accomplished.

His whole body sagged, and he slumped into one of the guest chairs, exhausted.

"That was close," he said.

Stottlemeyer sighed. "Do you think we can get back to the Officer Milner homicide now?"

"Water," Monk said to me.

I reached into my big purse for a bottle of Sierra Springs. It's the same purse I used when Julie was a baby and I had to lug around diapers, milk, and wipes. Now I carry wipes, rubber gloves, Ziploc bags, and bottles of Sierra Springs, the only water he'll drink.

I gave Monk the bottle, and he opened it up and took a long swig.

"Who cares if Officer Milner arrested Bertrum Gruber eight months ago?" Stottlemeyer asked.

"Gruber is the witness who came forward and identified the Golden Gate Strangler," Monk said.

"Aka the Foot Fiend," Disher said.

"Thanks," Stottlemeyer said.

"Gruber said he was going to the community garden to check on his strawberries the morning of the murder," Monk said. "He claimed he saw Charlie Herrin coming out of the park with the victim's shoe in his hands. Gruber even got a partial plate from Herrin's car."

"It was another lucky break for you," Stottlemeyer said. "God knows you certainly get more than your share."

"Gruber was lying," Monk said. "He wasn't growing strawberries. It was the wrong time of year for planting them."

The strawberries again. He just couldn't let that go.

"So he lied. Gruber was probably in the park looking to score some drugs," Stottlemeyer said. "You can't really expect him to admit that to the police, can you? What matters is that his information was good. He did the right thing and helped you catch a serial killer."

"He cheated," Monk said.

"What?" Stottlemeyer said.

"He cheated," Monk said emphatically.

Stottlemeyer gave me a look. I shrugged. I didn't know what Monk meant, either.

"Fine. He cheated," Stottlemeyer said. "What does that have to do with Officer Milner's murder?"

"Everything," Monk said. "Because Bertrum Gruber is the guy who killed him."

21

Mr. Monk Drops the Other Shoe

Monk's declaration stunned all of us.

Stottlemeyer rubbed his mustache and glanced at Disher, who glanced at me, and I glanced right back at Stottlemeyer. I'm not sure what that round-robin of glances accomplished, or the message it conveyed, but we did it one more time for good measure.

"What could possibly make you think that Bertrum Gruber shot Officer Milner?" Stottlemeyer asked.

"It's obvious," Monk replied.

"Only to you," Stottlemeyer said.

"It's right here on the arrest sheet." Monk got up from his seat and handed Milner's arrest record to Stottlemeyer, who briefly scanned it.

"I still don't see it." Stottlemeyer handed the paper to Disher, who scrutinized it.

"Me, neither," Disher said, handing the sheet to

me, as if I'd know what I was looking at. I gave it a quick once-over, but it was all meaningless to me.

"Officer Milner arrested Bertrum Gruber eight months ago for buying drugs in the same park where Charlie Herrin murdered a woman last week," Monk said.

"Yes, you said that," Stottlemeyer said.

"It's on his arrest sheet," Monk said.

"I know," Stottlemeyer said. "I can read."

"So there you go," Monk said.

"There I go?"

"You aren't bothered by the coincidence?"

"*What* coincidence?" Stottlemeyer said.

"That all three of them were in the park at one time or another?"

"Potrero Hill was Officer Milner's beat," Stottlemeyer said. "Bertrum Gruber lives in Potrero Hill. Charlie Herrin dumped a body in a park in a neighborhood where Officer Milner works and Gruber shops for drugs. I don't see a coincidence here. I see a logical explanation for how their lives intersected. What I don't see is a motive for Bertrum Gruber to murder Officer Milner."

"Me, neither," Disher said. "I'm with the captain on this. Captain Stottlemeyer that is, not you."

I was in agreement with Stottlemeyer and Disher, but I also knew that Monk was never wrong about this stuff. In my opinion, they should have just gone out and arrested Bertrum Gruber and worried about how Monk figured it out later. Trying to follow Monk's thinking was giving me a monumental headache. I believe if your brain isn't wired like Monk's—and whose is?—trying to think like him makes all your neurons fire in the wrong direction. It can be hazardous to your mental health.

"Milner was one of the officers who secured the crime scene after the body was found in the park," Monk said. "Two days later Bertrum Gruber came forward, lied about seeing Charlie Herrin in the park the morning of the murder, and won a two-hundred-fifty-thousand-dollar reward for information leading to the capture of the Golden Gate Strangler."

"You don't think Charlie Herrin strangled those women?" Stottlemeyer said.

"Oh, he definitely did it," Monk said. "He's the guy."

"I'm so confused," Disher said, taking a seat.

"Then what did Gruber lie about?" Stottlemeyer said.

"About being in the park that morning," Monk said. "He wasn't there. He didn't see anything. He cheated."

My head was splitting. "Then how did Gruber get all the information about Charlie Herrin?"

"Officer Milner told him," Monk said.

Stottlemeyer, Disher, and I did another round-robin of glances. It didn't help my headache. I started rummaging around in my big purse for some Advil or a mallet.

"How did Officer Milner know?" Disher said.

"He knew about the shoe because he was at the crime scene," Monk said. "I don't know how he found out the rest."

"Assuming you're right—and that's an assumption of biblical proportions," Stottlemeyer said, "why wouldn't Milner arrest the Strangler himself? It would have been a career-making arrest; he would have gotten all the glory."

"But not a penny of the two-hundred-fifty-thousand-dollar reward," Monk said. "As a city employee, he was ineligible to collect it. You said it yourself, Captain: Money was tight for him. The reward would have done his family more good than making the arrest."

"So he recruited Gruber to be his front man, fed him the information, and they split up the money," Stottlemeyer said. "Only Gruber got greedy and decided to keep it all for himself."

"That's my thinking," Monk said. "Which is also the way it happened."

"How do you know?" Disher said.

"The magazines and brochures in Milner's police car," Monk said. "He was looking at cars, homes, and vacations he couldn't possibly afford."

"That's all you've got?" Stottlemeyer said. "That's the basis for your entire theory?"

"Pretty much," Monk said. "And the strawberry thing."

"What strawberry thing?" Stottlemeyer said.

"You don't want to know," I said, dry-swallowing two Advils.

"Gruber also got his mom's birthday wrong," Monk said.

"Excuse me?" Stottlemeyer said.

"Gruber claimed he remembered Herrin's partial plate because it matched his mother's birthday, M-five-six-seven for May fifth, 1967, but for that to be true, she had to give birth to him when she was ten years old, which I find highly unlikely."

"What if she adopted him?" Disher said.

Stottlemeyer looked at me. "Is that Advil?"

I nodded.

"The math still doesn't work," Monk said. "If his mother was born in 1967, she's forty. He's thirty."

"Maybe she adopted him when she was twenty and he was ten," Disher said.

"Toss me the bottle, would you?" Stottlemeyer said to me. I did.

"It still doesn't add up," Monk said.

"I'm not so sure," Disher said. "Does anyone have a calculator?"

Stottlemeyer put some tablets in his mouth, washed them down with a sip of coffee, and tossed the Advil bottle back to me.

"Okay, Monk, here's how I see it," Stottlemeyer said. "You've got absolutely nothing connecting Bertrum Gruber to the murder of Officer Milner."

"How can you say that after everything I just told you?"

"Because none of it makes any sense," Stottlemeyer said.

"It couldn't be more sensible," Monk said.

"We may be experiencing a historic moment here," Stottlemeyer said. "This could be the first time you're wrong about the solution to a homicide."

"I'm not," Monk said.

"Hey, you don't have to convince me," Stottlemeyer said. "I don't sign your checks anymore.

You're a captain in this department. If you think you've got something, prove it."

"I don't want to step on your investigation," Monk said.

"Trust me, you won't," Stottlemeyer said.

"You're sure?"

"Monk, I guarantee it. The Bertrum Gruber angle is all yours," Stottlemeyer said. "Run with it with my blessing."

"Okay." Monk headed for the door. "I will."

Monk went back to his interrogation room office. I went with him and closed the door. He paced back and forth in front of his desk.

"Can you believe that?" Monk said.

"It's shocking," I said.

"I couldn't have been any clearer if I had Bertrum Gruber standing in the room making a confession."

I didn't say anything. Monk paced some more.

"The facts are indisputable and the conclusions are logical and inevitable."

Monk paced back and forth. I kept my mouth shut.

"How could anyone listen to that explanation and not be thoroughly convinced that I'm right?"

After a moment Monk stopped and looked at me. "*You* are convinced, aren't you?"

I was hoping he wouldn't ask me that question.

"Frankly, Mr. Monk, no."

"How can that be?" he said. "What part don't you get?"

"Everything after you said Bertrum Gruber killed Officer Milner."

"Okay," Monk said. "I'll go over it again."

I held up my hands in surrender. "Please don't. The Advil hasn't kicked in yet, and I'm afraid my head might explode."

Monk nodded and started pacing once more, counting to himself.

"What are you counting?" I asked.

"The number of times I pace," he said.

"Why?"

"I want to make sure that when I'm ready to quit I end on an even number," he said.

"Why don't you just pick a number to pace to and end then?"

"That presupposes that I will know when I want to quit pacing."

"Don't you?"

"I'm thinking," Monk said. "I'll finish pacing when I'm through thinking, and I'll do it on an even number."

"So you might have to pace past the point when you've finished thinking."

"Usually I can time it so they happen at about the same time," Monk said. "I just walk slowly or think faster."

"Gotcha," I said, and debated to myself whether the two Advil I'd already taken would be enough. "How are you able to keep count and talk to me at the same time?"

"I'm counting in my head," he said.

"While you're talking," I said.

"Of course," he said. "Can't you do that?"

"No," I said. In fact, I could barely think at all. It felt like my brain was trying to break out of my skull.

"That explains why you couldn't follow my simple solution to Officer Milner's murder."

"Simple?" I shrieked. Yes, shrieked. I'm not proud of it.

"Simple," he said.

"How did Officer Milner figure out that Charles Herrin was the Golden Gate Strangler?"

"I don't know."

"What proof do you have that Officer Milner and Bertrum Gruber have even seen each other in the last eight months?"

"Gruber couldn't have known what he knew otherwise," Monk said.

"That isn't proof," I said. "That's a guess. So how are you going to establish that Officer Milner solved the murders and then told Gruber about it?"

"That's a niggling detail."

"No offense, Mr. Monk, but that seems like a big detail to me. Without that, how can you establish Gruber's motive for killing Officer Milner?"

"Why do you think I'm pacing?"

"The only two people who can tell you what you need to know are Officer Milner and Bertrum Gruber," I said. "Milner is dead and Gruber won't talk. So where can you go to find the evidence?"

Monk paced back and forth. And back and forth again. "I need a picture of Officer Milner. Can you get me that?"

"Probably," I said. "Why?"

Monk paced back and forth one more time and then stopped. "Twenty-eight."

"You're finished thinking?"

"I am," Monk said with a smile. "Now it's time for some action."

22

Mr. Monk Goes to Jail

Visiting a jail is a lot like going to the airport these days, only you're not allowed to bring any personal belongings with you. You have to walk through a metal detector, but even if you don't set off any alarms, a guard is still likely to run a wand around you and physically pat you down.

Unless you're Adrian Monk.

The guards at the county lockup were familiar with him and knew his strong aversion to being touched. So they did an extraordinary thing: They let him pat himself down.

Yeah, that's right. He gave *himself* a full body search, right there at the security checkpoint. And believe me, it was something to see.

He contorted his body this way and that, slapping himself as if he were covered with fire ants, while the guards looked on with stone faces.

But he was thorough.

"Uh-oh." Monk patted his pocket. He reached inside slowly, as if there might be a mousetrap in there that he didn't know about, and pulled out single, shiny quarter. "What was I thinking bringing this inside a jail?"

"What harm could a quarter cause?" I asked.

Monk shook his head and looked at the guards. "She's a newbie." He looked back at me. "This quarter could be carved into a tiny, but deadly, arrowhead."

"I've heard of prisoners making shivs, but never arrowheads."

"That's because the tireless diligence of these fine guards has prevented that from happening." Monk dropped the quarter in the basket that contained his wallet and other personal items.

One of the burly guards stepped forward to pat me down.

"Can't I pat myself?" I said.

The guard shook his head.

"But you let Mr. Monk do it," I said.

"He's a special case," the guard said.

I couldn't argue with that. I got patted down.

We were led into a windowless meeting room with gray walls and only a metal table and four matching chairs, all screwed to the floor.

"I like what they've done with the place," Monk said.

He wasn't being sarcastic. He really liked it. The table was in the center of the room, the four chairs spaced evenly apart, creating a perfectly symmetrical ensemble.

Monk walked around the table several times, admiring it, touching the four corners lightly with the tips of his fingers as he passed.

"It's beautiful," Monk said. "It's like a sculpture. I wonder if I could get one of these installed in my house."

"You want to furnish your place like a prison?"

"Remind me to get the name of the artist before we leave," he said.

The door opened and the guards brought in Charlie Herrin, who was in chains and wearing a bright orange jumpsuit. They led him to a chair and locked the chains at his feet into an eyebolt on the floor.

"Is that really necessary?" Monk asked.

"He murdered three women with his bare hands," I said.

"Knock on the door if you need us," one of the guards said. "We'll be right outside."

The guards left and closed the door. We sat down across from Herrin. He looked at me as if I were a Fudgsicle.

"Hi," Monk said. "I'm the guy you held hostage the other day. You might not recognize me because you were behind my back with your gun to my head."

"I remember you," Herrin said, his eyes going up and down my body. "Who is she?"

"Don't tell him my name," I said. "I don't want this monster knowing anything about me."

The last thing I wanted was to get letters, e-mails, or collect calls from Herrin and his buddies in prison.

"She's someone I know who goes places with

me," Monk said. "I'd like to ask you some questions."

"You can ask all the questions you want," Herrin said. "But I'm not answering them without an incentive."

"Like what?" Monk said."

Herrin smiled at me. "I want your left shoe."

"In your dreams," I said.

"That's my problem," Herrin said. "All I have are my dreams. They took my entire collection of souvenirs away. I have needs that aren't being met in here."

"That's the idea," I said.

Herrin shrugged. "No shoe, no answers."

Monk looked imploringly at me. "Give him your shoe."

"No," I said.

"It's an old shoe," he said.

"I don't care," I said.

"It's all scuffed up and dirty," Monk said.

"That's not the point," I said. "You know why he wants this shoe. You know what this shoe means to him. Do you really want to indulge his sick, twisted desires?"

"Do you want a murderer to go free?" Monk said.

He had to put it that way, didn't he? I reached down, pulled off my shoe, and dropped it on the table.

"Happy now?" I said.

Herrin picked it up delicately, as if it were a glass slipper, and brought it up to his nose. He inhaled deeply and closed his eyes in rapture.

Monk grimaced in disgust and so did I.

"My God," Monk said. "You're so, so, so sick."

"It may be a long time before I get this close to another shoe," Herrin said. "I want to savor it."

"Hurry up and ask your questions," I said to Monk. "I want to get out of here."

"Me, too," Monk said. "Give him your other shoe."

"What?" I said.

"Give him your other shoe," Monk said.

"I don't want her other shoe," Herrin said.

"Give it to him anyway," Monk said.

"I'm not giving him another shoe."

"She can keep it," Herrin said.

"You're only wearing one shoe," Monk said to me. "Be reasonable. You can't walk out of here with just one shoe."

"Yes, I can," I said.

"No, you can't," he said.

"I'm not giving him my other shoe," I said.

"What are you going to do with just one shoe?" Monk said.

"I'll have it and he won't," I said.

"I don't want it," Herrin said.

"All that shoe will do is remind you of the shoe you gave to him," Monk said. "Do you really want to be reminded of that?"

I looked at Herrin, who was lovingly sniffing and stroking my shoe. No, I didn't want to be reminded of that.

"Fine." I took off my right shoe and smacked it down on the table. "Enjoy it, you creep."

"Why would I want a right shoe?" Herrin slid it toward me. "It's incomparable to a left shoe."

"Take it." Monk slid the shoe back to him using the very tip of his index finger.

"No." Herrin pushed it away.

"Yes." Monk slid it back again.

"No." Herrin pushed it away.

"Either you take the right shoe or I'm taking back the left one," Monk said.

"No, you won't," Herrin said.

"Yes, I will," Monk said.

"Then I won't answer your questions," Herrin said.

"Shoes come in pairs!" Monk slammed his fist on the table, bolted up from his seat, and glared at Herrin with a righteous fury I'd never seen in him before. "It is the natural order of the universe. It's bad enough that you've murdered three women, but you will *not* mess with the natural order of the universe. Do I make myself clear?"

Herrin swallowed hard, cradled my left shoe to his bosom with one hand, and reluctantly took my right shoe with the other.

"That's better." Monk settled back into his seat and took a deep breath. He rolled his head, adjusted his collar, then reached into his jacket pocket and took out a photo. "Have you ever seen this man before?"

It was a picture of Officer Milner.

Charlie Herrin glanced at the picture and nodded. "Yeah, I've seen him."

Monk was right: There *was* a connection between Milner, Gruber, and Herrin.

"Do you know who he is?" Monk asked.

"The cop who pulled me over," Herrin said. "It

was the second time I thought I was going to get caught, but I was on a winning streak."

"What do you mean?"

"I was driving home on Saturday. It was all foggy; I should have been paying attention to my driving, but I was totally distracted by the shoe. I had to keep touching it, looking at it, smelling it," Herrin said, doing all of that now to what had once been my shoe. "Who could blame me? I'm only human."

"I'm not so sure," I said, disgusted.

"I looked away from the road for one second and accidentally blew through a red light," Herrin said. "I got clipped by this Hispanic guy going through the intersection. It was only a busted tail-light, but that could've been the end, right there, if he called the cops. But he was an illegal alien. Barely spoke English. He didn't want trouble any more than I did. We both walked away from it like it never happened."

"So where does Officer Milner fit into this?" Monk said.

"Sunday I'm driving to work and he pulls me over. I had that incredible shoe in my lap. I tossed it in the backseat, but I knew I'd been caught. I knew that was the end. He walked up to the car, leaned into the window, and asked if I knew how fast I was driving. I didn't. He told me I was speed-ing, going thirty-five in a twenty-five-mile-per-hour zone, and that he was going to give me a ticket," Herrin said. "He took my license, went back to his car, and sat there for the longest time staring at me."

I could imagine what was going through Milner's mind as he sat in his car, pondering what fate had mischeviously dropped in his lap.

The instant he saw that left shoe in the backseat of the car, he knew he'd pulled over the Golden Gate Strangler in a random traffic stop.

What were the odds of *that*?

But more important, what the hell was he going to do about it?

Milner knew his duty was to arrest the murderer. It would be a career-making, headline-grabbing arrest that would make him a national hero.

For the rest of his life, Officer Milner would be known as the brave young cop who singlehandedly caught the Golden Gate Strangler.

So what was stopping him?

The $250,000 reward. By all rights it should be his, too, along with the glory.

But it wouldn't be.

All he'd get from the mayor was a firm handshake and a photo op. The check would stay in the mayor's pocket.

The mayor was willing to give the check to any schlub off the street but not to a cop, not to someone who risked his life every day and worked overtime just to scrape up enough to pay for groceries.

How unfair was that?

I could certainly sympathize with Milner's moral quandary.

He was torn between going for the glory and going for the cash. Both options had a powerful allure.

So while Charlie Herrin sweated it out, Officer

Milner sat there in his police car, silently struggling with a choice that, either way, would irrevocably change his life.

Ultimately, greed won out over duty.

Or, to put it more charitably, Officer Milner couldn't resist the immediate opportunity to provide a better life for his family over the less tangible, potential long-term rewards of making the arrest.

"I was sure he was just waiting for backup to arrive," Herrin said. "But no, he got out of the car, handed me my license, and let me off with a warning. Can you believe that? What a break. He didn't see the shoe. He didn't know who I was."

"Actually," Monk said, "he did."

"Then why didn't he arrest me?"

"There are two hundred and fifty thousand reasons why he didn't," Monk said.

23

Mr. Monk Feels Queasy

The guards didn't let Herrin leave the room with my shoes, but there was no way I was taking them back. I wasn't going to touch them, either. I told the guards to toss them in the trash. I walked out of the jail and all the way to my car in my stocking feet.

Monk and I both thoroughly disinfected our hands in the car with his wipes, but it would take a lot more than that to make either one of us feel clean again.

We stopped on the way back to headquarters at a Shoes for Less store, where I bought a pair of twenty-dollar running shoes just to have something to wear for the rest of the day, though considering how poorly they were made, I had my doubts they'd last that long.

From there, we went straight to Stottlemeyer's

office and filled him and Disher in on what we'd learned from Charlie Herrin.

Stottlemeyer listened without interruption until Monk was finished, then asked Disher to bring in Officer Milner's personal effects.

Disher stepped out of Stottlemeyer's office to get them from the evidence room.

"You want to know what I don't get?" Stottlemeyer said.

"What?" Monk said.

"Everything," Stottlemeyer said. "How is it that I can look at the same evidence you do and see nothing at all, and you see who the killer is and what he had for breakfast?"

"It's a gift and a curse," Monk said.

"Thanks," Stottlemeyer said.

"I was talking about me," Monk said. "I see too much. You can walk outside and just appreciate the day. I see everything that doesn't fit and I can't let it go."

"It makes you a hell of a detective, Monk."

"But I miss a lot of nice days."

Disher returned with a box filled with plastic bags containing all the items Officer Milner had on his person at the time of his death.

Stottlemeyer searched around in the box and removed a bag containing Officer Milner's ticket book. He opened the bag up and started flipping through the citations. It didn't take him long to find the one he wanted.

"Here it is," Stottlemeyer said. "He never finished writing up the citation, and didn't submit it when he got back from patrol. But all the information is here. The date and time of the traffic stop. The make, model, plates, and description of the car, even Herrin's name and address."

Stottlemeyer handed the ticket book to Monk, who glanced at the citation.

"But we still don't have anything tying Gruber to Officer Milner's murder," Disher said. "All this proves is that Officer Milner met the Foot Fiend."

"Who is the Foot Fiend?" Stottlemeyer said.

"Charles Herrin," Disher said.

"He's the Golden Gate Strangler," Stottlemeyer said. "Not the Foot Fiend."

"He is to me, sir. And I'm pretty sure that's how he's going to be remembered in the annals of crime."

"What 'annals of crime'?" Stottlemeyer said.

"The ones that everyone reads," Disher said.

"Name one," Stottlemeyer said.

"Um," Disher said. *"The Annal of Crime."*

"I've never seen it," Stottlemeyer said.

"It's on all the newsstands. You just have to look really, really hard to find it, like behind *Dog Fancy* or *Rubber Stamp Journal.*"

"Yeah, I'll do that." Stottlemeyer turned his attention back to Monk. "Randy is right about one thing: You haven't made that final connection. You can't prove Milner fed Gruber the information on Herrin, and without that, you've got no motive for murder."

"On the contrary, Captain." Monk held up the ticket book. "The evidence is right here."

* * *

I called Bertrum Gruber and told him that Monk had a few more questions he needed to ask in order to wrap up the investigation. He balked, until I reminded him that one of the requirements of the reward was that he cooperate fully with the police, and if he didn't, he risked immediate revocation of all the funds he'd received. It was a lie, but Gruber invited us to meet him at the marina, where he was looking over a sport yacht he was interested in buying. Stottlemeyer, Monk, and I went to see him.

I don't get to the marina very often, which is a shame, because it's one of the most picturesque spots in the city. Birthday-cake houses with their brightly colored stucco frosting line the wide boulevard that faces the Marina Green, a grassy park that curves around the boat slips, a forest of bobbing, white masts cast against the dramatic backdrop of the Golden Gate Bridge. Kite fliers, joggers, bike riders, and sunbathers fill the park year-round, regardless of the weather, giving it a festive feel that not even the prospect of seeing Bertrum Gruber could ruin for me.

Stottlemeyer, Monk, and I walked down the gangplank from the park to the dock. Monk clutched the wooden handrail as if caught in a violent gale. But the gangplank wasn't moving at all. *He* was, bobbing in rhythm with the masts.

"Relax, Monk," Stottlemeyer said. "We aren't even on a boat."

"I'm getting seasick just looking at them," Monk whined.

"So don't look at them," I said.

We walked down the dock until we spotted

Gruber standing underneath the spoiler of a thirty-five-foot white sport yacht. The boat had an aggressive, arched-forward design that made it look like it was speeding even while it was moored in its slip.

Gruber wore a white yacht cap with gold leaf on the black bill, a blue-and-white-striped crew shirt, a red ascot, a windbreaker, white pants, and brown leather Top-Siders with tassles over his bare feet. He looked ridiculous, as if he were dressing up for a costume party.

"Ahoy, mateys. Isn't this baby gorgeous?" Gruber said. "You should see inside. Flat-screen satellite TV, granite countertops, handcrafted cabinets, and ultraleather upholstery. It's sweet. Come aboard."

"We'd really rather not." Monk looked queasy at the thought of it. "This is Captain Stottlemeyer. He's taking part in the investigation now."

Gruber climbed down off the boat and joined us on the dock. "That makes all three of us guys captains."

"It does?" Stottlemeyer said.

"I'm Captain Gruber, and this is my vessel." He stroked the smooth hull while looking at me. "It's my lady. I'm calling her the *Lust Boat*."

"What's a dinghy like this cost?" Stottlemeyer asked.

"Please." Monk groaned. "Could we speed this up?"

"Just south of two hundred Gs," Gruber said.

"That's a big chunk of your reward," I said.

"I'm only giving them a down payment," Gruber said. "But they know I'm good for the rest. I've just optioned my inspirational life story to NBC-Universal."

"Good for you," Stottlemeyer said.

Monk swayed and swallowed hard. "We need to double-check a few points in your statement. Can you go over it again as fast as you can?"

"I went to the garden to tend my strawberries. I saw the guy coming out of the park with a shoe in his hand. He got into a Ford Taurus with a busted taillight and a dented bumper. Part of his license plate was M-five-six-seven."

"There's just one problem with that," Monk said, pausing to clutch his stomach and take a deep breath. "Charlie Herrin didn't break his taillight and dent his bumper until *after* he left the park."

"No way." Gruber shoved his hands in his jacket pockets and shook his head. "I know what I saw."

"You didn't see anything," Stottlemeyer said. "You were just repeating the details Officer Milner gave you when you agreed to his scheme for a cut of the reward. Only you decided to kill him and take it all, didn't you, Bert?"

"Could we continue this conversation up on the street?" Monk said. "Where the waves are less rough?"

The dock was as firm as the sidewalk. The only thing moving was Monk.

"As we speak, we're searching your apartment and taking your clothes back to the lab to test for gunpowder residue," Stottlemeyer said. "While we're ransacking the place we might even find the murder weapon."

"You won't," Gruber said.

It happened so fast I didn't see where the gun came from. One second Gruber was standing there; the next he'd grabbed Monk and put a gun to his head. He must have had the gun in his jacket pocket the whole time. Maybe he planned to ditch it at sea.

Stottlemeyer got his gun out almost as fast, leveling it at Gruber. I was no longer part of the play. I'd become a member of the audience. All I could do was watch.

It was a surreal. It was probably even more so for Monk.

"Oh, God," Monk said. "Not again."

"Back off or he dies," Gruber said to Stottlemeyer.

"I don't feel so good," Monk said.

"This isn't a very bright move, Bert," Stottlemeyer said.

"The two of us are getting on this boat and going," Gruber said. "Anybody follows me and he's shark bait."

"Everybody stand still," Monk said, looking nauseous. "You're shaking the dock."

"You want Monk," Stottlemeyer said. "You can have him."

I looked at Stottlemeyer. "You're not serious."

"What can I do?" Stottlemeyer put his gun back in his shoulder holster. "He's got us beat. Besides, I think being stuck on a boat with Monk may be worse punishment than death row anyway."

Gruber backed toward the boat, pulling Monk along with him. "We're getting on the yacht."

"I can't," Monk groaned.

"Do you want to die?" Gruber said.

"Yes," Monk said. "Put me out of my misery. Please."

Stottlemeyer slowly bent down and tied his shoe. I couldn't believe how casually he was taking all this.

"Shut up and move," Gruber said.

"Don't say move," Monk said. "I can't even think about motion right now."

Gruber dragged Monk with him. "You're getting on the damn boat."

"Someone please shoot me," Monk said.

"Shut up," Gruber said.

Suddenly Monk heaved forward and threw up on the dock. Surprised and revolted, Gruber let go of Monk for an instant. Stottlemeyer whipped out a tiny gun from a hidden ankle holster and shot Gruber in the shoulder.

The impact slammed Gruber against the boat and knocked the gun from his grasp. He slid to the dock, whimpering in pain, clutching his shoulder.

He wasn't the only one whimpering. So was Monk, who was on his knees at the edge of the dock, gagging over the water.

I went to him and gently stroked his back until his gagging subsided. He was in misery.

Stottlemeyer snatched up Gruber's gun, then called for backup and an ambulance on his cell phone, but that wasn't necessary. The gunfire had drawn a crowd in the park, and I could already hear sirens coming.

"It's all over, Mr. Monk," I said.

"I know," he rasped. "You can find my will in the top drawer of my nightstand."

"You're going to be fine."

"Don't humor me," he said, shivering. "Can't you see I'm in my death throes?"

"You were great, Monk," Stottlemeyer said, keeping a careful eye on Gruber. "I knew you'd make a move, and I just waited for it."

"I wish Wyatt had been here," Monk said. "At least he would have had the decency to shoot me."

24

Mr. Monk Learns a Life Lesson

Monk didn't want the paramedics to treat him. He didn't want to move at all, for fear the motion would make him vomit again. He suggested we call the medical examiner and a mortuary instead and have them wait in the parking lot until he expired.

"It shouldn't take long," he said.

Even for Monk, this seemed extreme. He was being a big baby. If Julie was even slightly nauseous, she'd throw up as casually as some people sneeze and feel better right away. Me, I'd rather be nauseous for hours than throw up. But still, it wasn't a big deal. Everybody throws up in their lives. Surely this wasn't Monk's first time.

"Mr. Monk, aren't you overreacting a bit?" I said. "Haven't you ever vomited before?"

He gave me a withering look. "If I had, we'd be having this conversation over my grave."

I got the sentiment of the remark even though the logic didn't quite track.

Despite Monk's protests, Stottlemeyer instructed the paramedics to take him to the hospital anyway. Monk gagged a couple more times on the gurney and on the drive to the hospital.

By the time we got to the ER, he was convinced that he was seconds away from death. Monk demanded to sign a DNR form while he was still lucid.

The doctors started an IV drip to restore the fluids he'd lost, and gave him an injection of something to stop his queasiness. The doctor told me that it was possible Monk experienced some seasickness, perhaps even some stomach poisoning from something he ate, but it was more likely that his symptoms were self-induced, the result of a panic attack. He said I could take Monk home as soon as he'd calmed down.

It didn't take too long for Monk to relax. I don't know whether it was the drugs, the fact he was no longer on the pier, or the fatigue, but within an hour he was back to his usual self. He sat up on the gurney in the exam room and discussed his ordeal, now that it was safely in the past.

"I've only been that close to death once before," he said, "when I was buried alive in a coffin."

"I remember that," I said.

"When I was in the coffin, I saw visions of Trudy," Monk said. "It was like she was with me, preparing me for my journey to the other side. This experience was different."

"For one thing, you weren't dying," I said. "You were just sick to your stomach."

"I saw a long tunnel with a bright light at the end," Monk said. "It may have been God."

"Or a train," I said.

"I guess it just wasn't my time," Monk said.

"You're probably right," I said.

"I've learned a very important life lesson from this," Monk said. "I'll take Dramamine before going on the high seas again."

"You were ten yards from the shore, Mr. Monk."

"I was on the water," Monk said.

"The pier is secured to posts that are driven deep into the floor of the bay," I said. "You weren't actually on the water."

"I was in the Pacific Ocean," Monk said. "It was *The Perfect Storm* on a dock."

Stottlemeyer came into the exam room. "How are you feeling, Monk?"

"Lucky to be alive," he said.

That much was true. Monk may not have been in any danger of dying from seasickness, but a bullet in the head had been a real possibility for a while.

"There are a lot of cops who'd like to shake your hand," Stottlemeyer said. "But don't worry: I told them not to."

"Thank you," Monk said.

"How is Gruber doing?" I asked.

"He'll live to serve a nice, long life sentence," Stottlemeyer said. "Ballistics matched the bullet recovered from Officer Milner to the gun Gruber held to Monk's head."

"Case closed," I said.

"Was there ever any doubt?" Monk said.

"There's still one thing that's bothering me," Stottlemeyer said. "Was Officer Milner's wife really in the dark about what he was doing, or did she lie to us?"

"It doesn't matter. Her husband was killed," I said. "She's suffered enough."

"But let's say Monk didn't have his brainstorm," Stottlemeyer said. "If she knew the truth and didn't tell us, Gruber would have gotten away with murder and literally sailed off into the sunset."

"Then it's a good thing Monk figured it out," I said.

That was when we had a visit from a very unexpected guest. Mayor Smitrovich stormed in, slamming the door behind him. All those veins were bulging on his forehead again, which reminded me of those people in the movie *Scanners* who could make someone's head explode just by thinking about it.

"Tell me you didn't just shoot the man I announced on television was a great citizen and a shining example of what it means to be a San Franciscan," the mayor said to Stottlemeyer.

"I did," Stottlemeyer said proudly.

"The man I gave two hundred and fifty thousand dollars of taxpayer money to reward him for his courage?"

"That's the one," Stottlemeyer said.

"What possessed you to do *that*?"

"He murdered a police officer," Stottlemeyer said. "He also put a gun to Monk's head."

The mayor turned his fury toward Monk. "How could you let this happen?"

"Would you have preferred that I didn't solve the murder?" Monk said.

"Are you absolutely sure that he's guilty? Isn't it possible that you may have made a horrendously stupid mistake?"

"No," Monk said.

"But this simply isn't possible," the mayor said, almost pleading. "How could the man who turned in a serial killer end up being a murderer himself? It *can't* be true."

"Fate is a funny thing," I said.

"I'm not laughing," the mayor snapped at me.

"I am," Stottlemeyer said. "But only a little. It's more like a chuckle."

"The picture of me shaking that cop killer's hand and handing him a check is going to be spotlighted on every newscast, newspaper, Web site, and blog in the country."

"Maybe the world," I said.

Mayor Smitrovich pointed accusingly at Monk. "You knew all about what Gruber and Milner were doing before the press conference. You set me up."

"No, I didn't," Monk said.

"Don't play dumb with me. You've been shrewdly manipulating events from the start." The mayor glanced at Stottlemeyer. "You were working hand in hand the whole time with your good friends in the police union. And I fell for it."

The mayor was even more paranoid than Cindy Chow, and just as adept at weaving complex conspiracy theories. I couldn't decide which of their paranoid conspiracies was the most insane: her belief that extraterrestrials and the CIA were conducting mind-control experiments on unsuspecting people, or his notion that Monk was a political mastermind who had intentionally tricked the mayor into giving a murderer a $250,000 reward. One thing was clear: Both the mayor and Chow should be heavily medicated at all times.

"I won't forget this, Monk," the mayor said, the implied threat quite clear.

"I doubt the voters will, either," Stottlemeyer said.

The mayor scowled at all of us and left even angrier than he'd been when he arrived. If his head was going to explode, for his sake I hoped it happened while he was still in the hospital.

Monk sighed. "It's so sad."

"How do you figure?" Stottlemeyer asked.

"He still doesn't realize that the podium was his undoing," Monk said.

The police department dominated the news that night and the following morning.

The Tuesday-night newscasts all led with the story that Bertrum Gruber, the hero who led police to the Golden Gate Strangler, had killed police officer Kent Milner; and, as Mayor Smitrovich predicted, footage of the press conference was used to illustrate the story. They also reported that police and city negotiators were working through the night at an undisclosed hotel to reach a deal in the ongoing labor dispute.

The front page of the Wednesday-morning edition of the *San Francisco Chronicle* led with a two-column picture of Mayor Smitrovich and Bertrum Gruber shaking hands over the $250,000 check. But this time the news was a bit different. Mayor Smitrovich had managed to spin the story in a more flattering and totally fraudulent light.

MAYOR AIDS POLICE IN CAPTURE OF COP KILLER

When Barry Smitrovich bestowed a $250,000 reward on Bertrum Gruber for providing information leading to the arrest of the Golden Gate Strangler, the mayor was actually acting a role in an elaborate con staged by the San Francisco Police Department to ensnare one of their own.

"It was a calculated risk, but I was glad to do whatever I could to help law enforcement," the mayor said in a statement issued by his office. "Unfortunately, things went tragically wrong."

The mayor was referring to the shooting death of police officer Kent Milner, who allegedly concocted a scheme with Gruber to defraud the city out of a quarter of a million dollars.

Police sources reveal that Milner pulled Golden Gate Strangler suspect Charles Herrin over on Saturday for a routine traffic violation. Milner realized he'd stumbled on the serial killer but, instead of arresting the suspect, he gave Gruber the information needed to claim the reward, which they were going to share. Milner was a city employee and thus ineligible to claim the reward himself.

The police were on to the scheme but lacked the evidence to make any arrests.

"Giving Gruber the reward was part of a complex cat-and-mouse game to gather the necessary evidence," the mayor said in his statement. "I worked closely with the police on this critical law enforcement operation. I participated without ever considering what the short-term personal or political consequences might be to me. Seeing that justice was served was my only priority then and remains so now."

What the police didn't count on was the depth of the greed of the criminals they were pursuing. Before the police could make their case, Gruber allegedly killed Officer Milner to keep all the money for himself.

I scanned the rest of the article, looking for a quote from somebody in the police department refuting the mayor's lies. There wasn't one.

I'm not a politician or a conspiracy theorist, but I had a feeling there was a good reason the police chose not to contradict the mayor's account of events. The mayor's embarrassment may have given the police considerable leverage in the negotiating room.

All of this was swirling around in my mind as I drove Monk into headquarters on Wednesday morning for another day at work. The first thing I noticed was that the place was full of cops. It seemed like most of the force had recovered from their bout of Blue Flu.

The homicide squad room was packed with detectives, leaving no room for Monk's team, who'd been relegated to standing room in the back. But Chow, Porter, and Wyatt weren't being ostracized.

They were talking animatedly with their fellow cops and sharing laughs.

Disher spotted Monk and yelled out over the din of conversation, ringing phones, and general office hubbub, "There he is!"

Suddenly all the detectives rose to their feet, faced us, and applauded. Monk was startled and embarrassed by the attention.

Stottlemeyer stepped out of his office, and the applause died down so he could speak.

"We all wanted to thank you for what you did for Officer Milner," Stottlemeyer said. "He may have been a flawed individual, but he was still one of us."

"I would have done the same thing for anybody," Monk said. "No murder should go unpunished."

Batman couldn't have said it better. But Monk didn't stop there.

"Whatever I accomplished I owe to my team of detectives, Cindy Chow, Frank Porter, and Jack Wyatt," Monk said. "You can thank me by showing them the respect and appreciation they deserve."

The assembled detectives turned and gave Monk's team a round of enthusiastic applause. I whispered to Monk, "Great speech, Mr. Monk, and you didn't need any notes. Speaking in front of an audience isn't so hard."

"This isn't an audience," Monk said, clearly touched. "This is family."

Stottlemeyer motioned Monk and me into his office and closed the door behind us after we came in. He didn't invite Disher to join us, nor did the lieutenant try to worm his way in.

That wasn't a good sign.

25

Mr. Monk and the Status Quo

Monk didn't seem to share my trepidation. He was still moved by the standing ovation.

"That was really something," Monk said.

"Yes, it was," Stottlemeyer said. "Nailing that cop killer erased a lot of hard feelings toward you and your team."

"I'm so glad to hear that," Monk said. "Now we can all work together in harmony."

"Not quite," Stottlemeyer said, taking a seat on the edge of his desk. "We had the mayor over a barrel on this Gruber thing, so our union reps used that to our advantage in negotiations. They were able to close a deal last night that's pretty close to what we wanted."

I knew it. That explained why everyone was back at work and in such good spirits—but not why we were having this closed-door conversation.

"That's terrific," Monk said.

"For the rank and file," Stottlemeyer said. "But not so much for you. Part of the deal requires the department to promote from within for any detective-grade openings and above."

Monk nodded. "So I'm not a captain anymore. I can live with that."

Stottlemeyer sighed and looked at me. I got the feeling he was asking me for my support. Or was it my forgiveness? Before I could work it out, he shifted his gaze back to Monk.

"I hate to say this, Monk. But you aren't a cop anymore, either," Stottlemeyer said.

Monk didn't say anything. He didn't have to. The heartbreak was written all over his face and in the way he slumped his shoulders.

Stottlemeyer looked at me again, but he didn't find whatever he was hoping for. What he got was my disgust. How could they do this to Monk after everything he did for them? If the union had the mayor over a barrel it was because *Monk* put him there. And this was how they thanked him? Some family.

Then again, maybe it was the mayor's doing. Maybe yanking Monk's badge and shattering his dream was the mayor's way of getting back at Monk for his own public humiliation.

But the police let the mayor do it.

"You have to pass the psychological evaluation and meet all the reinstatement qualifications that the mayor let you skip over," Stottlemeyer said. "But even if you did all that, with this hiring freeze in place you still couldn't get in. I'm sorry, Monk. I truly am."

"Did you even fight for him?" I said.

"Who am I going to fight, Natalie? I wasn't in the negotiating room. I didn't make the deal, and I certainly don't have the power to change any of the terms. I've got no standing in this."

"Thanks a hell of a lot," I said.

"That isn't fair," Stottlemeyer said. "This isn't my doing."

"You're *doing* nothing, and that's worse. You should all be ashamed of yourselves."

I glared at Disher in the squad room. He felt my anger and turned away. There was no reason he should get out of this untouched. They were all culpable.

Monk cleared his throat, tipped his head toward the squad room and asked quietly, "What about my team?"

"They're out, too," Stottlemeyer said.

"Do they know?" Monk asked.

Stottlemeyer nodded. "I told them before you came in. They've already turned in their badges."

Monk reached into his pocket and took out his badge, handing it to Stottlemeyer without even looking at it.

"I feel terrible about this, Monk."

"Me, too." Monk shuffled out of the office.

I stepped in front of Stottlemeyer. "This is wrong, Captain. You know it is."

"Be realistic, Natalie. The men out there may have forgiven him because he caught a cop killer, but Monk and the others are still scabs. Nobody is going to reward them for crossing a picket line, whether there actually was one or not. That's just the way it is."

"It sucks," I said.

"It does," Stottlemeyer said. "But let's be honest—it's not like we didn't see this coming from the start."

He was right. We all saw it—me, Dr. Kroger, and Stottlemeyer—but it didn't make the reality any easier to accept, or what they'd done to Monk any less wrong. It didn't have to happen the way we knew it would.

Monk did his job, he proved himself as a cop and a leader and probably saved some lives along the way, and it didn't matter to anyone. The police and the politicians used him and gave him nothing in return. In fact, he was supposed to be grateful that nobody harbored any hard feelings toward *him*.

Can you believe that? How about his feelings? Didn't they matter to anyone?

Apparently not.

I walked out and found Monk talking to Chow, Porter, and Wyatt.

"I wasn't expecting my badge back," Porter said. "But it's damn nice to go out a winner. Thank you for that, Mort."

"It's Monk," Sparrow said.

"Where?" Porter said, looking all around.

"He's right in front of you, Grandpa," Sparrow said.

Porter looked at Monk as if seeing him anew. "Are you still afraid of milk?"

"Terrified," Monk said with a smile.

Chow spoke up. "Thanks to you, Monk, we scored a major victory against the alien shadow government. They can try to bury what we've discovered, but the truth has a way of bubbling to the surface. I'll make sure that it does."

She handed Monk a tiny electronic device that looked like an iPod crossed with a flashlight.

"What's this?" Monk asked.

"You use it to scan for bugs," Jasper said. "It's like a radar detector for audio or video surveillance devices."

"You have one of those?" I asked.

"Of course," Jasper said. "Don't you?"

I was beginning to wonder if he'd become as nutty as Chow, but then he winked at me and I felt a lot better.

"You're going to be under surveillance now by the Omega Agency for the rest of your life," Chow said to Monk. "Consider it a badge of honor."

"I will," Monk said.

Wyatt stepped forward and scowled at Monk. "You're a wuss."

"Yes," Monk said. "I am."

"But in some ways, you may just be the bravest man I've ever known." Wyatt handed Monk a bullet.

"What's this for?"

"It's the bullet you saved me from using," Wyatt said. "Even though it never tore through your flesh, it still feels to me like it's yours."

"Thanks," Monk said.

"Come visit us sometime," Wyatt said.

"Us?" Monk asked.

"The three of us are opening a detective agency," Chow explained. "There will always be a job there for you if you want it."

"I'm a lone wolf," Monk said. "A rebel. A rogue. A loose cannon."

"I thought I was too," Wyatt said. "But things change."

"I'm not a big fan of change," Monk said.

"Then this is a good thing," Wyatt said.

"What is?"

"Not getting your badge back," Wyatt said. "Think of all the changes there would have been in your life."

Monk thought about it for a second, and then his entire demeanor changed. He stood up straight. His eyes widened. He smiled. The disappointment he was feeling seemed to completely evaporate.

"You're right," Monk said. "Whew, what a relief."

Mad Jack Wyatt, messenger of happiness and enlightenment, and without firing a shot. Who would have believed it?

The three detectives started to leave. I grabbed Jasper by the sleeve and gestured to Sparrow and Arnie to step to one side with me for a moment.

"Let's stay in touch, okay?" I said.

"Sure," Jasper said.

"That would be great," Arnie said.

"We'll have lunch," Sparrow said.

What they meant was, *We'll never see one another again.* "No, I mean it. I have a job I thought nobody understood. But then I met you. We're all basically doing the same thing. We've got a natural support system here. It would be a shame not to take advantage of it now. We can really help one another."

"Jasper is already helping me," Sparrow said with a lascivious grin. Jasper blushed. Arnie glanced meaningfully at me.

"I don't need that kind of help, Arnie."

"I'm a happily married man," he said indignantly.

"Good," I said. "Let's keep it that way."

"We'll stay in touch," Jasper said, and this time it felt like he meant it.

I almost mentioned my brilliant idea of forming our own union, the International Association of Detectives' Sidekicks, but I didn't want to scare them off.

The three of them walked out, Sparrow and Jasper hand in hand, following the detectives they worked for. But I knew that the relationship between each of them was more than employee and assistant, like it was for Monk and me and, I suppose, Stottlemeyer and Disher, too.

We all needed assistance, even the assistants.

I didn't know if I'd ever see them again, but it was comforting to know they were out there if we needed them.

26

Mr. Monk Goes to Traffic School

There are some things in life that I'm pretty sure everybody hates to do, regardless of their sex, race, religion, or nationality—like flossing your teeth, cleaning your bathroom, and attending traffic school. You could pick anybody off the street and they'd agree that those tasks suck.

Everybody, that is, except Monk.

He flosses his teeth hourly. He cleans his bathroom several times a day. And even though he doesn't drive, he insisted on going with me to traffic school, which was fine with me. I would have made him go with me anyway.

The only reason I had to take the class was so I could burn off the totally bogus speeding ticket I got driving him around during the Blue Flu. It was Monk's fault I got the ticket, so the least he could do was endure the eight hours of torture with me.

The class was held not far from my house, in a

storefront that used to be a mom-and-pop travel agency, until the Internet drove them out of business. The walls that were once decorated with pictures of exotic, faraway places were now covered with various road signs and posters urging people not to drink and drive. Three rows of folding chairs were lined up facing a simple, gunmetal gray desk, two file cabinets, and a dry-erase board.

As soon as we arrived, Monk started rearranging the chairs into four rows with an even number of them in each. I shrugged my silent apologies to my fellow students as they stood around and waited impatiently to take their seats.

I wanted to sit in the back, where I hoped to get a little sleep, but Monk insisted we sit in the front row.

"I don't want to miss anything," Monk said.

"I'd like to miss it all," I said.

"Then you won't learn from your mistakes."

"People don't come here to learn, Mr. Monk. They come here to take their punishment."

"Punishment?" Monk said. "This is a perk."

"You're kidding, right?"

"Double yellow lines, crosswalks, and left-turn-only lanes. Speed limits, traffic lights, and clearly defined parking zones. It's beautiful. It's perhaps the finest expression of our humanity."

I stared at him. "Traffic lanes and stop signs. *That's* what you think expresses the best of mankind?"

"It's peace, order, and equality," Monk said. "If only sidewalks and hallways had lanes. It would mean an end to the chaos."

"What chaos?"

"Have you seen how people walk?"

He tipped his head toward the happy people passing by out on the sunny street outside. That was where I longed to be, and the class hadn't even started yet. It didn't seem like chaos to me. It seemed like freedom.

"They go to and fro, every which way; nobody walks in a straight line anymore," he said. "Everybody is weaving and dodging, trying to avoid a collision. Some are running; some are strolling. It's anarchy. But if we all had to walk in lanes, travel at a set rate of speed, and signal our intentions, it would revolutionize society. I daresay it could even lead to world peace."

I looked into his eyes. I thought I saw tears.

This was supposed to be a miserable experience for *both* of us. It wasn't right that I would be spending the day in agony while he was in bliss. I was tempted to do something really evil, like take off my belt and miss a loop or two on my pants when I put it back on, just to drive Monk insane for the next eight hours. But I would only be torturing myself, since I was the one he'd be pestering all day.

I was still trying to come up with a way to make this experience as hellish for him as it was going to be for me when a door opened in the back of the room and in walked our teacher with the bearing, imperiousness, and dour solemnity of a Supreme Court justice. He was in his fifties, wore a tweed jacket and a bow tie, and carried a copy of the California Vehicle Code as if it were some kind of sacred text.

Monk stood. I yanked him back down into his seat.

The teacher set the California Vehicle Code on his desk and turned to the classroom.

"I am Mr. Barnaby Merriman, your traffic school instructor. You are traffic offenders. You are here because you didn't respect the laws of the road. If it were up to me, you'd all be serving time in jail. Instead, thanks to the mercy of the court, you are here in my classroom. You will not leave here today until I am satisfied that you not only *know* the law; you *embody* it."

Monk applauded. Merriman glared at him.

"Are you trying to be funny?" Merriman asked.

"No, sir," Monk said. "I am in complete agreement with you."

"So why did you break the law?"

"I didn't." Monk motioned to me. "She did."

"I was speeding," I said. "Twenty-eight miles per hour in a twenty-five-mile-per-hour zone. Lock me up and throw away the key."

Merriman shifted his gaze back to Monk. "So why are *you* here?"

"Personal enrichment," Monk said. "It's been a while since I've had a chance to really explore the California Vehicle Code."

I thought Merriman would assume Monk was a smart-ass and throw him out of the classroom. But he didn't. He must have seen the genuine excitement in Monk's eyes.

"Very well," Merriman said. "But no funny business."

"Absolutely not," Monk said as if he were taking a vow. He despised funny business.

We began by taking a multiple-choice traffic law quiz, and then we went over the answers in detail, one by one, with the teacher. The first question was:

> If a person is crossing in the middle of the block, you must stop your vehicle:
> a) Only if the person is in the crosswalk.
> b) Only if the person has a white cane.
> c) When necessary for their safety.

"What is the correct answer?" Merriman asked the class.

Monk was the only one who raised his hand. Merriman sighed and pointed to him.

" 'D,' " Monk said.

"There is no 'D,' " Merriman said.

"There should be."

"There isn't."

"It's a trick question," Monk said.

"No, it's not" Merriman said. "The correct answer is 'C,' when necessary for the person's safety."

"The correct answer is 'D', make a citizen's arrest," Monk said.

"Why would you want to do that?" I asked.

"The person is jaywalking," Monk said. "That's a crime."

"We're discussing the vehicle code," Merriman said, "Not the penal code."

"The law is the law," Monk said. "I was a crossing guard for seven years. Take it from me. I know the mean streets."

"Moving on," Merriman said. " 'If your car gets into a rear-wheel skid, you should, "A," Turn the steering wheel in the same direction as the skid, "B," Hold the steering wheel absolutely straight, "C," Turn the steering wheel in the opposite direction of the skid.' "

Monk raised his hand. He was the only one. Again. Merriman picked on a teenage girl in the second row who was doing her best not to be noticed.

"The correct answer is 'A,' " the girl said.

"Wrong," Monk said. "The correct answer is 'D,' pray."

That was more than Merriman could take. He threw Monk out of the classroom, closed the door, and locked it.

Oh, how I envied Monk. I remained trapped in the living hell of traffic school while he was free.

He could have gone anywhere and done anything. He could have taken a walk. Visited a museum. Read a good book. Eaten an ice-cream cone. Fallen in love.

Instead, Monk remained right outside the window, happily directing the foot traffic on the sidewalk, separating people into invisible lanes, and doing his small part for world peace.

Every so often he'd smile and wave at me. It was a very, very long day. But the punishment worked. I vowed never to speed again.

Read on for an excerpt from the next book starring Adrian Monk, the brilliant investigator who always knows when something's out of place . . .

Mr. Monk and the Two Assistants

Coming in hardcover from New American Library in July 2007

The doctor had already given Julie a preliminary exam, and she'd just returned from having her arm x-rayed when Monk finally joined us. He opened the curtain surrounding Julie's bed in the ER as if he was stepping out onto a stage.

Ladies and gentlemen, give it up for Adrian Monk!

He'd managed to find a hospital patient gown to put over his clothes, rubber gloves for his hands, and a surgical mask to cover his nose and mouth.

It was quite a sight and well worth the wait. He brought a smile to Julie's face when she needed it the most—not that he meant to.

"What?" Monk asked us, totally oblivious to his clownish appearance.

"Don't take this the wrong way, Mr. Monk," Julie said, "but you look silly."

"I think what you mean is 'sensibly dressed.' "

"You're right," she said, sharing a glance with me. "That's exactly what I meant."

"I'm relieved to hear you say that," he said, then wheeled in a cart containing gowns, gloves, and masks for us both. "It may not be too late to save you."

"From what?" I said.

"You name it," he said. "The Black Death, Ebola, scurvy."

"You can't catch scurvy," Julie said. "You get it from not eating enough oranges."

"That's an old wives' tale," Monk said, handing out our garments. "From wives who later died of scurvy."

That was when the doctor came in. He had such a grim expression on his youthful face, I was afraid he was going to tell us Julie had a brain tumor.

"I'm afraid you have a broken wrist," the doctor said. "The good news is that it's a clean break. You'll only have to wear a cast for a couple of weeks."

If that was it, why did he have to look so serious? Maybe he thought it made him appear more learned and mature so he wouldn't get a lot of flack from patients for being so young. Actually, it made him look like he'd eaten something for lunch that decided to fight back.

"Do I get to pick the color for my cast?" Julie asked.

"Absolutely," he said and waved over an ER nurse.

The nurse walked behind Monk and held up a

chart with a dozen sample plaster colors for Julie to see. There was something vaguely familiar about the nurse, but I couldn't place her.

She had thick, curly brown hair with blond highlights, and stood with attitude. By that, I mean she had a certain rough confidence about her—the kind that's like a scar. It's a toughness you can only get on the streets, and not the ones you find in suburban housing tracts. Growing up in suburbia, you end up with a pampered confidence that comes from knowing you have mutual funds earning money for you.

"We have a wide selection of colors to choose from," the doctor said. "Or you can go with white and rent your arm out for advertising."

"Really?" Julie replied. "What does that pay?"

I was taken aback by the question. When did Julie become so entrepreneurial?

"I'm kidding," the doctor said.

"But it's not a bad idea." Julie looked at me. "We could go around to local businesses, like the pizza parlor or the bike shop, and see if they'd be interested in using my arm as a walking billboard."

This broken wrist was revealing a whole new side of my daughter to me.

"You have a deal," I said.

"You could offer them a special rate to advertise on both arms," Monk added.

"But I don't have a cast on my left arm," Julie said.

"You will," he said, nodding.

"No, I won't," she said.

"It's what they do in these situations."

The nurse was starting to fidget, tapping her foot on the floor in frustration.

"But my left wrist isn't broken," Julie said.

"It doesn't matter," he said. "It's standard medical procedure."

"You want me to put a cast on her left wrist?" the doctor asked Monk incredulously.

"Doesn't that go without saying?"

"No," the doctor said, "it doesn't."

"You can't put a cast on only one wrist," Monk said. "She'll be off-balance."

"The cast isn't that heavy," the doctor said. "I can assure you that her balance will be just fine."

"It will if she has a cast on both arms." Monk turned to me. "Where did this guy go to medical school? If I were you, I'd get a second opinion."

The nurse's face was growing tense, and a flush was rising on her cheeks. She looked like she might hit Monk with that display board she was holding.

I knew what she was feeling all too well. I had to bring this ridiculous debate to an end before Monk needed medical attention.

"Julie is not getting a cast on her left wrist, Mr. Monk," I said, "because it's not broken."

"You aren't thinking rationally. You're clearly in shock over Julie's injury. You ought to have a doctor look at you." Monk glanced dismissively at the doctor. "A *real* one."

"I don't want a cast on both wrists," Julie said to me.

"Don't worry, honey," I said. "It's not going to happen."

"Of course, it is," Monk said. "She can't leave here imbalanced."

"You mean unbalanced," the doctor said, "not imbalanced."

"What do you know?" Monk said.

"I know you're imbalanced for thinking she's unbalanced," he said, smiling at his own cleverness.

Monk was not amused. "You're under arrest."

"For what?" the doctor asked.

"Impersonating a doctor."

"Are you a police officer?"

"I'm a consultant to the police," Monk said. "I investigate homicides."

"I haven't killed anyone," the doctor said.

"Not yet," Monk said, "but if you keep practicing medicine like this, you will."

The nurse suddenly threw the display card against the wall in a fit of anger, startling us all.

"That's enough, Adrian," she said. "Believe it or not, the whole world doesn't revolve around you and your special needs. This poor girl has been through enough today without having to deal with you too. So shut up and let us do our jobs."

Monk jerked at the sound of her voice, his eyes going wide with shock.

The nurse took a deep, calming breath and then looked at me. "I'm sorry about that, but this is an argument you can't win. Trust me. The only way any of us is going to get any peace is if we put a cast on Julie's left wrist."

Before I could object, the nurse stepped up to Julie. "Don't worry, honey. After the cast dries,

I'm going to cut it off, put some Velcro straps on it, and give it to you. That way, you can put it on whenever Adrian is around and take it off the instant he leaves. Problem solved."

Adrian? Hearing Monk addressed that way by a person I assumed was a complete stranger to him startled me a bit. I'd never heard anyone but Monk's brother and his shrink refer to him by his first name. Perhaps assuming that familiarity was simply a calming and controlling technique nurses and other medical professionals used to deal with emotionally or psychologically disturbed individuals.

"Or I could have this guy committed," the doctor said, narrowing his eyes at Monk. "That would solve the problem too."

"I appreciate the offer, but I think we'll go with the second cast," I said, turning to Julie. "If that's okay with you."

"Yeah," Julie said. "I just want to go home."

The nurse smiled. "Don't we all. I'll be right back."

She left to get whatever she needed to make the cast. Monk hadn't moved since she'd spoken. I don't think he'd even blinked. I was impressed with the decisive way she'd handled the situation, and I appreciated it, but I couldn't figure out why her speaking up had shocked Monk into silence.

The doctor said something about us coming back in a couple of weeks, gave me a prescription for painkillers for Julie, and then left to treat another patient.

I looked at Monk. He seemed frozen in place.

"Would you mind staying with Julie for a minute?" I asked him.

Monk nodded ever so slightly. He wasn't going anywhere.

I caught up with the nurse at the supply cabinet. "Excuse me," I said. "I just wanted to say thank you for helping out. Sometimes my friend can be difficult to handle."

"I'm used to it," she said, her back to me as she scrounged around for her things.

"You must meet a lot of people like Mr. Monk."

She sighed wearily. "There's nobody like Adrian."

She'd done it again. She'd called him Adrian. There was something about the way she said it, with her strong New Jersey accent, that gave me a pang of anxiety in the pit of my stomach. I suddenly had an ominous inkling what the explanation for her familiarity with him might be.

"You've obviously had some experience with him before," I said, fishing.

"That's one way of putting it," she said, turning to look at him again, almost affectionately. "I used to have your job."

And that was when I saw the ID badge clipped to her uniform and my suspicions were confirmed. *Sharona was back.*